Praise for *Wish You Were Here*

USA Today Bestseller
Cosmopolitan September 2017 Pick
Goodreads Best Romance of August 2017
HelloGiggles, "17 Books We Can't Wait to Read in August 2017"

"With a surprising cast of lovable and relatable characters, witty banter, and some utterly romantic scenes, Renée Carlino's *Wish You Were Here* is about more than just finding love—it's about rediscovering what love is. Just remember to have tissues on hand."

—Karina Halle, *New York Times* bestselling author

"Readers will enjoy meeting Charlotte's family, be charmed by Charlotte and Helen's friendship, and will be eager to uncover just what's going on between Charlotte and the mysterious Adam—all while swooning over the sexy parts."

—*Booklist*

"If you loved *Before We Were Strangers* and *Swear on This Life*, then Carlino's latest, *Wish You Were Here*, will be a no-brainer addition to your to-be-read list as she's outdone herself. *Wish You Were Here* will have readers laughing, crying, crying some more, and basically running a gamut of emotions in this beautiful, heart-wrenching story. The relatable heroine finds herself not only at a crossroads in her life, but torn between two great guys. Furthermore, this is a memorable story where readers will fall in love with both men. It would not be surprising if readers picked *Wish You Were Here* as one of their top reads this year."

—*Romantic Times* (4.5 stars, Top Pick)

"An absolute must-read. One hundred percent feelings, beginning to end."

—*USA Today*

"There's an unwritten rule that you must read at least one sticky-sweet romantic book per summer. And we suggest *Wish You Were Here*."

—*HelloGiggles*

"If you loved *Me Before You*, then you have to read this book!"

—*Aestas Book Blog*

"Another Carlino masterpiece! Emotional and heartbreaking comes to mind when I think of *Wish You Were Here*. . . . This book and story grabbed my attention from the get-go and I couldn't stop reading, addicted to the words and frantically trying to finish to see how it would all end."

—*Shh Mom's Reading*

"Beautiful. Absolutely, stunningly beautiful. And spectacular, and powerful, and heartbreaking. . . . I just don't have enough adjectives to describe my feelings for this book!"

—*Night Owl Reader*

"Beautiful and heartfelt, and once again, Renée Carlino has delivered the touching prose she does so well! *Wish You Were Here* is a thought-provoking, poignant, and remarkable story about self-discovery and love."

—*Totally Booked Blog*

"I absolutely love this woman's ability to tell a story and pull me right in."

—*Girl Plus Books*

ALSO BY RENÉE CARLINO

Sweet Thing
Nowhere but Here
After the Rain
Before We Were Strangers
Swear on This Life
Wish You Were Here

BLIND KISS

KISS

A Novel

RENÉE CARLINO

ATRIA PAPERBACK

New York   London   Toronto   Sydney   New Delhi

ATRIA
PAPERBACK

An Imprint of Simon & Schuster, Inc.
1230 Avenue of the Americas
New York, NY 10020

First Atria Paperback edition August 2018

ATRIA PAPERBACK and colophon are trademarks of Simon & Schuster, Inc.

For information about special discounts for bulk purchases, please contact Simon & Schuster Special Sales at 1-866-506-1949 or business@simonandschuster.com.

The Simon & Schuster Speakers Bureau can bring authors to your live event. For more information or to book an event, contact the Simon & Schuster Speakers Bureau at 1-866-248-3049 or visit our website at www.simonspeakers.com.

Manufactured in the United States of America

10 9 8 7 6 5 4 3 2

Library of Congress Cataloging-in-Publication Data

Names: Carlino, Renée, author.
Title: Blind kiss : a novel / Renée Carlino.
Description: First Atria Paperback edition. | New York : Atria Paperback, 2018.
Identifiers: LCCN 2018004996 (print) | LCCN 2018011019 (ebook) | ISBN 9781501189630 (ebook) | ISBN 9781501189623 (paperback : alk. paper)
Subjects: | BISAC: FICTION / Contemporary Women. | FICTION / Romance / Contemporary. | FICTION / Romance / General.
Classification: LCC PS3603.A75255 (ebook) | LCC PS3603.A75255 B55 2018 (print) | DDC 813/.6—dc23
LC record available at https://lccn.loc.gov/2018004996

ISBN 978-1-5011-8962-3
ISBN 978-1-5011-8963-0 (ebook)

For my best friend, Angie

*"Cutting people out of your life is easy,
keeping them in is hard."*

—Walter Dean Myers

BLIND
KISS

1. Present Day

PENNY

In my dreams, I danced. It had been a decade since I had laced my pointe shoes and glided across a stage, let alone a studio, yet in my dreams I felt strong. Flexible. In control of my body. I felt like myself.

In reality, I was like every other suburban housewife in Fort Collins, Colorado, though lately I'd been allowing myself to indulge in old dreams by going down to the studio where I used to dance as a girl. Now it's a Subway restaurant. What a travesty. I often sat on the bench just outside of its double doors and wished that I could afford to pay the lease on the space to reopen the studio: it had always been my goal, but life changes. We get sidetracked. Some of us get lost in the details of domestic life, and before we can blink again, we're thirty-four and our dreams are unattainable.

That particular morning, I turned on the TV to see what the weather would be like. It was spring and the ice had melted, but it was going to be a gloomy day. Instead of the news, the movie *Groundhog Day* filled the screen. *How apropos*, I thought, though I didn't necessarily want my own cycle to break. My fourteen-year-old son, my only child, was going off to MIT in the fall. How I raised a genius kid, I'll never know, but it seemed too soon for him to be leaving. To be leaving *me*, alone, in a life that seemed unrecognizable, in a marriage that was slowly, and quietly, dying.

I paced around the house, making sure everything was perfect, as always, until Milo came down for breakfast.

"Do you want blueberry waffles or pancakes or eggs or—"

"Don't worry about it, Mom," Milo said with his back to me as he made himself an espresso. "I don't eat breakfast anymore."

"Since when do you not eat breakfast? It's the most important meal of the day. It's why you're so smart."

"That's not why I'm smart, Mom. It's because I was born this way. It's because of Dad and Grandpa and you."

"And Gavin and Ling and Kiki and Grandma," I added, reminding him of my two best friends from college, my sister, and my mother—the small village that had helped me raise Milo.

"What are you going to do today?" he asked.

"The weather looks bad but . . . maybe I'll go down and check out the studio again. Try to talk to the owner of the strip mall if he's in his office."

"You mean sit outside the Subway and daydream?" Milo said teasingly.

"Don't be a smartass. A girl can dream."

"I think it's good for you, Mom. You need to get dressed, get out, and breathe in some fresh air."

His words stung. *Had I really been moping around that*

much? When had I stopped getting dressed? I looked down at my pajamas and ran a hand through my hair. I imagined what I looked like to my son.

I approached him for a hug, and he swooped me up and squeezed me hard. "I love you," I said.

"You were the best mom."

"I'm still your mom. You should let me hold you like a baby on the couch, while I still can."

"I haven't let you do that since I was, like, five," he said, laughing.

"You were seven. But I guess you're three inches taller than me, so maybe you should hold *me* like a baby?"

He laughed again. He was so handsome, just like his dad. I thought to myself how much the world was going to love him, and how I was going to lose him.

"That would be really weird, Mom."

"I know. I'm just gonna go shower and head out. Text me later, okay?"

"You got it." He threw back the espresso, picked up his backpack, and headed for the front door.

As I walked up to my room, I heard the door close and felt a deafening silence descend upon the house, as it did every morning when Milo left, only to lift once again when he returned in the afternoons. But I could see its invisible shadow trailing across the horizon of my future: a silence that would stay forever.

I SAT AND watched the college kids from Colorado State passing through the doors of Subway with their five-dollar footlongs. It made me nostalgic for my own college days, though I couldn't say why—I could never eat like that when I was a student. I guess I just envied them their spark. Their buoyancy. Their untouched futures.

I heard the familiar purr of a car engine and turned to see Gavin pulling into the parking space directly in front of me. Our eyes connected through the windshield as he shook his head and laughed. I smiled and gave him a little wave.

Gavin was always handsome and tall, with a full head of messy, dark-brown hair, and a heavy brow that made his green eyes seem even more penetrating and brilliant. He had full lips that naturally turned up at the corners, even when he wasn't happy. His hands were rough, thick, and scarred from his work as an auto mechanic, though I knew he was still deft with a guitar. Even though I'd told him his sideburns were lame and out of style, he wore them long anyway, and he never shaved his face with a real razor, only the electric kind that leaves a permanent five-o'clock shadow. He also wore bracelets, which drove me a little crazy. I told him they made him seem feminine, but the truth was there was nothing feminine about him. At all.

"Hey! Surprise, surprise," I said as I stood up to hug him.

"You look fantastic, P. Do you always get dressed up to hang out in front of Subway?"

"Ha! I was hoping to meet the strip mall owner. I'm thinking about converting this place back into a dance studio once Subway's lease is up, but I'm not sure if I have the funds."

"That would be amazing. Can't you guys sell one of your cars or something? Or maybe a Tag watch?" He smirked. It was true that my husband brought home good money, but what Gavin didn't know was that the cars were leased—and MIT was going to cost a fortune.

"Oh, shut it. Let's grab some lunch. You keep saying you want to catch up, but I haven't seen you in so long. We can walk across the street to that little pub by Bank of America, if you want to?"

"You just read my mind. I'll drive by the way," he said, smirking.

I looked at him suspiciously. "Big news?"

He shook his head. "Let's get a drink first."

WE SAT AT the bar of the pub as I continued to stare at him, a mixture of curiosity and fear boiling in my gut. He ordered a beer, and I ordered Chardonnay with beer-cheese pretzels.

"That's different for you."

I usually stuck to salads, an old habit from my dancing days, but I had lost a lot of weight in the past few weeks. "Don't think you can distract me so easily. Tell me what's going on. Did you break up with Briel?"

He took a long pull from his beer and stared straight ahead. "Don't be mad, okay?"

I stared at him, wordlessly, the fear fully boiling over. And then he dropped the bomb on me.

The next few minutes were hazy as Gavin, the bar, and my glass of Chardonnay swam together before my eyes. I tried to reach for the glass but found it suddenly empty. *That's weird. It was full a minute ago.* I motioned to the bartender for another, then poured it down my throat in a steady stream.

I was breathing fast when I slammed the glass on the

bar, shattering my fugue state—and bringing Gavin into sharp relief. I was reeling.

"Shit, Penny! Be careful. You almost broke your glass!" He practically yelled.

"You're moving to fucking France?!" I yelled back.

The bartender jerked his head toward the door, and within minutes Gavin was forcibly dragging me out of the bar by the arm. I slipped out of his grip and bolted to the parking lot, seething and very much drunk. I was fully freaking out when he caught up to me. "So do you love her?" I asked.

"Briel? What kind of question is that?"

"Just answer me."

"Fuck, Penny. That's not what this is about. I don't really have a choice here, though, do I?"

"You always have a choice."

He glared at me. "That's fucking rich, coming from you."

I shook my head vigorously. "Totally different situation."

"Like hell it was."

"When do you leave?"

"In two days."

"WHAT?!"

He ran up and shook me by the shoulders. "Jesus, if I knew you were gonna take it like this, I wouldn't have told you in public. Pull yourself together."

I screamed at the top of my lungs and then made a guttural sound as I hunched over and held my stomach.

"First Milo, now you?"

"Don't you put that on me. I'm not the reason why you're about to be alone and unhappy."

"Fuck you, Gavin!"

"Fuck you, Penny!"

He didn't turn around—he just stormed off in typical Gavin fashion: petulant, recalcitrant, and a total shithead. People in the parking lot were gawking, appalled, covering their children's ears. But no one made a move to leave. When Gavin and I got like this, we were like a car wreck by the side of the road, impossible to look away from.

Gavin slid into his '67 Chevelle and fired up the engine. I hated that car because he loved it so much. It had a black leather interior, a flawless paint job, and tinted windows, like it belonged to some kind of celebrity—which Gavin definitely wasn't. It was his only possession worth a dime, besides his garage, a few guitars, and a Zippo lighter he swore River Phoenix had given to him at the Viper Room the night of his death.

I ran to the exit and stood in the middle of the lane, daring him to run me over as he ripped out of his parking spot and raced around the corner toward the exit. "We're not done talking, you coward!"

He slowed but let the car idle while he revved the engine. "I *dare* you!" I yelled.

He stuck his head out the window, leaned his tattooed arm against the door, and actually *grinned* at me.

So smug. What a dick.

"You look ridiculous standing there. Get out of the way!"

I walked toward his window and noticed that his demeanor had completely softened. There was even humor in his expression. He wanted me to block him, and he knew I would.

"Can't you have a proper fight without running away?"

"You were lecturing me, yet again. I have a mother,

thank you. You have a child you can order around . . . and a husband you can control. I don't need your shit, okay? Don't you realize that I'm freaking out, too? I'm going through the hardest time of my life, and you're making this all about you."

"You've been going through the hardest time of your life for the whole fourteen years I've known you."

"And as my friend, do you think you're helping my situation right now?" he spat back, his mood shifting once again.

"Don't even. Don't you dare act like I haven't been a good friend to you. You've put me in the most awkward situations, you've bolted on me, you've stopped speaking to me for weeks at a time, but still . . . I make myself available to you. I've been *here* for you, always. And now you're moving thousands of miles away when I need you most?"

He shook his head slowly. "That's right, Penny. You *have* been here. You've been right by my side, lecturing me, rolling your eyes at me, pressuring me to get serious about Briel, all so I could go and fuck up my life even more while you sit in your nice house, with your KitchenAid mixer, your Oracle espresso machine, and your fucking Yellow Lab."

"Don't talk about Buckley that way! He's a good dog. And you love our espresso machine."

Gavin's lips turned up at the corners. "You're so messed up, Penny. You definitely have a chemical imbalance."

I pointed to my chest, shocked. "Me? Look who's talking? Please, pull into a parking space. I don't want to stand here anymore, making a spectacle of myself. Some parent from Milo's school is probably watching this whole thing. There'll be whispers at the next PTA meeting. Is that what you want for me?"

"Don't pretend like you go to PTA meetings. And look around: Everyone's gone. It's just us."

He was right. The parking lot had cleared out. Gavin was sitting in his idling car while I was standing outside his window like a moron.

"I resent you for saying I pushed Briel on you. And yes, for your information, I do go to PTA meetings."

"*You* encouraged me to go out with her, then you needled me about it until I finally did."

"You were horribly depressed! I thought you were gonna jump off a bridge. I told you to go out with her and to have some fun. She's a nice girl. I didn't say turn your life upside down, pack up, and run away with a foreigner! You're thirty-six years old, Gavin. I think it's time you grew up." I shook my head. "God, I can't believe you."

He jerked his head back and squinted. "Great band but not totally PC to call someone a foreigner, Penny." His voice was low.

"Are you going to become a French citizen now, too? You better brush up on your French."

"Everyone speaks English there."

"No, they don't! People always say that, but you'll see. They might be able to communicate to a degree, but it's not conversational English."

Why am I still standing here, screaming about French people?

I needed to tie this conversation up in a pretty little bow. I needed closure. I couldn't say good-bye to my best friend without it. He was leaving, going to France to chase a girlfriend I knew he didn't love. I was losing him. And it was my fault. We couldn't leave each other angry.

"I'll figure it out," he said. "Try not to make me feel worse about my situation, though I know that's hard for you."

"Your situation? It's always *your* situation. What about *my* situation?" He just stared at me. He was hurting; I could tell. But I was hurting, too. "Listen—"

"What?"

"Don't interrupt me." I cleared my throat. "Gavin . . . it's just . . . I'm going to fucking miss you, okay? I'm having a hard time right now, and life is about to get a whole lot harder the second you leave." I started to cry.

He hated it when I cried, but he didn't ask me, "Why are you crying?" He never had to ask.

He took a deep breath in through his nose, then released it forcefully in a burst of frustration. A second later his car stalled. He put it in gear, got out, and swooped me up in a bear hug. "Penny, Penny, Penny . . . my crazy girl," he said as he rubbed my back. I was wiping my snot-covered nose on his black T-shirt and he didn't care one bit.

He held me for a long time. When he started to release me, I said, "It's not enough."

He picked me up again and squeezed me harder. Tucking his face into my neck, he said, "It'll never be enough."

"Why?" I said, fully bawling against his shoulder.

He brushed a strand of my hair, damp with tears, behind my ear. "I have to go, and so do you. You need to be with your family now."

I felt the lump in my throat growing. "You don't have to constantly remind me that I have a family. I love my family. But you're a part of it, too, and that's why I'm here. That's why I'm fucking crying in the parking lot in front of Bank of America."

He pulled away and we stood there, two feet apart, staring at each other, as if we were committing each other to memory. Allowing one another to really look at and take the other person in, stripped down to our bones, without scrutiny.

"Is this it?" I asked.

"This is it, P."

I shook my head, leaned up on my toes, and wrapped my arms around him. We hugged again for a long time before he got into his car. I tried to hold on to the feeling of having him in my arms, or maybe I was trying to hold on to the feeling of being held in his.

He started the engine as I stood there, waiting for him to leave.

"We'll talk on the phone or email or something, okay?"

"Okay," I told him.

He swallowed nervously. Looking up at me from the car window, he said, "I wish it were you, Penny."

That was my bow. He knew I needed it, good or bad— no matter what feelings it shook loose from our long and complicated history together.

2. Fourteen Years Ago

PENNY

If you had asked me, at the age of sixteen, if I saw myself living at home at twenty-one, I would've laughed in your face. Yet here I was, at the beginning of my senior year of college, still waking up in my childhood bed and having breakfast with my parents and little sister, Kiki, every morning.

I had spent my entire life in this house. My dad was a microbiologist at a pharmaceutical company in Fort Collins, which paid just enough to send me to college but not enough for me to live in the lap of luxury in my own apartment, according to my practical father. *We live five minutes away from Colorado State—and you have a perfectly good bed here.* He wasn't wrong, but still—it put a major damper on my social life.

My mom's job was doting on Kiki. My sister was twelve years younger than me—definitely an *oops* baby. Even though my parents had always wanted a second child, they had given up all hope after ten years of trying, and then,

"Oops! Here comes Kiki." Where I was dark-haired and olive-skinned, like my dad, Kiki was blond and fair-skinned, like my mom. I always thought my mom liked Kiki better because of that.

Keeks had been on the pageant circuit ever since she was a baby, so the poor kid acted like a trained Pomeranian. Though I had nothing against pageants, I couldn't understand why my mother was so determined to be a stage mom to my little sister when I was practically begging her to come to my ballet recitals. Mom had been a beauty queen when she was younger, but still . . . it never made sense to me why she couldn't relate to ballet, too.

We ate breakfast together every morning in the kitchen, at the round wooden table, on country-style chairs. Dad would read the paper, Kiki would do her voice exercises, and Mom would cook and serve us, wearing the same apron she'd had since I was born. I would just sit there and wonder how I'd spent my entire life in the same city but had no social life to show for it.

"Why don't you get involved in a school club or a sorority?" Mom asked as she slid runny eggs onto my plate. I grimaced. She was a terrible cook. I mean, how can you fuck up eggs? Especially when you make them three times a week?

"I have dance rehearsals every day, Mom. And right now, that's enough." I lied. It definitely wasn't enough, but who was going to pledge a sorority as a senior?

"Well, why aren't you friends with any of the girls in your program?"

I threw a look at Dad, but he ignored the conversation and instead shuffled through his newspaper quietly as Kiki continued trying to improve her vocal range.

I didn't want to answer my mother's question. The truth was that the girls in the program were absurdly competitive, and few of us had formed honest friendships. If I had said that, my mother would have come back with "Well, you chose dance as a major." She liked to remind me of that fact, as if it were the worst decision of my life. We all knew I would've been at Juilliard or in a dance company by now if I really had the chops. But I loved dancing. I wanted to build my life around it, in any way I could.

All my high school friends had gone off to college in other cities, other states, and other countries, but I was stuck here, floundering on the Fort Collins social scene. I hadn't had a boyfriend since high school, and aside from a few one-night stands my freshman and sophomore years, I'd been dateless. I needed to find something to do outside of school and dance. I needed to make friends and I knew it. But it was hard as a commuter, and as a senior. Everyone had already found their cliques long ago.

My sister's voice was getting higher and higher. "God, shut up, Kiki, please! Mom and I are trying to talk."

"Don't be rude to your sister," Mom snapped. "She has a pageant this weekend. She needs to prep for it."

Kiki looked over at me like I was an alien. I pushed my eggs around the cobalt-blue plate.

My father looked at me over his specs. "Sweet Pea, clean your plate," he said quietly. "It's not that much food."

Dancing was my life, but the rigor had taken its toll. There was pressure to be both skinny and strong, and I was always confused about what size I should be. I was definitely not the skinniest, and I wondered if that's what had kept me from being an elite dancer.

While taking the tiniest nibbles of gross, slimy eggs to appease my father, I asked Kiki, "Do you even like being in beauty pageants?"

She smiled one of her sparkle-toothed smiles. "Of course I do." I smiled weakly back at her. Poor thing.

"You'd think the people of Colorado would have learned their lesson by now," I said.

My dad shot me a look of warning.

"What?" Mom said, wide-eyed.

"Mom, come on. You parade her around like she's a miniature adult. Did you actually bleach her hair?" My mother glared at me. "This is JonBenét-level insanity."

She turned her back on us and walked across the kitchen, dumping the frying pan into the stainless steel sink with a clang. She stormed into the living room, sniffling, as my dad glared angrily at me.

"What? She's hard on me, too," I said.

He shook his head. "That was horribly insensitive, and frankly, in poor taste. That poor little girl, JonBenét—"

"You're right, you're right. I'm sorry, I'm sorry. I shouldn't have brought it up." Growing up an hour away from Boulder in the nineties, I'd had my fill of JonBenét talk.

"Who's JonBenét?" Kiki asked.

"Don't worry about it, Keeks." I patted her on the head and got up to go after my mom.

I found her sitting on the edge of her bed, crying. She was so fragile. So vulnerable. I looked around the room awkwardly while she sobbed into her hands. Her bed, with the floral comforter and frilly bed skirt, had been perfectly made like it had never been slept in. Her room was straight out of the show *Dynasty*. She even had one of those breakfast trays with little flowerpots on it, which sat perfectly in the center of the bed. It had never been used. She tried so hard to hold everything up and maintain appearances. I should have admired her determination more, but there was something desperate about it. Something that rubbed me the wrong way—especially since she had the bad habit of making biting comments about every single one of *my* choices. I never felt good enough for her, and I felt like I was constantly spoiling the image she was trying so hard to cultivate.

"I'm sorry, Mom. I just think the pageant thing is a little over-the-top. Aren't you afraid Kiki will burn out before she's even a teenager?"

She looked up and scowled. "I never burned out on it when I was in pageants. When are you going to burn out on ballet?"

"I'm not unless I catch on fire." I smiled.

"You're so much like your father. Everything is a joke to you. Maybe things will be different when you graduate and realize you can't keep chasing impossible dreams. Your dad will have to get you a job at the pharmaceutical company in the warehouse or something."

It wasn't the first time she had hurt me. It wasn't even the first time that day. Why did she have to constantly make me feel like I was delusional for feeling passionate about ballet? "You don't think I'm a good dancer, do you?"

She opened her mouth but hesitated. Time stood still as I waited, prepared for another not-so-subtle insult. "I think you're a good dancer, Penny. I've always thought that."

"Then why are you making me feel like my only option is to work in some warehouse?"

"Because dancing is not a job," she said firmly.

"What are you grooming Kiki for? Twirling a glitter-filled baton across a stage while singing the National fucking Anthem? I'm athletic and I'm one of the best dancers in my program. Don't tell me that doesn't count for something."

"You think the pageants are for nothing? How about public speaking and confidence?"

I laughed bitterly. "You're right. Forget I said anything. I have to go, I'm gonna be late." She'd win the argument no matter what. There was no point in drawing it out further.

"You're still my daughter, and you're still living under my roof. You need to show me some damn respect and clean up your language."

That was as bad as her language got. The lone exception was when she'd had too much champagne at our neighbor's Christmas party one year and said *shit* and *piss* in the same sentence. My dad had nearly choked to death on a cocktail weenie.

As I headed for the door in my warm-up sweats, slippers, and coat, my father stopped me.

"Sit down for a second," he said. He took the duffel bag from my shoulder, set it on the floor, and gestured toward the chair beside the front door.

When I sat down, he knelt in front of me and removed one foot from its slipper. He began bending my toes forward and backward. He did this often to loosen up my feet. Without looking up, he said, "Are you going to be on pointe today?"

"Probably."

"How much time do you have right now?"

"About three minutes," I told him.

He pulled a tube of arnica cream from the side of my bag and began massaging it into my foot. I noticed in that moment that he was getting old. His hair was turning gray and he was getting an old-man belly, just above his belt.

"Sweet Pea, they look bad. You lost another toenail," he said. "You also need to be wearing your boots out there, not slippers. It's cold. It's supposed to snow today."

"I can't wear the boots. They hurt too much. I'll skip the studio this afternoon. Maybe go to the library and study."

"Good."

For some reason his kindness toward me made me emotional. He was the only one who believed in me. I found myself getting choked up and looked away as he continued to rub cream into my feet.

"How's that feel? Better?" he asked.

I nodded and stood, put my slippers back on, and hugged him. "Thanks, Dad." He always hugged me well.

"I'm proud of you, little girl."

I couldn't speak. He knew my mom was hard on me. It was nice to have one parent who knew how to be soft.

ONCE AT SCHOOL, I practiced a romantic modern dance routine with my usual partner, Joey. It was a beautiful piece, choreographed by Professor Douglas, a young, fun, easygoing guy who came onto the scene at CSU the year before. Douglas was his first name, but everyone started calling him P-Doug by the second semester of my junior year, and he just went with it. He jokingly said he'd base our final grades solely on our hip-hop routines. He had been a professional dancer until he tore his meniscus and had to have three surgeries before he could dance again. He'd never be a pro, so now he was our instructor.

The song he chose for Joey's performance and mine was a "Wicked Games" cover. It was evocative and perfectly suited for the choreography. We had gotten the routine down pretty well except for the lifts, which wasn't Joey's strong suit. He was a graceful dancer, long and lean, but he liked to do solo work more than partner work. He wasn't into girls, which shouldn't have mattered, but it did to him. He'd never have a career in dance as long as he appeared physically repulsed by women. Most of the gay partners I'd had understood that acting was a part of dancing, unlike Joey.

Doug was sitting in the audience while we rehearsed onstage. "Do the second lift again," he said. "Your line looks off, Joe."

Joey had a crush on him, but I think Doug was straight, which made Joey extra sensitive to his remarks.

"My line?" Joey pointed to his chest.

"Yes," Doug confirmed.

"That's a hard lift and Penny wasn't holding it."

"Excuse me?"

"You feel heavier to me," he said. "You feel shaky."

I looked at Doug. "I'm five-foot-six and a hundred and thirteen pounds—and Joey thinks I'm too heavy for this lift?"

Doug shook his head. "Joey, you're just off today, man."

Joey crossed his arms, huffed, and then stormed offstage.

Doug and I were silent for a moment, until he started to cue up the music for my solo piece. "Doug, do you mind if we call it? I need to let my feet rest. I'm taking the night off from ballet, too."

"Sure, Penny. You danced beautifully today. You were holding the pose with strength. You don't need to be concerned about your weight."

"Thanks, Teach." I smiled before skipping back to the locker room.

3. Fourteen Years Ago

PENNY

While making my way to the library, I decided to stroll through the psychology building to kill time. I hated the library; everything was too quiet and static, though it was easier to study there than at home. As I passed through the entryway to Clark Hall, I ran into Ling, a psych major I knew, pinning fliers to a bulletin board. I caught the words BLIND KISS printed in big block letters.

"Hey, Penny!" she called out. "We're offering a twenty-dollar Java Hut gift card for this one." She knew I was down to participate in most psych studies if I could get free coffee or a lunch out of it.

I looked at the flier and back at her. She didn't smile at all; she was all business. "I don't know. 'Blind Kiss?' Sounds suspicious."

I felt someone come up behind me. I turned to see another girl reading the flier intently. "You have to kiss someone you've never seen or met with a blindfold on? That's crazy. I would never do that. What if you get a total dog?" She rolled her eyes and walked away.

I didn't think I wanted to kiss anyone blindfolded, even if I was getting free coffee out of it.

"Come on, Penny, it's for our senior project. We already have five volunteers. We just need five more . . . girls." She said the last word under her breath.

I laughed. "So you got five guys to agree but haven't been able to get *one* girl to do it? Shocker."

She leaned in close. "Look, I'm not supposed to tell you this, but I would make out with any of the dudes who signed up. They're all hot. I swear." Somehow I found that hard to believe. "Take a walk with me," she said. "I have to put up the rest of these fliers."

Ling wasn't the friendliest but I admired her fortitude. She was basically the only girl I knew who wasn't in dance. I also liked her style; on that particular day, she wore combat boots with a floral-print dress.

"Say I *do* agree. What's going to happen?"

Her eyes lit up. "You're gonna do it? I'm so —"

"Hold on—" I put my hand up. "Just tell me about it."

We were walking through Clark, trying to dodge people as classes let out. Ling was small, but she had a formidable presence. "Out of my way!" she snapped as she zipped through the crowd. "Penny, listen. All you have to do is kiss a guy. No big deal."

It wasn't a big deal, though it had been a while since I'd been kissed. "What exactly are you studying?"

"We're gonna blindfold you, put you in a room to-gether, and ask you how you feel about kissing a person you've never seen or met. Then we'll pair you up and you'll talk for a little while . . . and then you'll kiss. Afterward, you'll talk about how it felt and then we'll take the blindfold off."

"What's the point?"

She stopped walking and faced me. "You don't get it?"

"Not really."

"We want to know if people can feel attracted to another person without ever seeing them. It's about separating looks from physical attraction. Also, we're trying to measure the power in a kiss. What you transmit, what you feel." She giggled. "It's very romantic."

"Sounds terrifying. Even if everyone is good-looking."

"Then don't do it, Penny. Why are you following me around?"

"What about *actual* blind people?"

"That's different. Our culture, our generation, is obsessed with looks. It's a good sensory experiment. Our hypothesis is that imagination is what drives sexuality; projection fuels intimacy between people. That's what this experiment is all about. But it's complicated. Just forget it."

She was pinning another poster to a bulletin board when a little crowd formed. "We have plenty of guys," she said to the crowd. "We just need girls. We'll compensate with forty-dollar gift cards to Java Hut."

"You told me twenty," I whispered near her ear.

"Shhh," she said. "I have to up the ante. This thing is supposed to happen tomorrow. We have a videographer booked and everything. I'll give you a forty-dollar card too, okay? Just be quiet." She directed her attention back to the crowd. "This girl is doing it. We just need four more."

"You are?" a few girls murmured with looks of disgust on their faces.

"For the sake of science," I said. I also didn't want to disappoint Ling. "Come on, when you're all seniors, you're gonna need volunteers for your projects."

We got four other girls to agree after a lot of pleading. After the crowd scattered, Ling turned to me with a huge grin on her face. "Thanks for helping me out today, Penny. Once this whole thing is over, I promise I'll come and watch you dance, okay?"

I smiled. Ling and I were going to be friends.

By that point, the library sounded even less appealing. I needed to dance. I would have to skip ballet the following day to do Ling's experiment, so even though I'd told my dad and Professor Douglas I'd take it easy, I decided to go to the ballet studio anyway to get in some toe time.

Walking through the CSU parking lot toward my '94 Honda Accord, the chill in the air was strong. I was moving fast on my numb, bruised feet.

The Honda was my dad's old car he'd sworn would run for three hundred thousand miles. I pumped the gas as I turned the key over and over but there was nothing. "Dammit." I hit the steering wheel and looked at the odometer. It only had a hundred and ten thousand miles.

Slouching in my seat, wondering what to do, I was startled by a rap on my window. I looked up to see Lance, a microbiology major who knew my dad.

"You flooded the engine," he yelled.

I got out of the car. "My dad said I'd get three hundred thousand miles out of this piece of junk."

"I can give you a ride home," he offered.

"Um. Can you give me a ride to my dance studio? It's about two miles away. My dad can pick me up after he gets off work."

"Yeah, no problem. I totally dig your dad, by the way. His last lecture was amazing." My dad was a frequent guest lecturer so all the microbio kids knew him.

"Yeah, he's great."

I locked up my car and got into Lance's Toyota Corolla. The inside was pristine and smelled like coconuts. "Penny, have you ever swabbed your steering wheel?"

"Huh? No." The stench from my dance bag was starting to overpower the coconut scent.

"When I knocked on your window, it looked like you had your mouth on the steering wheel."

"What's your point?" I'd only been resting my face on it, but he seemed grossed out. I wasn't in the mood for his judgment.

"You should swab it and bring it into the lab. You'd be amazed by how much bacteria is on a steering wheel. It's dirtier than a toilet seat." I seriously doubted his claim, but whatever, he was the scientist.

"Interesting." I pointed to the next stoplight. "Make a left up there."

"So, what are your plans after graduation?" He was driving exactly the speed limit, which either meant he was trying to make the ride last as long as possible or he was an old man.

"I was thinking about opening a studio and teaching dance. How 'bout you? Do you have an internship lined up?"

"Definitely something in pharmaceuticals, but I was actually thinking about going into sales instead of research and development. More money, you know?" He turned toward me and wiggled his eyebrows. Lance was a dead ringer for Tobey Maguire. A lot of girls liked him. He was sweet and charming, confident but not arrogant. He would have been perfect boyfriend material—if I were looking.

"Well, you didn't need all this schooling for pharma sales."

He laughed. "It was in the contract. I had to go to college in order to collect a trust fund my grandmother had left me. I'll be able to buy a house as soon as I graduate. But I'll still need to work. And as much as your dad inspires me, and as much as I love the lab, I don't want to do that every day, you know?"

"Yeah, I do know, actually. Oh, you just passed the driveway."

"Whoops." He did a very cautious U-turn and pulled into the parking lot.

Slinging my bag over my shoulder, I jumped out and turned to look at Lance through the open door. "Thanks a lot. This was really nice of you."

He smiled and seemed to hesitate for a moment before continuing. "I know this might seem out of the blue, but do you want to go out sometime?"

"With you?" *Oh man, why did I say that?*

He huffed. "Yeah, with me."

"Oh sorry. You just caught me off guard. Yeah, maybe. I just have to get through exams. Maybe during Thanksgiving break or something?"

"Okay, cool. Let's keep in touch."

"Sure. Do you want to exchange numbers?"

"Yeah, let me see your cell phone. I'll put my number in it."

Embarrassed, I said, "Oh, I don't have one. You'll have to call my house number. Here, give me yours and I'll put it in."

"You don't have a cell phone?" He was shocked as he handed over his.

"I'm probably gonna get one for Christmas."

"Oh. Okay. I'll call your house then."

"Cool, thanks again for the ride."

The studio where I had practiced since I was a kid was starting to look run-down. It was in a small strip mall and the landlords hadn't painted the exterior or trim in twenty years. It was brown and dingy, and several roof tiles were missing. Whenever it rained or snowed, which was a lot in the winter, there would be leaks, which damaged the hardwood dance floor. I wished Nancy, the owner, could get some help but she seemed so overwhelmed all the time.

I reached for the glass studio door but it wouldn't budge. It was locked, though I could see Nancy inside at the front desk, talking to a man and a woman. She saw me, stood up, and came to let me in. "Sorry, Penny, just having a little meeting. Come in, come in." I nodded at the man and woman as I headed for the locker room.

That day I practiced my *grand jeté* in front of the floor-to-ceiling mirrors, a beautiful but difficult move in which the dancer leaps forward, legs turned out, hips squared, with the front leg pointed forward and the back leg turned upward. Everything has to come together; your shoulders have to be pulled back, your neck has to be long, and your arms, extended in clean, graceful lines. I leapt twice to get power and force off the ground. While I was in the air, Nancy walked the floor and yelled, "Extension, Penny!"

I hit the ground hard with a thud. Not very graceful.

"Again," she said. "Again! Again!"

Each time it was getting better. I was feeling lighter and stronger and landing softer. My legs and feet were aching, but I wanted it to be perfect.

At the end of my practice, Nancy came up to me. "Great work today, Penny."

"Thanks, Nance. See you next week."

She smiled but said nothing.

4. Fourteen Years Ago

PENNY

At home that night I went down to our basement studio and practiced the *grand jeté* over and over. At some point my dad came in but I hadn't noticed. The lights were dim and I was doing the jump with my eyes closed; I liked to practice that way to prepare for the effects of stage lighting. When I stopped the music, he was holding his hand to his cheek, sitting on the bottom stair. I couldn't see his expression so I turned on the light. He was crying.

"Are you okay, Dad?"

"Ahh, I'm just old and emotional."

"Tell me," I said.

"You're such a beautiful dancer. It takes my breath away." He started tearing up again.

"God, you *are* getting old and mushy." We both laughed. He used to be the funny guy, but he had been more sad than funny lately. "Is everything okay with you and Mom?"

He wiped tears from his face. "Why do you ask that?"

I gave him a look. "I don't think you're just crying in the dark because I'm a good dancer, Dad."

"We're fine, Sweet Pea. Marriages go through phases."

"Dad, the pageant shit has to stop."

"Penny," he chided.

"I'm serious. She's gonna screw up Kiki."

"It's all she has right now," he argued.

"No. She has you and she has me."

He smiled weakly. "Go get some rest, Penny. You need to eat dinner and then soak your feet. They look terrible."

"Dancer's feet, Dad."

"Yeah, yeah, but they're my baby girl's feet."

THE NEXT DAY I headed to Ling's study, my stomach tied in knots. Why had I agreed to do it? Lapse in sanity, I guess. But I had promised Ling, so after Professor Douglas's dance class, I showered, dried my hair, brushed my teeth, and dabbed on a bit of lip gloss before heading to Clark. I was wearing jeans, my UGG slippers, and a hoodie from my old dance studio. It was a blind kiss, after all; it's not like I had to impress anyone with my fashion choices.

Once I got there, I knocked on the classroom door. Ling answered without a word and ushered me in. There were four girls all chatting next to a table of juice and cookies.

"Go ahead and have a snack." Ling leaned in and whispered near my ear. "I have a flask with rum in it, if you want." Why did everyone in college drink rum? It has to be the most disgusting liquor. Also, Ling was more nervous than usual, which made me more nervous.

I smiled. "No, thank you. I'll just wait."

There was a connecting room with paper covering the window in the door. Ling spoke to someone on a walkie-talkie and said, "Okay, ladies, we're gonna go in and show you the studio. The boys are waiting in another room on the other side of the studio." She pointed to each girl in front of me and said, "You're one, you're two, you're three, you're four, and Penny, you're five. That's the order you'll go in."

"You're not matching us up based on looks, are you?" one tiny blond girl with a pointy nose and pursed lips said.

Ling stared at her for an uncomfortably long time. "Are you serious, girl?" Ling was so awesome.

"Well?" Pointy Nose said.

"No, it's totally random and looks are subjective. That's the whole point!" Ling practically shouted at her.

We went into a large classroom where all the chairs had been pushed to one side to create a staging area. There were four students in the room: one guy behind a camera propped on a tripod that faced a small makeshift stage, another guy, and two girls standing near the stage with clipboards.

"Hi ladies, I'm Tracy. Ling and I are heading up this study." Tracy was all business, complete with brown hair in a low bun and a pair of glasses on the end of her nose. I noticed the heater had been cranked up really high in the room.

I whispered to Ling, "It's hot in here."

"Just wait until people start making out."

"No, seriously, I might puke."

"That would be really gross, Penny. Please don't do it on camera. When it's cold, people's nerves go haywire, so we're trying to make everyone comfortable. Take off your sweat-shirt if you have to."

I only had a dancing tank on with no bra, not that I needed one. "Umm. Well, okay it's not like he's going to see me."

"Exactly," she said.

I tore off my sweatshirt and threw it on a nearby desk. The students showed us where we would be walking and standing, so once we were blindfolded we wouldn't feel disoriented. Afterward, we were led back into the first room to wait.

Girl number one, a tall, gangly thing with mousy hair, wearing basketball shorts and a T-shirt, was called in first. We waited and waited and then finally Pointy Nose said, "Jesus, are they fucking in there?"

When the girl came out we all bombarded her with questions. She was quiet. She just said, "That was really weird. He was all right, I guess."

"What took so long?" a girl dressed in a club outfit and stilettos asked.

"They ask a lot of questions when you're blindfolded and then after . . . when you're just staring at each other awkwardly."

Girl number four, who looked like every other hoodie-clad college girl, stood up and said, "Fuck this, I'm outta here."

"No, please," Ling said as she came back into the room to usher in girl number two.

"I'm serious, I'm not doing it. Keep your stupid Java Hut gift card." The girl stormed out.

Ling turned to me. "Well, Penny, I guess you'll go fourth. I'll tell guy number five he's been cut."

"Um, Ling—"

Ling pointed at me. "No, you're doing it. I said I'd watch you dance. You're doing it, Penny! And you're going to win the award for best guinea pig at CSU."

"Is that really a thing? I don't think I want that." *What'd I get myself into?* "Let me just take a breath."

I opened the door that led to the hallway and saw girl number one pass by me. She waved to a guy coming out of the adjoining room on the other side of the studio area, and he waved back. I assume it was the guy she had just swapped spit with. He was not attractive at all. I felt bad for thinking it, but it was going to be hard for me to not picture that guy when it was my turn. He was at least four inches shorter than me, which made basketball-shorts girl easily a foot taller than him. He seemed nice but he had pretty bad skin and fairly greasy hair. He was definitely a freshman, if not a devious seventh grader who had found a way to sneak in.

When Ling came after me, I was scowling. She handed me the flask and I took a large, disgusting swig.

"They're not all good-looking." I cocked my head to the side. "Liar."

"You might be off the hook," she said.

"Thank you, God!" I shouted. Clubbing Girl and Pointy Nose turned and glared at me.

"Yeah, so it looks like we're actually missing two guys, but we still need to give it a few more minutes."

"I'm so happy to hear that. I can't believe you told me they were all hot."

"Honestly, I never even saw them. That was Tracy's job, not mine, I just had to get the girls."

"You are such a liar!" I poked her in the shoulder and glared at her.

"It's just a kiss. Jeez, it's not like we're asking you to sleep with him."

I dry heaved. "Have another swig." She handed me the flask and some breath mints.

As the hour went on, the other girls cycled in and out like it was no big deal. I was gathering my things, getting ready to leave, when Ling walked in. "Not so fast. Your guy was late—that ass—but he's here and they're blindfolding him now."

"Oh God, did you see him?"

"Just chill. The other girls handled it like pros. What's your deal?"

"Those girls *looked* like pros."

"Penny, shut up and turn around. Just let me blindfold you."

"I hate this study so much. You have no idea. Did you see him? Why'd you call him an ass?"

"I didn't see him but Tracy said he was bitching about only getting a ten-dollar Java Hut card."

"Why is he only getting ten?"

"Because he said yes the second Tracy asked him to be in the study." She huffed. "You should be happy. You're getting forty dollars' worth of coffee. It's basically liquid gold during finals."

She used a dark floral scarf as a blindfold and triple checked it to make sure I couldn't see a thing.

"Take my arm, I'll guide you," she said.

I linked my arm through hers and followed her into the makeshift studio. "I'm nervous."

"You'll be fine. Okay, step up." She led me to a spot on the small stage where I felt a pencil on the ground. "Keep one foot on that. That's your mark. The guy will be here in a minute."

I heard his voice first. It was deep but soft, grounded in his chest but not husky. "Wait, where the fuck am I? Oh shit." When I heard him trip, I started laughing.

"Hey, woman, are you laughing already? I haven't even kissed you yet." Everything was black but for some reason his demeanor instantly put me at ease. I could feel him standing opposite me now.

"Reach out and take each other's hands," said the guy behind the camera.

Ling guided our hands toward each other. His were warm and large; they swallowed mine up. "Tiny little hands," he said.

"Ha!"

Ling started in. "Okay, we're going to ask you a few questions and then ask you to kiss. You can take as long as you want. You don't have to force yourselves to stop or continue, just let it happen organically." I couldn't imagine how that would be humanly possible.

He squeezed my hands in a way that was calming.

"So, girl number four," Ling said, "are you nervous?"

"Uh, yes."

"What about you, guy number four?"

"Not really."

"Why did you agree to this?"

He spoke first, "Free coffee."

"What about you?" Ling poked me in the shoulder.

"Um, yeah. The coffee, I guess."

"So what do you think this experiment will give you? You go first." She poked my arm again.

"Herpes simplex one."

The guy chuckled. "No, I'm good," he said.

"What about you?" Ling asked.

"I don't know. An experience." He didn't seem nervous at all. "Like, what can you feel from just a kiss?" He ran his thumb over the center of my palm. It sent shivers down my spine. "Or by touch alone. I mean, I do wonder, you know . . . like, if it's different, if I'll feel nothing because I don't know what she looks like."

I huffed and tried to pull my hands away but he held them tight. "Where you going, lady?"

I didn't respond.

Ling poked me again. "Tell him your name and what you like to do."

"Penny. I'm a dancer."

"Tiny little *T. rex* dancer."

"You're funny."

"You smell good."

"Stahhhp!" I was embarrassingly turned on by his little thumb strokes on my palm.

"Now you go, dude. Tell her," Ling said.

"I'm Gavin, and uh . . . I don't know, I like to play guitar and work on cars. I'm an engineering major."

It was unusually quiet in the room after that. Even without sight, I could tell Gavin was tall, just based on where the sound of his voice was coming from. We were close. He smelled like mint and cardamom soap. I could feel the specific heat of his body even in the warm room.

"Ling?" I said.

"One sec, Penny. Josh is changing a setting on the camera."

She was far away now. I could sense that only Gavin and I were on the stage.

"Are you really nervous, Penny? Your voice is shaking," Gavin said, only loud enough for me to hear.

"Yeah." He clasped my hands together between his and brought them to his chest. I could feel his heart beating. I could tell he had a strong, lean body. "I'm nervous, too," he whispered.

"You don't seem like it. Why'd you say you weren't?"

"I was trying to impress you."

"Go ahead, you guys," Ling said.

"What?" I asked.

I felt like I was going to pass out, and then Gavin's hands were on me, one on my back and one on my waist. I was acutely aware of everything. He was wearing a T-shirt. He was warm. I felt safe. My hands naturally went to his broad shoulders. I couldn't speak. He pulled me flush to his body and moved a hand from my waist to caress my cheek. We were acclimating ourselves to the space and to each other's bodies. My hand went to his face and felt his scruff.

His hand on my back was strong, pulling me up and in, and then his mouth was on mine. Slow and gentle at first. He laid playful slow kisses on my bottom lip until I opened to him and we were kissing harder, faster. Our tongues were dancing, gently teasing. He was a good kisser. I knew that immediately. I had no awareness of my surroundings, only a feeling of wanting more, as if we had kissed before. Nothing awkward, no teeth clanking. His hand went to my neck and then he pulled away and trailed kisses down my jawline to my collarbone. I was going to spontaneously combust. If he was the ugliest guy in the world, I would have still been attracted to him. It was an easy decision standing there on the stage, blindfolded, while Gavin nibbled on my ear.

He slowed and stopped just after placing one last delicate kiss on my lips.

"Whoa!" Ling shouted. "It just got way hotter in here."

Gavin and I laughed nervously. We were no longer touching. It felt odd. I wanted to bury my head in his chest.

I was still standing motionless when Ling said, "Not yet, Gavin. We have some questions first before you take off your blindfold."

He clapped his hands together. "I'm just dying for that gift card, you know?"

I could tell he was being sarcastic.

"Okay, Gavin," Ling said, "what do you think Penny was trying to tell you with that kiss?"

"Tell me? I think I did most of the talking. Wouldn't you agree, honey?"

I laughed abruptly and nervously.

He went on. "Confidence, maybe."

No one had ever said that to me.

"What about you, Penny?"

"It was . . . sensual."

"Yes," Gavin agreed, nonchalantly.

"Okay, you can take off your blindfolds."

I pulled mine over my head. He did the same. We saw each other. He was gorgeous, with warm green eyes and an angled jawline. His full lips were slightly parted. He was staring at me, squinting, and then he said softly, "Hi, beauty."

"Hi."

"Do you two feel closer now, or is it strange?" asked Ling.

I shrugged absentmindedly as I stared at Gavin.

He smiled. "How 'bout I buy you a coffee? I have connections around here, you know?" He winked. We were lost, and totally ignoring Ling.

"You guys," Ling said. We both turned and looked at her. She had her hand on her hip. "We're not done yet."

"Okay," I mumbled.

"Penny, are you more nervous now than you were before? Look at Gavin and answer the question."

I turned to face him. "Yes." Oh my god, his eyes were like truth serum to me.

There was a small, tight smile playing on his lips. "Why?" he asked.

"I don't know . . . I like you." *Did I just say that? What is wrong with me? He's stunning me with his lips. My brain is not working. I've been drugged.*

Now his smile grew into a wide grin. I looked down and noticed my nipples were hard and obviously peeking through my thin, tight tank top.

He followed my eyes, then looked back up at my lips. I crossed my arms over my chest.

"How about that coffee to warm you up?" he said.

That's not why my nipples were hard. "Maybe."

For the first time since I had removed the blindfold, I looked around the room. The four other psych students were discussing something in the corner while Ling scoured her clipboard.

"Are we done?" Gavin asked.

"Yeah, I guess we can call it. I'll walk you guys out," Ling said.

Gavin took my hand unselfconsciously and led me off the stage. Our hands were clasped like it was the most normal thing in the world. In the holding room, Ling looked down at our linked fingers and scribbled something on her clipboard. She came over to my ear and said, "He's hot," loud enough for him to hear.

Gavin laughed.

"Here're your coffee cards." She handed four to me but only gave one to Gavin. They were ten dollars each.

"Hey, why'd you get four?"

"I'm a good negotiator," I said.

"Guess you're buying."

I had told P-Doug I'd come back after the study to run over our partner routine again at four, and it was already three fifteen.

"I don't have much time. I have a dance practice at four."

"Well, let's get goin', Boo."

The tension was dissipating. How could a guy be so confident while also being so natural and casual? It was charming. He led me toward the hall. "Bye, Ling!" I said.

She was looking at us with a wicked smile. "Bye, you two."

When we were about halfway down the hallway, we heard Ling and the other psych students clapping and cheering. Apparently they got what they needed.

"That was by far the weirdest thing I've ever done," I told Gavin.

I let go of his hand to put my sweatshirt back on. He walked quickly in front of me and pushed the glass doors open. The cold air blasted my face. He turned, grasped my neck with both hands, and kissed me again.

When he pulled away, his eyes were open. He was staring at my mouth. "It's freezing out here, huh?" he said.

"Again," I said.

He pushed me up against the building wall and kissed me, harder this time.

When he stopped, he asked, "Do you have a boyfriend?"

"No."

"Come on then. I don't want to be late for our first date."

"I . . . I mean, I have to . . ."

"Come on, Java Hut awaits." He was fun, spontaneous, full of life.

Inside the Java Hut, we went to the counter and Gavin pulled out his coffee card. "I'm treating, even though you managed to swindle four of these out of those poor psych majors. I mean, we both know I did most of the work back there."

"Hey, I wasn't so bad."

His expression turned serious. "No, you definitely weren't bad. Now what'll it be, little dancing queen?"

"I'll have a green tea."

"Ahh, she's healthy, too. I'll take a large quadruple caramel macchiato with whole milk," he said to the cashier, and then looked at me and smirked. "It's like liquid crack. I'm gonna be so high at dance practice."

"Wait, what?"

"Come sit," he said, changing the subject.

I noticed the design on his T-shirt for the first time. It was orange with an illustration of a pickle wearing sunglasses. Underneath the pickle were the words *Dill With It.*

I laughed as I sat down beside him. "What are you laughing about?" he asked.

"Your T-shirt's funny."

"Thanks." He took my hands and held them across the table. It felt like we were on a real date, which was giving me whiplash. I'd known him for less than an hour. I slipped my hands out of his grasp and clasped them in my lap.

"Penny, we practically had sex with our mouths while wearing blindfolds. I mean, baby, you did *not* hold back."

"Neither did you."

"You know I knew you were pretty before I agreed to do the experiment, right? Tracy told me so."

"Oh yeah?"

"Yeah, but I had no idea you'd be so uniquely beautiful. You're transcendent. You really are."

My stomach did a somersault. "Th-thank you."

"You're welcome." He smiled. Gavin had a childlike quality about him. I liked the way he lied about not being nervous, and then easily admitted he was. He wasn't afraid to tell the truth, and he didn't seem to get embarrassed easily.

"I don't think coming to dance practice will be very exciting for you."

"I do," he fired back.

"Well, um—"

"Please?"

"Um . . . okay, but no critiquing me."

"You're my best friend, I would never insult you," he said with a serious look.

"Ha! Funny."

"It's true. At the moment, you're my best friend in the world."

"You're an interesting guy, Gavin."

"Interesting in a handsome and charming kind of way?"

"Yes." The truth serum was still in effect. Maybe it always would be with him. *Why was I thinking of always?* "How old are you?" I asked.

"Twenty-three. Don't say it! I'll do it for you. Yes, I'm on the five-year plan. This is my last year but I did change my major three times, so you know . . . that kind of extended my glorious time here."

"What came before engineering?"

"Ahh, you were listening. English, then music."

"Wow, you're all over the place."

"Thank you, Penny. You're not the first to say so." He shook his head in mock irritation.

"I didn't mean to—"

"I'm kidding. I don't get offended by it. It doesn't matter how long it takes me. I'm an only child, and the first of all my cousins to go to college, so I get points for that."

"Actually, I'm all over the place, too. I'm conflicted about dance and how I'll turn it into a career."

Gavin took a sip of his coffee and started to choke. "There are a lot of ways to make a career out of dance."

"I've done ballet and contemporary dance my whole life, but my parents . . . well, my mom actually wanted me to have a degree in something more solid. And maybe . . . probably I'm not good enough to be a professional dancer."

"Why do you have such a low opinion of yourself?"

"I don't. I mean, I don't know."

He shook his head and then looked at the clock. "Shit, it's almost four. We gotta go," he said. I liked how he said *we.* I liked his concern for me.

He grabbed my hand. "Let's walk and talk. So where do you live, Penny?"

"Five minutes away . . . with my parents."

That didn't seem to faze him. "Yeah, my dad lives in town, too. I used to live with him but couldn't stand it, so now I share an apartment off-campus with my friend, Mike."

"How do you pay for rent?"

"I work at Pete's, that gas station garage in town. I work on cars and do oil changes and pump gas and stuff, mostly at night. It pays the bills."

"I wish I could work, but practice is too demanding."

We were walking into the performance hall. Professor Douglas was talking to Joey at the front of the stage.

Gavin and I walked down the aisle toward them. "Hey guys," I said. "This is my friend, Gavin. He's gonna stay to watch practice so he can give me a ride home. My car's still broken down."

Gavin looked at me and squinted. I guess I had surprised him with that.

Joey rolled his eyes. "Now you're bringing boyfriends to practice?"

"He's just a friend—"

"Yes," Gavin said. "She is."

Professor Douglas turned his attention to Gavin. "Welcome. Have a seat anywhere you'd like."

"Does this mean I can bring friends to practice, too?" Joey asked.

"She needs a ride home," P-Doug argued.

"I bet she does." Joey was scanning Gavin up and down.

I looked out of the corner of my eye at Gavin and watched him wink at Joey. When I elbowed him, he said,

"What? I'm gonna help you out here and kill the little prince with kindness. I think he likes me anyway."

"I'm sure he does. He thinks he can convert anyone."

"Get warmed up, Penny," Professor Doug said.

"I gotta get up there. Sit by Doug. He's cool."

Gavin nodded and took a seat.

5. Fourteen Years Ago

GAVIN

What was I doing chasing this girl around? Until an hour ago, I literally believed we were put on this planet to eat and fuck. Now all I wanted to do was wash her hair and suck on her ears. What was happening to me?

I was currently hungover and tweaking from coffee. And this girl, Penny, the dancer with the almost black eyes and silky hair, was making me crazy.

I want to swim around in her dark oceans. I'm gonna fuck her. No, I want to cook breakfast for her in my underwear. I want to kiss her with a mouth full of hot chocolate, then fuck her.

I was confused.

"Hey man, so what do you think?" the professor asked.

"She's amazing." That was a gigantic understatement. She was warming up, and I was observing her flexibility. Joey had his hand on his hip, staring at us from the edge of the stage. I waved at him and batted my eyelashes. He looked embarrassed. I could tell he was jealous of Penny. She danced beautifully. It was impossible to take my eyes off her. Not to mention I could see her nipples through her tank top.

"She and Joey have been partners for two years. They really are the best we have here," Doug said.

"What's his problem?"

"A crisis of confidence, perhaps. Not unusual for seniors."

Penny was doing this insane jump across the stage while Joey Jackoff was just standing there.

"She's so good," I said.

"Yeah, almost too good for this place."

Joey took his eyes off Penny for one second and seemed to miss his mark where he was supposed to catch her and fall back, shielding her from hitting the stage. She fell to the floor with a thud and landed on her knees.

"Are you fucking kidding, Joey?" she yelled.

"Settle down, Penny," Doug said.

My little firecracker had a temper and I liked it.

Doug went to the front of the stage and ordered Penny to stay on the ground. "Penny, straighten your legs and stretch them out. Just rest for a bit, I'll get you some ice." He turned toward Joey. "You're out today. Get it together. Let's hope this isn't a serious injury."

Joey shrugged and pranced off the stage like he didn't care. Just before he was out of view, he turned and looked at me. I flipped him off.

I walked toward Penny as she sat with her knee propped up. She was watching me.

"That guy is such a fucking baby. I'm sick of his shit," she said.

Penny didn't seem to be in pain, though she did look extremely pissed. Doug ran off to get ice.

"Are you okay?" I asked her.

"Yeah, but he could have really messed up my knee."

She stood up easily and began stretching, bending over right in front of me as I watched her with intense focus. I'm not gonna lie, I was embarrassingly turned on.

Doug had a strange look on his face when he returned with the ice. "Do you even need this?" he said to her.

"No, I'm fine. I just wanted to get rid of Joey. He's ruining this routine for me, Doug."

"I'll have a talk with him. He'll get it. The level of difficulty on his part is minimal, but we all know how he is. He doesn't like to be in the shadow."

"Put a goddamn spotlight on him if it's going to patch up his ego. I don't want to get hurt." She was so assertive and smart and witty. I was totally into it.

Doug kept looking at me like he was sizing me up. I smiled.

He put his attention back on Penny. "Can you continue, or do you want to call it a night?"

"No, I want to try the jump a few more times. I want to work through this bruise, otherwise I'll be sore in the morning."

Doug looked at me again.

"You're not thinking . . . ?" Penny said.

"Well, he looks strong."

Before I even let the conversation go any further, I said, "I can't dance to save my life. Seriously, two left feet. Just awful . . . a spectacle, really." It wasn't entirely true. Back in Hollywood, where I grew up with my mom, she had taught me how to dance, but I wasn't about to jump around on a stage in a pair of tights.

"No, we just need you for the lifts," Doug said.

I would get to hold Penny? My eyes lit up. "Lift?"

"But he won't have the form, Doug."

"No faith in me, Little P?"

She smiled. "It's more complicated than that."

"No, Penny. He's got the strength and I want to get you off your feet. Work on balance for a bit."

If my roommate Mike were here witnessing this, I'd definitely get an earful. He was always heckling me about falling in love in five minutes, then out of love five minutes later.

Last month, after dating Kimber for only four days, I got the word *Kimbird* tattooed on my chest. Three days after that, she was sleeping with a guy from the basketball team and I didn't even care. A month before, it was Chelsea, who had a pet rat named Amadeus that sat on her shoulder like a parrot. Before that it was Lena, who liked to be spanked—hard—every time we had sex. I loved women, especially the weird ones. But Penny was more unique and talented and beautiful than any girl I had ever met.

I looked at my watch. I had to be at the garage in fifty minutes.

Screw it; give me the damn tights.

"I can help, but I only have about twenty minutes before I have to bolt."

"Oh, bummer," Penny said. "I was hoping you could look at my car in the parking lot. It's broken down and I actually do need a ride."

Doug was confused.

"Did I say twenty minutes? I meant an hour and twenty

minutes." Who cares if I was late? Pete could deal with it. I hadn't been to work late in over a week.

"Take off your boots," Penny said as she stretched.

"Gladly. Anything else you'd like me to take off?"

God, I couldn't stop looking at her underwear through her sheer tights, or were they pantyhose? Who cares.

She smirked. "Gavin, get serious. This isn't a social experiment. If you drop me, I'll kill you."

"I won't drop you."

"Work on the superman lift first," Doug said.

"God, that lift is hard," she said under her breath. She was nervous. "Okay, stagger your legs like this." She showed me and I mimicked her. "You need a solid center of gravity. I'll jump and you'll lift me over your head."

"Like *Dirty Dancing*?"

"Kind of, yes. Just don't drop me, Casanova. I'll handle the rest."

"I won't, I promise."

She placed my hands on her hips. "This is where you'll be lifting me from, which means most of my body will be over your head and back. If you lift me too hard and fast, I'll go flying and come crashing down, probably on my head. I could die or be paralyzed."

"No pressure," I said.

"How tall are you anyway?"

"Six-two."

"Great." She wasn't smiling. "I don't know why I'm agreeing to do this."

The music came on but it was different. I recognized it immediately. It was a cover of Bob Dylan's "Just Like a Woman," sung by Jeff Buckley. How fitting.

"God, I love this song," I said.

"I love him, too. You ready?"

"I can play this for you later if you want."

"I'd like that," she said.

"It's such a perfect song for right now."

"Why do you say that?" she asked.

"I'll tell you someday."

We were five inches apart. Our chests were heaving. And we liked the same music. How the hell was this happening?

"You ready to throw me in the air or what, Gavin?"

Right at the lyric, "She makes love just like a woman," she ran toward me, I picked her up, and a moment later she was over my head. I could feel her strength in my hands. We were steady. I knew she made love just like a woman; I could feel it in my fingertips.

Doug clapped. "Beautiful. Hold it. Beautiful, just beautiful."

It felt like she weighed nothing.

"Okay, Gavin, you're going to cradle her now. Watch her knee."

When I dropped her into my arms, she giggled, but I was frozen . . . mesmerized.

"What?" she said. "Why are you staring at me?"

"I don't know." I held her.

All of a sudden I didn't want to fuck her anymore. I mean I did, but more than that, I wanted to get to know her.

When I set her down, she said, "Well done. You're an old pro."

"That was easy."

Doug came onto the stage. "Don't worry, that was it,"

he told me. "We're not going to ask you to dance. I wanted Penny to test something. How'd you feel?" he asked her.

"Strong," she said.

"Good. Keep your head up. I'll bring Joey in for extra conditioning. He needs to regain his confidence."

Doug shook my hand and said, "Thanks a lot, Gavin. This whole thing is about trust. It seems like you two have it."

She trusted me?

"Penny and Joey have struggled with their lifts lately. It's not always easy to find the right partner. It requires a subtle alchemy. You know? A little bit of magic."

I looked over at Penny, who was squinting at me with the same peculiar look I'm sure I was giving her. I didn't take my eyes off her when I responded to Doug. "Well, she is my best friend, so yeah, the trust is there."

Penny laughed and shook her head.

After she gathered her stuff and we headed to the door, she turned to me. "Sure you don't mind taking a look at my car and giving me a ride? I live really close by."

Giving me a ride?

"I'm sure I don't mind. Let's hit it."

I was converting every word of our conversation into a sexual proposition. I needed to get a grip.

6. Nine Months Ago

PENNY

Checking my calendar for the fifth time that morning, it occurred to me that it was the first day since my son was born that I didn't have some obligation that had to do with raising a child, running a household, or being married. There were no soccer practices or guitar lessons after school. It wasn't my carpool day. I didn't have a grocery list to fulfill, or science project supplies to buy, or bills to pay, or laundry to do. I just had coffee to drink and a backyard to stare at.

I kissed my son good-bye for the day, came back inside, and took a bubble bath. I knew it would be the highlight of my day, so I took my time. It was fall but sunny and warm out. I decided to shave my legs on the off chance that someone would see them. My husband had been at work since before I even woke up, and he'd be away for the next two days on business in Michigan or Minnesota. Some place colder than Fort Collins, was all I knew. He stopped telling me where he was going, and frankly, I stopped caring.

My life was usually an exercise in completing the same list of responsibilities over and over again. It was mundane. I felt like I was losing myself, who I was, and what my dreams were. But I had my bed and a roof over my head—at least that's what my mother would tell me. And magically, there were only a few things to do today.

After turning up the heater to seventy-eight degrees, knowing it would piss off my husband, I walked around naked for a while and thought about masturbating, but I was too lazy. I weighed myself twice—once before I ate a bowl of cereal and once after. Then I went through all of Facebook . . . literally. I looked at the profile of every single person I was friends with from high school, and then I looked at the clock. It was only ten a.m.

I threw on a pair of tattered sweats, put on some music, stretched, and did some dancing in our loft, which my husband had converted into a tiny studio for me. My only outlet for creativity.

At eleven, Gavin texted me. This wasn't unusual. He always texted me in the morning. He lived an hour away, in Denver, where he owned a garage and made his own hours so he could come and go as he pleased. The man had two college degrees but preferred working on cars and living in a studio apartment above a tattoo parlor. If Gavin wanted to add a new tattoo to his collection on a whim, he could easily do just that. There was no cohesiveness to his ink, no well-planned sleeve. Though most of his forearms were covered, it was by piecemeal artwork. He didn't have health insurance but he had plenty of tattoos. That was Gavin.

Not that I could judge him. I was thirty-five and had never had a job. I'd had some very random luck with stock investments but that wasn't exactly a career.

Gavin: Hey . . .

                                        Me: What's up? I'm dancing.

There was a long pause, so I took my phone downstairs to pour myself more coffee.

Gavin: You're dancing?

                                        Me: I was, now I'm drinking
                                        coffee. What's up?

Gavin: I'm lost, P. I need you.

It had been a long time since Gavin had said anything like that to me.

                                        Me: Where are you?

Gavin: In your driveway.

I laughed in shock, then ran to the door and swung it open. It had been two months since I last saw him—almost the longest we'd gone since meeting each other fourteen years ago in Ling's psych study.

He was standing on the porch right outside, looking at me with sad, tired eyes. "What's going on?" I asked.

He leaned his body to one side to look past me into the house. "Where's whathisface?"

"You were in our wedding, you know his name, and he's away on business for two days. Tell me what's wrong?"

"Milo?"

"He's at school."

"I didn't want to impose."

"How long have you been out in the driveway?"

"An hour or so."

"Doing what?"

"Staring at your house."

"That's creepy. Get in here, dork."

I stood aside so he could come in. He didn't move. He was wearing his usual boots, jeans, and a T-shirt, with no jacket or flannel. He had his hands deep in his pockets, his arms pressed to his body, and he was shaking.

"What are you waiting for? Come in, you're cold." It wasn't that cold out but he was practically shivering.

He walked in and basically collapsed into my arms, his warm breath on my neck. "Fuck, Penny."

"What?"

"He's dying. For real."

I knew he was talking about his dad. He was the only man Gavin gave a shit about.

"Oh no. No, no." My heart was broken in an instant. Broken for Frank, Gavin's dad, whom I loved, and for Gavin, my best friend, whom I also loved.

His dad lived in the house at the end of our block, so when Gavin came to Fort Collins, he usually came to visit both his dad and my family . . . or his dad and me, rather. He loved Milo and got along fine with my husband, but when he came over, it was to see me. I knew that.

"I'm so sorry," I told him as I held him. He started to cry. "Talk to me."

I took his hand and led him to our living room. His eyes were puffy and red. He pointed to our couch and asked, "When did you get that?"

"Recently. Buckley chewed up the other one."

Buckley, our yellow Lab—think *Marley and Me*—destroyed everything.

"You have a white couch, P." It was a statement of fact as well as an accusation.

"Do you want coffee?" I asked him, ignoring the comment.

"Espresso, please, though I'm afraid I'll spill it on your white couch." He was still emotional, but now he was laughing a little as he sat down.

Inside the kitchen, I watched him as I turned on the espresso machine. He was running his hand over the white fabric.

"Are you making fun of my couch?"

"No. Well, kind of."

"I thought you were sad and lost. Not too sad and lost to make fun of my furniture, apparently?" I finished the drink and handed him the tiny mug of espresso.

"I am sad."

I plopped down next to him and crossed my legs. He took a sip and set the mug down on the glass table in front of us before glancing out the big back window. "You have a way better yard than my dad. I should have helped him more over the years, with his yard and everything. I should have been here. I'm mad at myself."

Gavin's dad had remarried a woman named Jackie

when we were in our mid-twenties. She and Gavin didn't get along. Gavin thought she was an alien . . . seriously. He said aside from her eyes being too big and far apart to be human, she also had no family and never shared her background with his dad. He got superstoned one night and called the FBI and reported her to them, saying she was using some woman's body as a host. The next day, when the THC had worn off, he called everyone who knew the story and apologized. But later, when he was sober, he told me he *still* thought she was an alien.

He didn't talk to his dad for three years. It was only after the divorce that they finally made amends. Gavin regretted shutting out his dad during the Jackie phase. His mom still lived in Los Angeles, but he rarely spoke to her. The tension between them was much harder to get over.

"Where is Buckley anyway?" he asked.

"In the garage. I put him in there when I dance; otherwise he'll jump all over me."

"I get it."

"I know. He's hyper but he's still a puppy. He'll calm down."

"No, I mean I get why someone would want to jump all over you when you're dancing."

I rolled my eyes. I either completely ignored his comments like that or I'd say something to shock him. "You wanna go fuck upstairs? I put these sweats on especially for you."

He looked at my tattered sweats and stained T-shirt. "You still look hot."

"Gavin." I gave him my typical "time to change the subject" look.

"Relax, I'm messing with you. Though you do still have that thing."

"What thing?"

"Transcendent beauty." He took a long breath and released it. "He has prostate cancer, stage four. It's spread all over. He didn't tell me. He fucking didn't tell me, Penny. Not until he knew he only had months or weeks to live."

"Why? Why would he do that?"

"Because he didn't want to burden me, I guess."

His face fell. He swallowed. His eyes welled up again and mine did, too. "Oh Gavin, I'm so sorry."

He fell into me again and buried his face in my chest. "He's all I have left. I have no family . . . nothing."

"But what about Jenn, and your mom?"

"My mom's a lost cause. In rehab again. Her stupid boyfriend is paying for it. And I broke up with Jenn. Six months ago."

"What?" I was shocked. All revelations to me. It had been his longest relationship to date. Three years, and they were about to move in with each other. "Why didn't you tell me? You tell me everything."

"I don't know. I thought you'd be mad. I knew you liked her."

"I *am* mad. She was sweet and kind and loving and—"

"She was a soul crusher, P. She was like the joke police. She never laughed at a single one of my jokes."

"You broke up with your girlfriend of three years because *she didn't laugh at your jokes?*"

"Yes, that's a deal breaker, don't you think? Move your legs, I want to lie down."

He put his head in my lap. I ran my fingers through his

hair. It was intimate, but we were intimately close friends. He was truly my best friend, and there were a million reasons why he was—more than Kiki, more than Ling, more than my own husband.

"What are you gonna do?"

"Move in with him and take care of him until he goes." A stray tear ran down his cheek. I wiped it away.

"What about the garage?"

"I'll hire someone to run it."

"And your apartment."

"Really, Penny? I'm pretty much the most untethered person you know. I could move to a mountain in fucking Bangladesh and no one would care. The garage runs itself. My apartment is a shithole. I'm moving here and taking care of my dad. The bonus is that I'll get to see you more. If there's a silver lining around this black cloud of doom, then that's it."

"I'd care," I said quietly.

"What?" He squinted.

"If you moved to Bangladesh. I'd care."

Having Gavin around more wasn't going to be easy on my family for obvious reasons. I never lied to my husband or cheated on him, but he was jealous of what Gavin and I had. And Milo didn't understand it either. Selfishly, I was happy Gavin would be down the street from me, but I could already feel the strain it would put on my family.

I rubbed my hand over his forearm and noticed a new tattoo right next to the figure of a dancer and the words *Pretty Girls Make Graves*. He never admitted it to me before, but I knew that particular tattoo was one of several he had gotten in reference to our relationship. The new tattoo was of a feather with an arrow through it, and it was still scabbing, like he'd gotten it a day or two ago.

"What's this about?" I asked as I rubbed my thumb over it.

"Nothing. I don't know. My dad likes archery." He closed his eyes. "I just wanted to hurt yesterday. More than I was hurting already."

"Did it work? Did you hurt more?"

"No. Nothing has ever hurt more."

"Then why do you keep getting them?" I asked.

"I guess I'm not as much of a quitter as you think."

"I never thought you were a quitter."

"You don't like my tattoos but half of them are about you." Confrontational Gavin pulled no punches. He spoke the truth.

"You've never told me that before."

"Did I have to?" He was choked up again. He took another deep, loud breath and released it like he was trying to blow pain out from the inside of his chest.

"You're not alone. You'll always have me."

"You have your own family," he said, his voice low and shaky.

It pained me to see him like this. "You're my best friend. You're my family, too."

He sat up and tried to collect himself. "Penny, why isn't your husband your best friend? Answer me that. I need to know."

He asked me this often, yet he referred to me as his best friend to everyone, including his girlfriend of three years. He had been calling me his best friend since the day we met. But he was angry and raising his voice at me, calling me out. "And why don't you have female friends, besides Ling? Why don't you hang out with your sister more? She lives right here in town."

"Come here." I put my legs over his lap and held him to my chest again. "Because I love you, and I'm allowed to love you."

"You didn't answer my question."

"Be quiet."

A few minutes later, his breathing slowed and he fell asleep on my chest. After five minutes, I shimmied out from underneath him, got up, and covered him with a blanket. He was exhausted.

There's no way to explain to people what Gavin and I meant to each other. It was socially unacceptable for a woman to share that kind of intimacy with a man after she'd been married for fourteen years to someone else, even if it wasn't sexual. Your husband is supposed to be your everything: your lover, your best friend, your financial partner, your confidant. I never understood that. How can you put all of that on one person? My relationship with Gavin had nothing to do with a single role my husband personally couldn't fulfill. Or an emptiness in our marriage. My relationship with Gavin was rooted in love. Maybe a kind of love people would never understand.

After tinkering around for a couple of hours, I left the house at two fifteen to pick up Milo, and when we returned, Gavin was gone. I tried calling him but he didn't answer.

Two hours later he sent me a text: my bow.

Gavin: I love you, too.

7. Fourteen Years Ago

PENNY

Gavin took his flannel off, tied it around his waist, and popped the hood of my car. He was leaning over it, inspecting the engine parts.

"Lance said I might have flooded the engine."

Still bent, he turned his head to look at me. There was humor in his expression. "Who's Lance?"

"A microbiology major my dad introduced me to."

"A microbiologist said you have a flooded engine?"

"Well, he's a student, but yes."

"Sounds like a genius. Can I see your keys?"

When I handed them over, he walked toward the driver's side to open the door.

"I have a bunch of dance stuff in there. It probably smells bad."

He looked back at me and smirked. His long legs barely fit in my tiny car. He turned the engine over once and there was nothing.

"It's your battery. I have jumper cables in my car. Do you want to walk over to the other parking lot with me, and we'll drive my car back?"

My feet were killing me at the moment. "Do you mind if I just wait here?"

"Actually, I do mind." He looked down at my slippered feet. "I'm not leaving you alone in a dark parking lot. Come on, I'll give you a piggyback ride."

Was he crazy? He bent in front of me. "Jump on."

Yes, he was crazy. When I jumped on his back, he popped me up higher like I was as light as a feather. "Thank you for doing this. Do you want my Java Hut gift cards or something?"

"I was hoping you'd let me take you out this weekend."

I tensed up. "Gavin—"

"Penny."

"I, um . . ."

He stopped walking so he could set me down and tie the laces of his Converse. He was still crouched when he looked up at me. Something in his expression made it impossible for me to say no to him.

"Okay, I'll go out with you, but I'm really slammed and . . . I don't really date . . . I don't really have time to . . ."

He motioned to his back, "Come on, get back on."

When he stood, he pulled my legs around his waist and said, "You're a tiny little thing but you've got some legs on you."

"I'm five-six. I'm not that small."

"So you made out with me, went on a date with me, let me throw you in the air in your underwear—braless, I might add—and then carry you across campus on my back, but you're still gonna put me in the friend zone?"

"I said I would go out with you."

"I heard a whole lot of excuses in there, though."

"I thought I was your best friend?"

"I mean, you are, but I was at least hoping for, you know, room to grow."

My heart was beating fast against his back. There were at least five reasons why I shouldn't have been messing around with him, especially when I was practically failing half of my nondance classes. I'd just put too much time into practicing dance. I had to. Maybe in some attempt to prove to my mother choosing dance would be worth it.

I liked Gavin and I wanted him to be my friend. I was finally making connections with people. I knew if we hopped into bed with each other, it would be over. I'd seen it a million times with the girls in high school. Guys get weird after you sleep with them.

He set me down in front of a beat-up old car with a mismatched paint job. "Okay, BFF, this is Charlize. Hop in."

"You named your car after Charlize Theron? This thing doesn't look like it can run, let alone start my car."

He chuckled. "Just get in."

The interior was pristine black leather, the dashboard was recently polished, and there were zero empty Big Gulp cups or Slim Jim wrappers in sight. He took care of his car well.

"It's nice inside," I said.

"I rebuilt the engine, too, and I'm saving up to get her painted. Black on black. When I'm finished, this car will be envied, coveted, and obsessed over by many."

The engine came purring to life. "What kind of car is it?"

"Charlize is a '67 Chevelle. She's my girl."

"Perfect. Then why do you need to take *me* on a date?"

When he came to a stop sign, he put the car in neutral and revved the engine. "Do you hear her singing, Penny? Do you hear that beautiful music?"

"This conversation is ridiculous."

We were both laughing by this point. He studied me for a moment, like he was trying to read my mind. "You like me, though. You *want* to go on a date with me." It wasn't a question.

"Cocky much?"

"Confident. Don't be mistaken."

"Why do you want to take me out so badly?"

"Fishing for more compliments, are we?" He'd caught me, but went on anyway. "Obviously you're beautiful. You have nice, you know, legs and . . . stuff."

"You're laughing. I don't think I'm really your type. I think you're messing with me. I'm not at all like Charlize Theron."

We pulled up to my car but he let Charlize idle before getting out. "You are so my type. Charlize—at least the actress—is not. I mean, she's gorgeous, in a blond, Amazonian, I-might-kill-and-eat-my-own-young kind of way, but I like your look better."

"Oh yeah? What's my look?"

"There's something dark about you . . . and interesting. Your creamy skin, your black hair. The way you move. Your mouth." He reached out to touch my cheek but I jerked away, breaking the seriousness of the moment.

"What do you mean I'm dark?"

He smiled and shrugged. "I don't know. Like I want to get naked with you and a Ouija board."

I burst out laughing.

"And your laugh . . . it's like the sound of someone squeezing the life out of a miniature trumpet. It's really cute."

"That is not a compliment. I have a nice laugh. And by the way, your voice is nasally when you're not trying to impress people."

He held his hand to his chest like he was offended, except he was still smiling. "I'm crushed. Penny, whatever your last name is—"

"Piper."

"Ha! Penny Piper? You've got to be kidding! That's either a children's book character or a porn star's name. Penny Piper picked a peck of pickled pep—"

"Stop! I know, trust me. I have to live with this name. My poor sister's name is Kiki Piper. Like we're fucking hobbits or something."

"Penny Piper is worse than Kiki Piper, hands down."

I cocked my head to the side. "Thanks."

"Just sayin'. What's your middle name?"

"Isabelle."

"I'm gonna call you PIP Squeak."

"Thank you. I can't wait."

"And by the way, I happen to have a deviated septum. That's why my voice sounds like this sometimes, you asshole. Now get out and help me with your car."

As we stepped out, he pointed to my Honda and said, "Try and start it when I tell you."

I stopped and turned to him. "What's your middle and last name?"

"Gavin Augusta Berninger."

"Regal," I said with a wink.

"I know, right?" He shrugged one arm like he was royalty or something.

"Is that French?"

"Yeah, my dad's family is French . . . sort of. Like, his great-great-grandfather came from France. No one in our family even speaks French."

"Hmm, not so regal anymore," I said.

"Whatever, Penny Piper."

Gavin did have that creamy French skin that I loved. God, I hated my name. My mom was seriously on quaaludes when she named us. She thought our names were cute, like we would be permanent children.

Once I was in my car, he hooked up the cables and revved the engine in good ole Charlize. "Go ahead!" he yelled.

My little Honda started right up. He got out and came over to my door as I was cranking up the heater. It was freezing and felt like it was going to snow. He motioned for me to roll down my window.

"So . . . not flooded. You can let your microbiologist friend know he should probably stick to amoebas and shit like that in the lab." He bent and looked through the window at some gauges on my dash. "Let it run for a few minutes."

I was shivering. "I hate the cold."

"You want me to get in there and warm you up?"

I ignored him. "Hey, aren't you gonna be late? Did you say you have to work?" I asked.

He looked at his watch. "I'm good. I'll unplug the cables and follow you home, okay? Just to make sure."

"You don't have to do that."

"I want to," he said as he was walking away.

Gavin really did follow me all the way home. After I pulled into the driveway, I got out and waved good-bye to him, but he rolled his window down.

"Wait, come here."

I jogged over to his car as it idled in the street. "What's up?"

"We're gonna hang out, right?"

I dug around in my bag for a pen. "Let me see your hand. Here's my house number and my email." I wrote it on his palm.

He kissed it before saying, "No cell phone?"

"Not yet. I asked for one for Christmas."

"You been naughty or nice?" He wiggled his eyebrows.

"Funny."

"Hey, by the way, thanks for making out with me," he said. "I gotta go. I need to get this tattooed on my hand." He pointed to my phone number.

I started laughing. "Bye, weirdo."

As I headed for the front door, he drove away and yelled out "Bye, PIP. I actually love your laugh. I want to hear it again tomorrow."

8. Fourteen Years Ago

PENNY

I didn't get a call or email from Gavin the next day, but I did see Ling the day after that. It was Friday, my dance conditioning day. It's basically a four-hour workout. No dancing, just strength training and stamina exercises. Joey was MIA of course, the piece of shit. Doug said he'd find him and let him know he was on thin ice, but I knew it would piss off Joey even more.

Ling was in the workout room, staring at all the male dancers while I finished barre squats.

"So, hot mama," she said as we walked into the locker room. "Looks like that Blind Kiss study wasn't so bad after all."

I was stuffing my dance crap into a bag on one of the benches. "Yeah, Gavin's pretty hot. He's a good kisser, too. I just don't have time for boys right now. I have to train hard until the end of the year and get the rest of my grades up. But, yeah, he's cool."

She was blinking at me through her glasses like she had no idea what I was talking about. "Um, helloooo, earth to Penny. Hot Kissing Machine is sitting on the curb outside, waiting for you. You didn't know that?"

"He is?"

"Yeah. I asked what he was doing and he said, 'Waiting for my BFF to finish conditioning.'"

"Oh my God." *What is he doing here?* "Oh Ling, I totally stink. I can't go out there. I mean, I smell really bad. I can't see him right now."

"I doubt he cares. Look at you." She waved her hand up and down my body. "Anyway, I thought you didn't have time for boys?"

"I don't. I need a way out. What are you doing tonight?"

"Going to a party in my building. You want to go to a stupid party with a bunch of my psych friends instead of hanging out with Hot Kissing Machine?"

"No. I mean yes. I want to go to the stupid party." I couldn't be alone with him; I knew that.

"Okay, suit yourself. Come by at eight. I live in those Greenwood Apartments with the red doors. Number twelve on the first floor."

"I'll be there."

"Cool," she said. "Have fun with your BFF. I can't wait to hear all about it."

"I'm not—"

She ignored me and left humming the "K-I-S-S-I-N-G" melody. My heart was racing. I walked out as Gavin was taking one last puff of a cigarette. He had an eye closed against the smoke.

"Hey, PIP," he said. "I missed you." He stubbed the

cigarette out in the planter and stood with his arms out for a hug.

I stared at him, stock-still, with my bag slung over my shoulder.

"Friendly hug?" he said, still holding his arms out.

"I smell pretty bad."

"Me too. We'll be perfect together. What did Doug call it? Alchemy?"

I hesitated and then finally gave in and hugged him, sort of the way I hug my dad: with my face in his chest, one arm slung over his shoulder and the other around his waist. The awkward one-armed hug.

He patted me on the head like a dog. "Okay," he said, "I'll take it."

I didn't want to lift both my arms and unleash my horrendous body odor. He was holding me when I mumbled into his shirt, "I just worked out for four hours, and I was gonna take a shower at home because the heater is broken in the locker room, and it's freezing in there, and I didn't feel like getting hypothermia on a Friday night, so I decided that I would just . . . you know take a shower later—"

"You're rambling, Penny Lane."

I pulled away to take him in. His hand was wrapped up and it looked like there was grease on the bandage. His longish hair was going everywhere and he was wearing black faded jeans, black boots, and a black T-shirt with a hole in the shoulder.

"Did something happen to you. Did you get hit by a car?"

"Ha ha, funny girl. No, I just came from work. I don't have class on Fridays so I usually work all day Friday. And now I've got the whole night free for you."

Oh God. "What happened to your hand?"

"Oh, nothing. I just had to cover some fresh ink."

"Huh?"

He grinned. "A new tattoo."

"Do you have a lot of tattoos?"

"I have a few. My roommate Mike is a tattoo artist."

That threw me. Not too many students I knew were living with tattoo artists. "How'd you meet Mike? Does he go here?"

"No. Ha! Mike is forty. We're in a band together. Nothing serious, just kind of a hobby band."

Who *was* this person? He was like a college mascot meets Eddie Vedder. "What do you do in the band?"

"I sing a little and play the guitar."

He wasn't smiling anymore. He was looking through me again.

"What?" I said.

"Nothing."

"So what's the tattoo of?" I asked, pointing to his hand.

"I already told you what I was getting. Your email and phone number, silly."

Oh, he was laying the charm on thick now. "I don't believe you."

He ripped the bandage off, and sure enough, he'd gotten my email and phone number tattooed onto the palm of his hand in my own handwriting. "Are you kidding? Is that real? Why would you do that?"

"I told you I would. I wanted to and I'm not a liar."

"But it's permanent."

"I didn't want it to wash off." He blinked and looked down at the ground. Was this Gavin being embarrassed?

"Well, you didn't *use* the number or email. I thought you'd call me?" I was trying to catch him off guard.

"I didn't have to because I saw your car and figured you were in there practicing. I thought I'd hang out here until you were done. See how the Honda's doing."

"How long have you been waiting?"

He shrugged. "An hour or so."

My eyes went wide. He had been waiting on the curb outside the dance studio for an hour. "The Honda is good, but that's not why you're here. I still can't believe you tattooed my number on your palm. What if my number changes?"

"I'll still call it just for fun, and tell whoever owns it that it used to belong to the most beautiful girl in Fort Collins."

"Oh geez, here we go."

"Do you want to go out with me tonight?"

"I actually have plans. I'm sorry." I was so glad I didn't have to lie. "I just told Ling I'd go to a party at her apartment."

"Really?" He was serious, like I had broken his heart with that information.

"Yes, really."

"Oh, well, I guess I'll have to try again some other time." His voice was low, almost a whisper.

"You have my number," I said.

He chuckled. "That I do. Can we at least grab a coffee or something before you go home? I'll have you back here in an hour."

"A coffee?" I said, squinting.

"A beer?"

"Okay, a beer sounds more like it." I needed the liquid courage. I wasn't blindfolded anymore.

"We're gonna get along, Little P, I can tell. We can go to New Belgium and share a flight or two."

"Okay," I said.

I left my things in the Honda and hopped into Gavin's car, where we were immediately greeted by The Smiths on the radio. Gavin knew every word to "This Charming Man," and he also had a pretty decent singing voice. There's something about a man who can sing and isn't too shy to do it in front of a girl he's just met.

"You sing pretty well."

"I can't actually sing that well on my own. It's like I can only do impressions or something. That's why our band does a lot of covers. Hey, do you mind if we run by my apartment so I can grab a T-shirt? One that doesn't have a giant hole in it?"

"That's fine," I said, though I was feeling a little uneasy about going to his apartment.

When we got there, I was surprised to find a very clean, two-bedroom upstairs apartment with big windows that looked out onto the street in front. I followed him into the living room as he pointed things out. There was a little dog following us, nipping at my heels. Some kind of terrier.

"That's Jackie Chan, Mike's dog. You can pick him up; he's nice." I'd always wanted a dog, but my mom wouldn't allow it in her pristine house. "Mike's not home so make yourself comfortable. Kitchen's there, bathroom's there. This is my room."

I stood in the doorway and looked in. There were three guitars in the corner: two acoustic and one electric. "You said you'd play that one song for me."

He was looking in his open closet for a T-shirt. "You already forgot our song?"

I hadn't, though I had a feeling he had. "'Just Like a Woman,'" he said as he glanced over and smirked. "I'll play it for you soon enough. We need to get those beers first."

He did remember.

When he tore his T-shirt off, I almost passed out. He was built—thin but defined, and he had random tattoos every-where.

His jeans were hanging low and I couldn't take my eyes off his waist. Grabbing a T-shirt off a hanger, he turned and faced me as he pulled it over his head.

"Whatcha lookin' at, P?"

Oh, just your perfect body, and your jeans hanging off your hips. "Nothing," I said.

"Nothing?"

"Well, actually, I'm wondering what all your tattoos mean?"

"A lot of different things," he said. He pointed to the word *Kimbird* on his chest. "This one was a mistake."

"Are they all about girls?"

He laughed. "No. Are you kidding? That would be a lot of girls. I feel like you're getting a bad impression of me."

"Well, I know nothing about you." *Which begs the question . . . why am I in his apartment staring at his half-naked body?*

"This one is definitely about a girl." It was the word *Carissa* in script on the inside of his arm, just below his elbow. "The only girl I've ever loved."

"What happened between you and Carissa?"

"Do you really want to talk about my exes?"

"Well, I'm asking about you." And yes, I did want to talk about his exes.

Taking my hand and pulling me toward the door, he said, "We can talk about Kimber and Carissa over beers—that's fine—but you have to tell me everything about you, too."

A FEW MINUTES later, we pulled into the parking lot of the New Belgium. "I've never been here. Do you think they'll kick me out for wearing sweats and slippers?"

"You make sweats look good. Anyway, look at me. I'm a grease monkey. And it's a brewery: they don't care."

Once we were seated, we ordered a flight of beer to split. "So tell me about Kim and Carissa."

"Kimber? Well, that tattoo was a mistake for sure because we only dated for five minutes. Impulse purchase, I guess you could say."

"Next week you're probably going to say that about my phone number on your hand."

He smiled. "Never." He swiveled on his barstool and turned to face me while putting his hand on my knee, like it was the most natural thing in the world. "Carissa was different. I would have married that girl, but we were young. She broke up with me on my twenty-first birthday. She invited me to a restaurant for my birthday dinner and—"

"Wait, when is your birthday?"

"November eighth. I'm a Scorpio, can't you tell?"

It was true, I would have guessed that. "Yes, Scorpio, I can tell. I'm a Taurus."

"We're perfect together!" he shouted, practically loud enough for everyone in the brewery to hear.

"No, I actually think those two signs are totally incompatible," I said.

"Anyway, so she invited me to a birthday dinner, and when I walked into the restaurant I found her sitting at a table alone. I thought she'd invite some friends to celebrate, but it was just her. She was also wearing a do-rag, which I found peculiar."

He was looking up at the ceiling in deep thought.

"And then what . . . ?" I asked.

He took a sip of beer. "And then she said, 'I'm sorry I can't be with you. I'm wearing this do-rag so you won't be attracted to me and won't be sad about us breaking up.'"

"What?" I said.

"Yeah, I swear. That's what I loved about her. She was a freakin' weirdo."

"So how did you react?"

"I just stood up and walked out, and then I went and got drunk and showed up at her apartment in the middle of the night. I thought I would serenade her with my guitar, but she called the police on me."

I started laughing but his frown didn't crack. "I'm sorry," I said.

"She ruined me. I mean, really broke my heart. I have no idea why she did it; she just said we were too young."

"How old were you?" I took a sip of beer.

"Twelve," he deadpanned.

Beer literally came out of my nose. "What?"

"I told you, it was my twenty-first birthday. Don't you listen?" He handed me a napkin. I wasn't even remotely embarrassed for some reason. He went on, "She graduated and wanted to move to Denver. She's a writer . . . so she's totally whack. She got an English lit degree and wanted to be a performance artist in the city. She'll probably write about how she broke my heart. Then she'll reenact it onstage dressed as a fucking grasshopper or something."

"I still don't get the whole do-rag thing."

"That was just Carissa. Everything had to be for the sake of something else. I'm telling you, she'll write a book about it. This extremely feminine and beautiful girl shows up to her boyfriend's birthday dinner to break up with him while she's wearing a dirty wife-beater, paint-splattered overalls, and a do-rag. She just wants to be able to tell the story over and over again with all the embellishments, you know? And, like, who the fuck does that?"

"And you liked this girl?"

"I loved her. The only one so far."

Maybe Gavin didn't have the best taste in women, which had me wondering what he thought of me. I needed to be responsible. I was not his type.

"I hate that Ouija board game, just FYI."

His eyes shot open. "Where'd that come from?"

"You mentioned it earlier. See, I do listen." He stuck his tongue out at me. "I think you might have me pegged wrong. I'm not this dark, interesting person. I basically have no hobbies, and even fewer friends—which is why I *have* to leave soon to get ready for Ling's party; it's already six, and I don't want to miss it."

"But you haven't told me enough about yourself to even peg you. That whole Ouija board thing was just about your look. Anyway, I can drive you home and then to Ling's, if you want? You probably shouldn't drive anyway. And aren't you starving? I'm starving. Let's grab a quick bite."

He was a fast talker, but not in a bad way. I loved that about him. I wanted to spend more time with him, but I didn't do well eating around other people. "I don't know . . ." I said.

"I know a burger place—"

"I don't eat meat."

"Are you a vegetarian?"

"No, I actually just don't eat red meat," I told him. My plan was not working. I needed to give in and just go with it or else I wasn't going to have enough time to get ready for Ling's party.

"Pizza?" he asked.

"Okay."

On the way to the local pizza joint, San Filippo's, he said, "So tell me about all your exes."

I laughed. "That's a short story. I've never really had a long-term boyfriend. I've just dated here and there. Anyway, like I told you, I'm not dating this year. It's just too intense with dance and finals and everything."

"You did mention that . . . like, five times. But here we are, Penny. Getting a drink and pizza . . . and now I'm gonna meet your parents in a few. I would call this a date."

If I brought Gavin home to my parents, they would literally have me committed. He'd tattooed our phone number onto the palm of his hand! That would be enough to put them off, never mind his other random tattoos and the fact that he was basically sex on two legs. I guess my parents didn't have to know that we met by sucking face blindfolded, though.

Once inside San Filippo's, I ordered another beer and a slice of cheese pizza. I never ate like this, but I didn't want to draw attention to myself by not eating. Gavin had a Coke. I guess he was committed to being my designated driver, but

I didn't want him to go to the party with me. Already, we had taken the day too far. Or at least I had let my imagination take it too far.

He was currently rambling on and on about something, but I wasn't listening because I was fixated on the flexing muscles of his forearms. I imagined how they moved when he played the guitar . . . and did other things.

I remember having *the* conversation with my dad when I hit puberty. Naturally, my mom avoided the topic because she wanted me and Kiki to be her dollies forever. But my dad wouldn't have his eldest daughter walking around with her head up her ass.

He sat me down and proceeded to drone on about periods and reproductive organs like he was giving a goddamn lecture at the university. It was all things I had learned in sex ed at school, but I appreciated the effort. It can't be an easy conversation for a father to have with his daughter. But one thing I do remember vividly is that when the topic of sex came up, he stopped talking about chromosomes and things you'd expect from a biologist and started talking about responsibility, love, and keeping my guard up against the kind of relationships that can be exciting and explosive at first. He said those relationships always fizzle out too soon, and that's why you have to use your brain when your body is sending you such loud messages. I understood exactly what he meant.

When I looked at Gavin, I knew he'd give me that explosive, mind-blowing kind of experience in the backseat of his old car. I knew he could light me up. He'd be professing his love for me by the end of the night, and then the next week he'd be onto the next, telling her how his palm tattoo was an impulse purchase.

"Penny? Are you listening? What's going on? Where'd you go?"

"I'm listening, I'm listening."

"So I moved back in with my dad in Fort Collins after leaving my mom in Hollywood. I saw enough of that place and enough of my mom for a good two years. She's come out to visit twice since then, but she's all swept up in her noncareer career . . . and booze."

He was really pouring his heart out to me, but I was still thinking about Kimber. I actually liked him and didn't want to be just a tattoo on his palm with a weird story behind it. Maybe I liked him too much already. Too much, too soon. *Explosive.*

"Gavin, we're going to be friends," I blurted out.

Jerking his head back, he squinted at me and then smiled. "We *are* friends, Penny. Best friends, remember? That's why I'm telling you my whole life story."

"No, I mean, for the first time in so long, I'm having fun. I'd like to keep it that way." I loved dancing but "fun" wasn't the word I'd used to describe the feeling of moving across the stage.

"Yeah, we can keep things fun," he said with a smirk.

I rolled my eyes. I'd have to dodge his advances for a while, but eventually he'd get that I didn't want more than this.

I was officially buzzed and suddenly feeling anxious about overeating. Gavin reached over and grabbed my hand. "You're a really beautiful girl and you have a perfect body. I hope no one has ever made you feel otherwise."

He knows exactly what to say.

"Thanks. . . . That's really nice of you. Dance is just really competitive. And you don't have to say that if—"

"I think you need to hear it."

"You don't know what I need. You just met me."

"You need a friend," he said.

My eyes started to water. I nodded. "I do."

"I'll be your friend, and . . . I'm going to take you to Ling's party, okay? If you want me to stay in the car at your house, I will. If you want me to wait outside of Ling's party, I will. I just want to be there for you. And when we're done hanging out today, I'll be there for you tomorrow, if you need me. That's friendship."

"So we'll be friends? You're not asking for more?"

"Yep. You know where to find me." He gestured toward me. "And I know where to find you."

Tied up in a nice little bow. I reached up, threw my stinky arms around him, and hugged him like I had known him my whole life.

9. Nine Months Ago

PENNY

It had been two days since I'd heard from Gavin after he stopped by to tell me his dad was sick. Pasta sauce was cooking on the stove for dinner, and Milo was upstairs playing video games when my husband came home from his two-day business trip.

"Hey, you," he said. He walked up and kissed me on the cheek. "I missed you."

"I missed you, too," I said as I set down a spoon to give him a proper hug. He held me longer than usual.

"So, Gavin's in town. I saw his car in his dad's driveway."

"I know," I said. "He came by here on Tuesday. His dad is sick. Stage four prostate cancer." I started getting choked up.

"Oh no. I'm so sorry to hear that." He was being totally sincere. We all loved Gavin's dad, Frank. "Should we take some food over to them? Is there anything I can do?"

"I'll text him and take them a couple of plates. I was

going to see Frank anyway. Milo misses you, so you guys should probably catch up."

He nodded. "Okay."

I didn't text Gavin, though, because I felt like he would say no. He didn't like me cooking for him. He thought it was too weird. I understood why. I made him avocado toast once and he looked at it for five minutes before taking a bite. When I had asked him what was on his mind, he'd said, "I was just thinking about what it would be like."

"How what would be like?" I had asked.

"If you and I had ended up together."

"Well, I'd expect you to pull your weight around here. It wouldn't be me serving you all the time. Count this as your Christmas present." It was July when I had told him that.

He laughed and said, "I don't want you cooking for me okay, P? Not even toast. Can you respect that?"

I did respect it. But this was a different situation. His dad was dying.

After I ate with my family, I made two plates out of the leftovers, threw on a jacket, and headed over to Frank's. Gavin's car was there and I could hear him on the porch, softly playing the guitar. Was it our song? His back was to me as I approached. The music stopped.

"Hey, P."

I walked up the steps to where he was sitting in the swing. "How'd you know it was me?"

"Because your ankles crack so damn loud when you walk. Your knees, too. I could hear you coming from four houses away."

I frowned. "Thanks." I hated that I had abused my body so much in my teens and twenties. It was funny, though, that Gavin noticed things like that about me. It added to the long list of comparisons I couldn't stop making between Gavin and my husband. Like how I could dye my hair orange and my husband wouldn't even notice, yet Gavin noticed whenever I bought a new T-shirt.

I held out the plates. "I brought you and your dad some pasta with chicken and salad."

"You didn't have to do that." He stood, put his guitar down, and kissed me on the cheek as he took the plates from my hands. "But thank you. Come on in, he'd love to see you."

There was already a hospital bed in the center of the living room. Frank was lying in it, watching TV. "Sweet Penny," he said, his voice strained. "I'm so glad to see you, honey."

I hugged him and kissed the side of his face. "I'm sorry, Frank."

"Well, I'm not dead yet. You don't need to go moping around here. Gavin has that covered." I turned around and looked at Gavin. In the light I finally noticed his eyes were puffy and bloodshot. It seemed like Frank was too young to be dying. He wasn't even sixty yet.

"Milo will want to see you, I'm sure," I said.

"Of course. Bring him down." Frank had occasionally helped me with Milo when I was in a pinch. My husband worked seventy hours a week most of the time. I could leave Milo with Frank when I needed to. The two got so close that he gave Milo his entire collection of baseball cards, and even took him to a Rockies game once. Gavin had never been interested in sports, so it was nice for Frank to have someone to bond with over baseball.

Gavin wrapped his arms around my waist from behind and put his chin on my shoulder. I went rigid.

"Sorry," he said, but he wouldn't let go. "Dad, are you gonna tell Penny your brilliant idea? Or should I?"

"I'll tell her. Why not? It's a great idea. Well, I just thought while Gavin's in town, you know . . . maybe you can introduce him to one of your friends? He'll have this house when I'm gone and . . ."

I jerked my head back, turned around, and glared at Gavin.

"Well, Frank—" I started to say, but he interrupted me.

"You know, ever since he screwed it up with that nice girl Jenn, he's been back on the market."

"Dad, I think we're putting Penny on the spot here."

That wasn't really the role I played with Gavin; we generally tried to stay out of each other's business in that way. The truth was that any matchmaking I did would end in disaster, especially while Gavin was dealing with his dying father.

"I know a girl. I'll talk to her," I said, just to make Frank happy.

Gavin laughed through his nose. He knew I was lying.

"Perfect," Frank said.

A few minutes later, Gavin walked me out to the porch. "So, this girl—"

"Ha. You know I would never subject anyone I know to your shenanigans."

"Just sit down with me for a sec, P."

"I have to get back home." I thought of my husband, waiting upstairs alone for me.

"Five minutes?"

"Fine." We sat side by side on the cold porch steps. The only light came from the TV inside; even the moon was nowhere to be found. "I think you need to fill me in on some things. Like, how you're going to inherit this house, and live on the same street as me."

"I'm not. This isn't my speed. You know that. I'll sell it once he passes." Oddly enough, that hurt my feelings. Was it *my* speed?

"There are still tattoo artists in Fort Collins, Gavin."

"You know what I mean. I don't know what I'm doing. I'm down, way down. I feel lost. I was driving the other day and had a weird impulse to floor my car and drive off an on-ramp."

This was normal Gavin talk. He was always being dramatic. But this time I felt like he had good cause. "Why is it okay for me to live here, but not you?"

"Did you hear me? I said I was going to drive off an on-ramp. Anyway, are you really going to do this to me right now? You really want to know why I can't live here? Because you have a kid and a husband, and I have no one. Not even a dog. You want to hire me to mow your lawn or some shit, or walk Buckley, or hang out with Milo while you go to five-star dinners with your husband?"

"Are you trying to hurt me now?"

"No, you're trying to hurt me by making me face these truths right now. Penny, you and I are not the same. Our lives are vastly different. I feel like I ruined mine. I'm lonely as fuck and my dad is going to die in this house, and I'll be the only one here for him. This is why I told you to have another kid. Milo will be it. It will all be on him. I know how it feels."

He was hitting below the belt now. "You know I tried to get pregnant again."

"Did you?"

I stood up to leave.

"Wait. I'm sorry. That wasn't fair."

"No, it wasn't, and by the way, I will be here for you. Me!" I pointed to my chest hard. "As always, Gavin. Maybe you can even order a hot nurse when your time comes."

"Not funny, Penny."

I smiled. He could see my face in the TV light, and I could see a small smile playing on his lips, too. "It's a little funny," I said. We were the only people we could be this way with.

He shook his head. "I'll walk you home."

"No, I'll be fine. You'll hear my ankles crack all the way down the street."

"Fine. Bye."

"Bye," I said. When I got to the bottom of the steps, he jumped and landed beside me, grabbing my hand at the same time.

Pulling me along, he said in his typical fast-talking way, "I'm walking you home so shut up. You're a sitting duck with those noisy ankles. There's wild animals around here, like Tanya Fairmore in that blue house and Barrette Kiels next door to her."

"We do have some weirdoes on this street."

"That's why I hate suburbia. We're safer in the 'hood. There's a nurse coming on Saturday. I doubt she'll be hot." He squeezed my hand. "But at least I'll have a break. You want to go see The National with me at Red Rocks? I have an extra ticket."

We were at the front door of my house. "You know I can't do that. Is it just you going?"

He nodded.

"Ask Mike," I said.

"Yeah, no, it's fine. I'll figure it out."

"But, God, I would love to see them there," I said.

"That's why I bought them, Penny," Gavin replied.

The door swung open, and the air grew thick with silence. We'd had many uncomfortable moments like this, with me and Gavin on one side of the threshold and my husband on the other. It was like getting caught kissing your boyfriend good night in high school. In this case, my husband was the strict dad who waits up all night. It wasn't fair to think of him that way, but in moments like these, I couldn't help it.

"Hi, Gavin. I'm so sorry to hear about your dad."

"Thank you, I appreciate that, man." They shook hands.

"So what did you buy for our Penny here?"

I answered for him. "Oh, Gavin has a nurse coming over on Saturday to cover for him, so he asked if I wanted to go see The National at Red Rocks with him."

My husband frowned. "What's The National?"

"A band," I said.

"Oh," he replied.

We were all standing in the doorway awkwardly. "Milo has that project thing anyway, so I told him I couldn't go."

"You can go," he said. "I'll work on the project with Milo. Why don't you come in, Gavin? Have a beer."

"I gotta get back to my dad." He pulled the tickets from his back pocket and said, "You know what? You guys take them. Milo can come and hang out with me and Frank . . . and Nurse Betty." He looked at me and winked.

My husband took the tickets and said, "Fantastic. Thank you, Gavin. We could use a date night."

I wanted to cry but instead I hugged him and said, "Thank you. Hang in there, buddy."

He whispered in my ear, "You'll be thinking about me when you fuck him tonight."

I pushed him off me. "Stupid," I said.

"I'm joking, lighten up. You're starting to act like Jenn." Milo was calling to my husband from upstairs, so he waved to us dismissively and walked away.

"Don't do that, Gavin. He already thinks our friendship is weird. Couldn't you tell he was pissed? And I can't believe you gave him the tickets. You love The National."

"He'll get over it, right? Tell him I whispered you had bad breath or something. He couldn't hear me. Anyway, I gave him the tickets because you like The National more, and I wanted you to see the show. So there. Don't say I never do anything nice for you."

He bent over quickly and kissed my cheek. "See ya, P."

10. Fourteen Years Ago

GAVIN

She was going to be the death of me.

I stood behind her as she unlocked the door to her parents' house. "Looks like no one's home," she said. "I think my mom took Kiki to some pageant bullshit. My dad must be working late. Come on in."

"This is your younger sister?" I pointed to a picture on the mantel as we walked through the living room.

"Yep, that's her."

"How old is she? Ten going on twenty-nine?"

"I know, it's ridiculous. My mother dresses her like that and makes her compete in beauty pageants. Kiki seems to like it, but I don't think she knows any better. Poor kid. She's sweet, though. Come back to my room."

Come back to my room? Shit. Why did I tell her we could just be friends? I tried to recall the promises I'd made and wondered how many were reasonable to break.

Penny's house was a standard three-bedroom postwar

suburban home. The décor wasn't what I would call gaudy, but it was definitely froofy. Kind of like a ten-year-old had been allowed to order anything she wanted from the Sears catalog. *Everything* had a damn ruffle on it. It didn't suit my idea of Penny.

When we got to the doorway of her room, I noticed how dramatically different it was from the rest of the house. Her bed was covered in a simple black comforter, and everything projected a modern aesthetic—sharp angles, cold, and minimalist. "Do you live in here with a vampire?"

"Ha-ha, very funny. You can sit there and wait for me." I sat at her glass desk in an office-style chair as she tossed clothes out of her bag and into a hamper. "Some of this furniture is from my dad's old office, so it's pretty sterile."

"Seems like you have different tastes from the rest of your family. No ruffles and flowers?"

"I like flowers," she said absently.

"What, like Venus flytraps?"

"If you grew up with all this frilly shit, you'd be over it, too. I mean, do you know any other families who still use doilies? Every surface is literally covered in them." She grabbed a shirt and jeans and headed for the door. "I'm gonna jump in the shower. I'll be out in three minutes."

"Do you need any help?"

"Be out in a jiffy," she sang as she danced out into the hallway. I waited a beat before getting up.

I snooped, okay? I'm not proud of it. I needed to know more about her. For instance: why was she so stubborn about not dating? Had someone broken her heart? This girl's room was literally devoid of anything girly that would indicate she'd even had a boyfriend before. No heart-shaped candy boxes, no folded love notes. No doodles of a guy's name written eight thousand times on the cover of a spiral notebook. All I saw were tights, toe shoes, and dance stuff; not a single ballerina music box, stuffed with all her best-kept secrets.

When I heard her coming down the hall, I bounced over to the glass desk and plopped back into her weird office chair. She was wearing an off-the-shoulder T-shirt, and her long black hair was wet and draped over her bare shoulder. She sat at the edge of her bed to put on her socks and boots as she winced in pain.

"Fuck, my feet hurt."

"Is there anything I can do?"

Even from a few steps away, I could tell they were red, swollen, and bruised.

"No, they're disgusting. Believe me, you don't want to touch them." She finished pulling on her shoes and stood up as if she were perfectly fine.

What I would come to learn about Penny was that even when she was clearly in pain or self-conscious about her body, it never showed. She moved with ease around the room, which must've come from years of performing onstage. She carried herself with grace and confidence. I wanted her to be healthy, to love her beautiful body, to take care of herself—even though we were still practically strangers. It was the first time I ever wanted something for someone else in a purely unselfish way.

I'd never wanted to be this guy before, fawning over a girl like a puppy. That wasn't me. Sure, I'd professed my love to a couple of girls, but I knew it wasn't real. In my ideal world, I was going to graduate, travel around the world, and have a girlfriend in every country. But Penny was flipping a switch inside me. Now, I couldn't imagine doing anything without her, her fucked-up feet, and her sopping wet hair. I felt born anew, baptized by her beauty.

"Gavin?"

Bathed in her voice.

"Gavin?"

Aching for her.

"Gavin? Where are you?"

"Uhhh, right here."

"What's going on?" She walked toward me. Before I knew what I was doing, I reached for her hips, pulling her closer to me. I had a strong urge to kiss her belly. "Isn't it clear what's happening, Penny? I'm really into you. If you let me, I'd jump right into bed with you and forget this whole friendship thing."

She pushed my forehead back. "C'mon. Stop."

"I can't help it. I have to tell you the truth."

She laughed but continued to push me away.

"Just let me kiss you," I said. "Let me kiss your belly?"

"No, weirdo."

I stood and braced her neck softly. "Let me kiss your mouth?" She didn't move. I bent and touched my lips to hers. She was still. I pulled away. "Kiss me back, jerk."

"No. We're going to be friends. We agreed."

"We *are* friends. Let's just be the kind that kiss each other," I said in all seriousness.

Something changed. She seemed sad all of the sudden. I ran my thumb over her cheek. *Who is this complicated girl?*

"We should get to the party."

I nodded. The mood had shifted.

As we were walking toward the front door, her mother and sister walked in. Penny didn't miss a beat. "Mom, this is my friend Gavin from school. He's driving me to Ling's apartment since I had a beer after dance class today. Gavin, this is my mom, Anne, and my sister, Kiki."

"Hello, Gavin," Anne said, reaching out to shake my hand. "Nice to meet you." She pointed to my arm. "Those are some interesting markings you have there."

Kiki chimed in. "Mom, those are tattoos. I think they're kinda cool."

An inscrutable look spread across Anne's face. "Interesting . . ."

"We don't want to be late to Ling's," Penny said, tugging me toward the door. "Gotta get going."

Anne looked uncomfortable. "Penny, can I have a word with you in the kitchen first?"

"Nope, gotta go, Mom. By the way, Gavin is the one who fixed my car. You can use that money for Kiki's professional airbrushed makeup this weekend and all the extra glitter." She tugged at my arm again. "Let's go!"

Anne shook her head. "Well, bye then. Be safe . . ."

Penny practically dragged me out of the house as Anne and Kiki gave us identical little waves from the doorstep like two beauty queens on a float in a goddamn parade.

I followed Penny to my own car and felt frozen for a moment.

"Something wrong?" she said as she stood near the passenger door.

Walking around to unlock her door, I said, "I got a weird vibe back there. Did you?"

"Well, they *are* weird. What can I say?"

"They seem really nice, though. Why didn't you want to stay and chat a bit?"

"Gavin, just get in the car. I'll tell you anything you want to know about them on the way to Ling's."

"What's the deal with you and your mom?"

She sighed. "It's complicated. Let's just say I'm closer to my dad."

"I actually get along better with my dad, too, though I'd never tell my mom that."

There was a beat of silence as Penny and I sat in my car. It was getting dark and I felt a burning need to get back to that moment we'd had in her bedroom. "So, when we did that Blind Kiss thing?"

"Yeah?" she said hesitantly.

"Well, didn't you feel it? You said you liked me, I think."

"Did I feel what?"

"Like, stars exploding? That kind of thing?"

"That's an interesting way of putting it, although a tad dramatic."

"Well?"

She sighed. "Yes, Gavin. It was a great kiss."

"So why are you so determined to keep things platonic between us?"

She turned her whole body toward me. "It was really one of the best kisses I've ever had. I told you that. But I want to get to *know* you, Gavin. You're like the first friend I've had where it doesn't feel like I'm in some kind of competition. And I'm afraid—"

"You're afraid if something happens, we won't be friends?"

"Yes. And I need to concentrate on school. I have to get

a job out of all this hard work I'm putting into dance. At least as a choreographer or instructor. I feel like if we date, we'll end up wasting our last semester drinking flights of beer."

"First of all, that's not how it would go—we would also have sexy times." I winked and smiled. It didn't work.

She sighed again. "Can you understand what I'm saying? What if I promise to be open, to go with the flow, and to work really hard at getting to know you? We don't have to decide anything right now." She looked at her watch. "We should get to Ling's."

"Okay, I guess," I said. I turned up The Cure's "Plainsong" and drove. Penny stared out the window. I forgot how emotional that song was until I thought about how she and I were trying to figure out how to be in each other's lives. What would we be to each other, and for how long? Would it be for a month? For a year? Would I ruin it by pushing her? I just wanted to be around her, but the girl had boundaries. Big ones.

When we got to Ling's, I walked Penny to the door.

Ling swung the door open and said, "Hi, HKM."

I looked around.

Penny mumbled, "Hot Kissing Machine. Ignore her."

"Well, ladies, I think this is where I leave you. Have fun at the party. Hey Ling, you have my number, right? From the experiment?"

"I prefer to call it a study, but yes, I do. Why, what's up?"

"Give me a call if our girl Penny needs a ride, or starts a girl fight."

They both chuckled. I grabbed Penny's hand and swung her around to face me. I bent, kissed her on the cheek, and said, "Bye, friend, have fun."

11. Fourteen Years Ago

PENNY

"Oh Ling, I'm so screwed."

She turned around and grinned at me. "I can see that. I mean, that blind kiss . . . it was like he was trying to put a baby in you. You guys stole the show. Like, you two need to bone, for sure."

"No, I actually like him."

"Precisely."

We were in Ling's bedroom, in her apartment, drinking Boone's Farm Strawberry Hill from the bottle, which felt like a crime, even back then. She was trying on different variations of the same outfit. I was thinking about why I was stopping myself from kissing Gavin a million times. I'd fall in love with him and end up pregnant at twenty-one, with no future and no hope of pursuing dance. He was a bad boy, good boy, bad boy, good boy. I was so confused.

Why, God? Why bring this guy into my life right now?

Ling finally chose an outfit, which was the first outfit

she had tried on. I was wearing an off-the-shoulder T-shirt, jeans, and boots. Nothing fancy. I wasn't planning to see anyone I knew, anyway; I just wanted to hang out with Ling and blow off some steam.

As we headed to the party in the building's courtyard, the first person we ran into was Lance, the microbiology major.

"You waiting for me, Lance?" I said teasingly.

"Hey Penny, didn't expect to see you here! You look pretty." He held out a full beer in a red Solo cup for me to take.

"You sure?"

He waved me off, like it was no problem.

"Thanks. You look nice, too, by the way. What are you up to?" Ling raised an eyebrow at me as she walked away.

"Actually, I've been creating a biosphere. I think your dad would flip out over it."

I smiled. "That's exciting." *Damn it, is he going to talk about science-y stuff now? Maybe I should've stuck with Ling.*

"So I created this really unstable environment and introduced these microorganisms, just to see if I could sustain them for any length of time. I mean, of course I had to provide energy sources. . . ."

I quietly chugged the beer as he went on. "I was shocked when I discovered an organism I hadn't introduced myself, and I . . ."

During Lance's lengthy explanation of his project, I got my hands on something stronger: a bottle of tequila. Thirty minutes, and several shots later, I was fully drunk. My eyes roamed around the party, looking for a way out.

Oh yes! Here comes Ling to save me!

"Ling! This is my friend, Lance! Have you two met?"

She gave me a weird look. "Why are you shouting?"

"I'm just excited to seeeee you! Meet Lance!"

She cocked her head to the side and appraised him, then fully turned to me. "So this is your type?"

"What?" I said.

She leaned in and whispered in my ear. "Are you into this guy? I didn't think he was your type."

I jerked my head back and scowled. I leaned forward and whisper-shouted, "No way! I'm not into annnnnyone. I'm shingle." I realized I was slurring and so did Ling.

She whipped her head around, looked at Lance, and then back at me. "Let's go, Penny. You need to call it. You've had a long day."

"Call who? Why? No I jusss fine. Ima goood."

Ling was glaring at Lance. "Did you roofie her?"

He held his hand to his chest. "Are you kidding? No! I would never. I'm not even sure how she's so drunk—she's had, like, one beer and a couple shots."

Ling glared at him even harder. "She's a dancer, genius. She's probably a total lightweight."

I could see Lance blushing through my double vision. "She can come to my apartment on the third floor and sleep it off. I live in this building."

"Um . . . noooo," Ling said. "I'm calling her dad."

"I'm standing riiiight here!" I yelled. "Ima big girl. I can take care of myself."

Everything about the next hour was a blur. I remember being back in Ling's apartment, and her trying to comfort me as I cried. She fed me a Hot Pocket and I threw it up in her bathtub. She gave me water and I threw that up, too.

She threatened to call my dad and I begged her not to. She tried to lead me to the couch but her cat had pooped on it.

Finally, I felt warm arms around me. "P, I'm gonna take you to my place, okay? You're safe."

"No, Gavin. I can't go with you. We're jusss friends." He was holding me up near Ling's front door.

"Maybe I should take you home then. Your parents will probably be worried if you don't come home, right?"

"Nooo, they don't care. They only care about Kikiiii." I pinched his arm.

"Ow!"

"No funny business!" I said.

He laughed. "No offense, but you have puke on your shirt and you're about to pass out. That's not really my thing."

It was weird that his admission hurt my feelings, but it also made me like him even more. I passed out in the car. I don't know how I got into his second-story apartment, or into his bed. All I know is that when I woke up the next morning, I was in one of his T-shirts and nothing else . . . and my hair was damp. *Did he give me a bath? Did he see me naked?* The sun was blasting me through the window, cooking my already injured brain with its Vita radiation.

Oh my God.

As I looked around, the only male in sight was Mike's dog, Jackie Chan, at the foot of the bed, staring back at me.

"Hello, Jackie Chan."

He cocked his head to the side.

"Did you strip me down and give me a shower?"

He cocked his head to the other side.

"Gavin!" I yelled.

A moment later, he was in the doorway, shirtless, wearing flannel pants. He grabbed the molding above the door and leaned into the room, showing off his ridiculous body. I could tell he had nothing on under his pajama bottoms.

"Hey, sleepyhead," he said.

I sat up and leaned against the headboard, crossing my arms over my flat chest. "I'm completely naked under this T-shirt . . . *your* T-shirt."

"I'm painfully aware of that." He glanced down at his crotch and back up to me, smirking.

"Please wipe that smirk off your face. I said no funny business. What happened last night?"

"Well, little firecracker, here's the whole story. I carried you into my apartment; you finally woke up and punched me in the chest about twelve times. Then you proceeded to strip off all of your clothes and throw them at me—at which point I tried to cover you with a blanket, but you tore that off, too. I did see every inch of your magnificent body, but that was all your doing—not that I minded. I begged you to take a shower, which you begrudgingly did, while I sat outside the door. Afterward, I went in with my eyes shut and toweled off your ungrateful but perky ass, and then put a T-shirt on you. You tried to kiss me about six times, so I threw you over my shoulder, gave your bare butt a little swat, and then threw you into my bed. You begged me to make love to you—your words, not mine—but I told you 'no way.' I covered you with a blanket and then ten seconds later you were asleep." He smirked.

I was mortified but I knew it was all true. Foggy memories were coming back to me in fragments. "Umm . . ."

"Nothing to say? You had a lot to say last night. You told me I had a nice body and a beautiful face." He laughed.

Oh god, I did say that.

"And that I was the smartest guy you'd ever met."

"I never said that!"

He squinted. "Well, I thought I heard you say it."

I tried to swat at him but missed. "What time is it? And do I smell pancakes?"

"French toast, actually. And it's noon."

"Oh my god, my parents are gonna kill me."

He held out his palm. "I called your mom and gave her my address. I asked if she wanted to come and get you, or if I should let you sleep it off. She said she was heading out the door, to the spray-tan lady, or some shit like that, so I just let you keep sleeping."

"Geez," I scowled. "She didn't even care?"

He walked toward me. "Penny—"

"Don't come any closer."

"I'm not gonna touch you. I slept on the couch, I swear. I left Jackie Chan in here to keep you company."

"I'm just warning you, I have the breath of a very sick dragon, and it feels like there are tiny sweaters covering my teeth."

"Yeah. I know, I can smell it from here."

"Thanks."

"You can use my toothbrush if you want." He looked like he felt sorry for me.

"She takes my sister to the spray-tanner for pageants."

"What?" Gavin came over and sat on the end of the bed. "You're kidding?"

"No, it's absolutely deplorable." I looked up to the

ceiling. "I still can't believe she wasn't worried about me sleeping at a stranger's house with his forty-year-old tattoo-artist roommate."

He picked up a guitar and starting strumming. "Well, she doesn't know that part, obviously. Anyway, Mike's out of town; otherwise, he would have gotten quite the show last night. You ready for some French toast? It's my very own recipe."

Who is this person?

He was strumming the song "Just Like a Woman," trying to work out the chords. "French toast sounds good, but I need my clothes."

"I'm washing them in the laundry room in the basement. They were in pretty bad shape, Penny."

"Oh god."

"My T-shirt's not good enough for you?"

"Well, I have nothing on underneath it."

"It fits you like a dress, and anyway, I saw everything last night. I mean *everything*." He wiggled his eyebrows.

I leaned over and socked him in the arm. "Don't do that to me. I'm embarrassed enough."

"You have nothing to be ashamed of, except for maybe your attempt at a half-naked pirouette in the hallway at three a.m."

I dropped my face into my hands and groaned. "Noooo. Ugh."

"It was actually really cute. You ran into the wall and starting cracking up."

The moment Ling had called, Gavin was still blurry in my mind. *Had he just come rushing over? Was he sitting around waiting for her call? Did he roofie me?*

"What were you doing when Ling called?"

"I was working on a paper and messing around on my guitar. I had just gotten into bed when she called."

Oh, the image of him getting into bed . . . "Working on a paper, my ass."

"No, I swear. I have to graduate, Penny. I'm twenty-three."

"What did Ling say when she called?"

"I believe her exact words were, 'Tiny Dancer can't hold her liquor and my cat pooped on my couch, so can you get your hot butt over here and help?'"

"And you just jumped in your car and came to get me."

"Yes. That's exactly right. You're welcome. Now come on, let's go eat." He put down the guitar and yanked me out of bed. As we walked through his apartment toward the kitchen, I shuffled behind him while tugging at the bottom of my T-shirt. He pointed to the couch. "That's where I slept."

There's no way his entire body fit on that couch.

"See, Penny? Already so many sacrifices I've made for our friendship. My feet hang two feet off that thing."

We moved toward the breakfast bar. I sat on a stool while he went around to the other side to serve up his homemade French toast. He'd already sifted powdered sugar and added sliced-up strawberries to the plates, which made my heart and stomach do a little somersault. "Impressive," I said.

"You don't have to eat all of it but you should put something in your stomach."

"Okay." My hangover was starting to really kick in. "This looks delicious but I feel awful."

"What were you drinking last night? Tequila?"

"And beer." I ate half the French toast and pushed the plate away. Gavin immediately grabbed it and set it in the sink.

"You need a little hair of the dog and a nap while your clothes dry." He started moving around the kitchen, whipping something up. A few minutes later, he handed me a glass full of tomato juice.

"Uhhh, what's this?"

He looked at me like I was an alien. "A Bloody Mary. Duh." I had never had one before. It looked disgusting but I drank it anyway while he went to the basement to put my clothes in the dryer. It worked. I started feeling more relaxed and my headache was fading. I walked around his apartment, looking at the random artwork everywhere. I finished the drink, used his toothbrush, then went into his room just as I heard him coming in the door. On his nightstand was a copy of an engineering magazine and the Kurt Vonnegut book *Breakfast of Champions*.

He reads.

Burying myself under the blankets on his bed, I feigned sleep. I could feel him as he entered the room. He didn't want to wake me.

He cares about me.

He tiptoed around the bed and grabbed a guitar. He reached down and straightened the blankets so they were covering my feet. I couldn't help but smile. He caught it.

"Faker," he whispered.

"Play me a song."

He grabbed the electric guitar instead and plugged it into a small practice amp on the floor. The volume was set very low. I could hear the string sound over the amplification. He started strumming softly, and I knew what he was playing: "Just Like a Woman," but the Jeff Buckley version. And then he started singing. It wasn't perfect but it was beautifully flawed. He held nothing back. He even changed some verses and lyrics, which made me laugh.

She dances just like a woman. Oh and she drinks tequila, not at all like a woman, but when she breaks, she breaks . . . just like a little girl.

The last line was so soft, so delicate—the way he delivered it, I thought he must believe it to be true. That I could break like a little girl.

When the song was over, he turned around and smiled sweetly.

"I liked your changes," I told him.

"I was going to add a line about your breath, but it seems to be minty fresh now."

Grinning, I said, "I used your toothbrush."

"So now your gross little sweaters are on my toothbrush?"

"You offered." I laughed, and then patted the bed next to me. "Want to spoon?" I yawned. "I need that nap."

In a flash he unplugged the guitar, put The Cure on his CD player on low volume, tore off his T-shirt, and slid in behind me, wearing only his flannel pajama. "God, I thought you'd never ask," he said. He wrapped his arms around me. Nothing hurt. Everything was right. We were spoons in a drawer. We fell asleep, his face tucked into the back of my neck.

I don't know what had come over me. Maybe it was the fact that my mom had prioritized taking Kiki to the spray-tanner over picking me up. I needed to feel something, to feel wanted.

It could have been days that we lay there tangled together—moving at times, always aware of each other's bodies. When we started to move together, I was curled in a ball with my back against Gavin's bare chest. He started dragging his index finger up my leg, making little circles on the outside of my thigh, pushing my T-shirt up until he was caressing my bare hip. I put my hand over his to stop him.

I didn't think what I was doing to him was fair, but I was scared we would become exploding stars if we gave in to each other. Our energy would be exhausted too soon and we'd have to float through space like lifeless rocks, bumping into each other, drifting through our own stardust.

"I'm sorry," he whispered, before kissing the back of my head. He rolled out of bed and threw his T-shirt on. When I looked back I noticed how turned on he was.

Catching me staring, he said, "It has a mind of its own." And then he laughed half-heartedly. "I'll go get your clothes."

"Yeah, I should get home. Thank you."

When he returned, we both got dressed quickly in front of each other. It wasn't weird at all.

HE WAS QUIET on the way to my house. It was around four p.m. when he pulled into my driveway. Shutting the car off, he turned to me. "You might want to go easier on the booze next time."

"Yeah, no kidding," I said.

There were unanswered questions lingering silently in the air around us.

"What do you have planned for tomorrow?" he asked.

"I'm gonna go to ballet class in the morning. That's it. Maybe study. You?"

"I have to finish that paper and study a bit, too."

"You want to come here and study around three?"

He smiled. "In your bedroom?"

"Yes, in my bedroom."

"Do I need to bring garlic or a wooden stake or anything like that?"

At first I thought he was flirting, but clearly he was teasing. "You're an idiot. Do you want to or not?"

"Yes, Penny. I want to study you . . . I mean *with* you. I'll be here."

Just before I got out of the car, my mom and Kiki pulled up. Kiki jumped out of my mother's blue Ford station wagon wearing a giant tiara. My mother was holding yet another giant trophy to add to Kiki's collection. I gave a weak smile and waved to both of them as they waited for me by the front door.

Gavin looked at me with wide eyes. "Wow. Kiki looks like JonBenét."

"No kidding. I better go."

As my mom opened the door, Gavin started up the car. He had his window down as he backed out of the driveway. My mother, Kiki, and I all watched him pull out of the driveway as he waved to us. "Congratulations, Kiki. See you beautiful ladies tomorrow!" he said.

My mom turned to me and asked, "Is he your boy-friend?"

"No, just a friend," I said, still staring at Gavin.

He looked right at me, blew me a kiss, and yelled, "See ya, Boo!"

My mom walked into the house, shaking her head.

12. Eight Months Ago

GAVIN

I could hear Penny's ankles cracking and the jingling of a dog collar before I saw her and Buckley coming around the corner.

Sitting on my dad's porch in the midday sun, I tried to pull myself together.

"Hey," she said from the sidewalk.

"How was the concert?"

She was squinting against the sun as she walked toward me. "It was great. Thanks again for the tickets and for watching Milo. Do you want me to give you some money?"

"No, I don't want your money."

Her expression fell. "What's wrong?" She sat down on the porch next to me.

"He's getting worse really fast. He can't even eat." My eyes started welling up.

"Gavin, I'm so sorry." She hugged me around my shoulders. "I want to go in and see him. Will you hold on to Buckley?"

"Sure."

"Sit," she told him before handing me the leash.

He was staring right at me. Once Penny was inside, I said to Buckley, "You were supposed to be our dog. *Our dog.*" He blinked. I let all the possibilities of what could have been rush through me. It made me sick. I had to push them away before she came back outside. "Your dad wanted to name you Sport. Aren't you relieved your mom has more sense than that?" I scratched him around the ears. "You're a pretty handsome dog, you know that? You get a lot a looks at the dog park? Those bitches be like—"

"Gavin," Penny interrupted from behind. "Please tell me you don't talk to Milo that way?"

"Don't be ridiculous."

She sat down next to me again.

"Your dad doesn't look bad, but he was sleeping so it was hard to tell."

I shook my head. "He's bad, believe me."

"I'm glad Milo got to hang out with him. He said they had a good time playing chess together." When she smiled, I noticed she had more frown lines than ever. I hadn't even asked about her life in the month since I'd been back. I was so swept up in my own drama.

"Yeah, I'm glad too." I stared off blankly.

"The nurse seems nice."

"Ha. Nurse Ratched? She has a curfew policy. Lights out at nine p.m.—for all of us, like I'm in prison. I'm about to fly over this fucking cuckoo's nest."

"Let's go get lunch. I have a couple hours before I have to get Milo."

"Okay." I got up. "You driving?"

"Yeah, I'll drive, then we can go straight to Milo's school."

I actually loved the kid, but I hated feeling like his stepdad. I didn't mind looking after him from time to time, but this weird pseudo-side-family Penny had created made me uncomfortable. I liked hanging out with Milo but not when she and I were alone together. It felt odd but I agreed anyway, just to get out of the house and distract myself from my dad.

I followed her and Buckley down the street as she walked fast. "Are you in a hurry?" I asked.

"Well, I have to do pick-up duty so I need to get to the school a little earlier today."

"What the hell is pick-up duty?" I felt ill already. "Like we have to take other kids home?"

She opened the front door as I followed her into the house. It was pristine inside, as always. "No, we just have to get out and direct traffic a little, maybe help kids to their cars and clear out the parking lot."

"That is a million times worse." I folded my arms over my chest. "I'm not going."

"Stop whining. It'll take half an hour with both of us."

"Won't it be weird, me and you there?"

Ushering Buckley into the laundry room, she turned on her heel. We were inches apart. "You've been to his school dozens of times, Gavin. Everyone thinks you're his uncle."

"Like . . . your brother?"

"Yeah."

"Oh god. Whatever, Penny."

Her voice softened. "You're kinda like a brother to me."

I grimaced. "Let's just go. I'm starving."

When we got out to the garage, I noticed Penny had a new car. "A white Mercedes SUV?" I shot her a disappointed look.

"It's four-wheel drive. You're always getting stuck in the snow. I can't get stuck in the snow. I have a kid."

"It's white. And didn't you just have a new car?"

"We lease them for two years. Just get in. I didn't pick the color."

"Obviously."

I got in and slouched down in the passenger seat.

"Where should we go?" she said, pulling out of the driveway.

"Odell's?"

"Nooo," she whined. "I'm not in the mood for food trucks."

"What about Horse and Dragon?"

"That sounds dreadful."

"It's not. It's actually very bright and cheery there. Jesus, Penny, you've really lost your edge."

We were at a stoplight. She turned and scowled at me, and then hit the gas a little too hard, forcing the car to lurch forward. "Fine, Horse and Dragon it is."

Once inside the restaurant, we took our seats at the bar. We always did that. It felt less intimate somehow. We were always trying to avoid intimacy in public.

"What's new with you, P?"

"Nothing. Same shit, different day. What about you?"

"Well, you know, I sit in my dad's house and watch him die. That's pretty much it. I'm putting together a slideshow of pictures for his funeral. I'm *already* doing that."

"I know you don't want to leave him alone, Gavin, but you need to get out more."

The bartender came over to take our order. "What can I get you two?"

"I'm not ready yet," Penny said, as she scanned the menu.

"Do you want to share a flight?" I asked.

"I don't want to drink beer in the middle of the day," she said absently.

I ordered one beer after another while Penny pushed lettuce around her plate. She wasn't skinny to an unhealthy degree, but she was very thin and probably borderline anorexic. I wished she'd eat more.

Four beers in and I was starting to feel bold. "Why don't you eat a hot dog or something? You've had four bites of lettuce."

"Thank you for keeping track," she said bitterly.

"Have you ever talked to the hubs about how you don't like to eat?"

"No. Drop it, Gavin. I do like to eat. This is just the size I'm used to. Let's talk about you," she said. "I know a girl I can introduce you to."

I turned and shot her a dirty look. "You pushing me on someone else now?"

"No, I mean a girl to have some fun with. Get laid or whatever. She's French—like, for-real French. She's traveling across the country, kind of hippie-ish. She's a singer in a band and works in that café where they used to do the open mic nights."

"Joe's?"

"Yeah."

"How do you know her?"

"Ling knows her from California. When she was out here last month, she introduced us. She's supercool. Her name is Briel. Very pretty, in a pixie-ish kind of way."

"What, like Tinker Bell?"

She elbowed me. "No, you know what I mean. She'll end up going back to France in a few months. Maybe you can just take her out. Have some fun."

"Fuck her at my dying father's house?"

"Oh my God. What is wrong with you? No. She's in Denver a lot, too."

Penny was getting frustrated with me. She had enough on her mind. I knew her marriage was suffering, even though she never talked about it. I could just tell. But she was the most loyal person I knew. Even to me. I sometimes called her Pennyloyalty for the *Unplugged* version of Nirvana's "Pennyroyal Tea." She loved dancing to it, and I loved watching her.

It's hard to understand how a woman could be loyal to two men, or how that even made sense, but it's possible. She always said, *There's room for secrets in a marriage, but not lies . . . not deception.* I think she had read that in some book. She was always fighting for individuality. She didn't want to be defined or labeled. She hated when I said she was married with children, like it was an insult. But she told me once, *I'm Penny. I have dimensions.*

She had to have her own life. Things he didn't know about her. Other relationships that didn't involve him. She was always trying to define those boundaries with him, but he was overly possessive. Penny was hard to cage, but the guy tried his damnedest to do it. And she loved him. I had to accept that, even though I never understood it. I had been accepting of that for a long time. I would take whatever she would give me as long as she was in my life.

"I don't want to take anyone out, P. I'm not ready yet. But thanks for trying." I pulled her to my side and kissed her cheek. She pulled away quickly.

"You have some pretty heavy-duty beer breath. I hope Uncle G doesn't make a scene at Milo's school."

"Have I ever made a scene?"

"Yes, pretty much every time I'm with you."

"Why stop now? Let's hit it." I clapped my hands together and stood up. She shook her head.

13. Fourteen Years Ago

GAVIN

We spent almost every day together. Even through the holiday break. When my mom came from LA to visit, I took her to see Penny dance. She said Penny was phenomenal, and I think my mother was even a bit jealous of her, but I didn't care.

Penny's partner, Joey, was still being a dick. I didn't know how she was able to put up with him, but she was patient. She practiced hard every day. And for me, there was nothing I liked more than watching her do what she loved.

I had Christmas Eve at her house, and her mom prodded me for details about our relationship. I'd been at their house a lot in the last couple of months, and Penny at mine, but we were still just being spoons in a drawer. Nothing went further. I felt like I deserved an award for my restraint. Both of us were studying hard for midterms, so I hadn't pushed her, but our exams were over now. We had time to figure *us* out before we had to go back to school. I got a tattoo the week before on the inside of my bicep between two larger designs. It was just the lyrics, *in my ears and in my eyes.* Penny knew.

Every time Anne trapped me in the kitchen, I'd try to change the subject from my relationship with her daughter, or I'd look for Penny's dad, Liam, to get me out of a pinch. I'd been hanging out with him a lot lately, too. He had a sense of humor when Anne wasn't around, but when she was there, especially with Kiki, talking about all the things they had to do for such-and-such pageants, Liam would get quiet and Penny would get judgmental, which would usually end in a fight among the whole family.

On Christmas Eve I was helping Penny set the table when Anne said, "So you guys have been inseparable lately."

"Uh-huh," I murmured.

"Penny?"

"Yes, Mom. We're friends. We like to hang out."

"Are you two being responsible?" she asked. I knew what she was getting at.

"You have no idea," I said.

Penny shot me a dirty look. "Anne"—I walked over and braced her by the shoulders—"your daughter is a saint. We really are just friends, though I wish it were more."

"Gavin," Penny chided.

Her mom giggled. She found me charming despite the stupid T-shirts, tattoos, and wild hair, which I knew she had judged, at first. Every time I came over I was helpful and complimentary toward her. I don't think I was the vision of her dream son-in-law, but she liked me. I knew that.

Later, in Penny's room, as Penny was brushing out her hair in front of the vanity, I walked up to her, wrapped my arms around her waist, and kissed her neck. She didn't move. I made eye contact with her in the mirror. "Why can't it be more?" I whispered.

She shook her head. I couldn't read her expression. "This isn't enough for you, is it?" she asked.

"I want all of you."

She broke out of my embrace and walked over to her dresser, where there was a small box giftwrapped. Handing it to me she said, "It's not much, but Merry Christmas."

I tore it open to find one of those silly half-a-heart BFF trinkets. Smiling bitterly, I said, "Did you want me to wear this around my neck or something?"

"No. It's just a symbol." She frowned.

"I guess I'm way out in the friend zone. Like in the farthest section of the friend zone. Like, in the outfield."

"More like in the stands in the nosebleed section."

I laughed even though her comment pissed me off. "Really, Penny? We're so close. We touch each other all the time. How can you say we're just friends?"

"I know what we are, Gavin, and I want to keep it that way. You can date other girls anytime you want."

"I want to date *you*. You can't tell me you wouldn't be jealous if I was taking other girls out?"

It came on slowly as I watched her in silence. She tried to hold back, but eventually she started to cry. "No." She sniffled. "I mean yes, I would be sad we wouldn't be hanging out as much, but I want you to have what you need." She was torn. I was pushing her too hard. I took her in my arms and hugged her. She tucked her head into my chest the way she always did.

"What do you need?" I asked.

"A friend. I need to get through this year. Everyone in my family doubts me. My dad has to work overtime every week to afford my tuition and all of Kiki's pageants. I can't fail them. I'll be worthless. I will turn to ash in your arms, Gavin, or bones and goo."

"That is a terrible visual, P."

"It's true. Will you wait for me?"

"For how long?"

"I don't know. Until the end of the year?"

I shook my head. "And then what?"

"And then we'll explore this. Just know I'm confused. And scared."

It was painful to see what a lonely person Penny was. She was really hanging on to us being friends because, other than a surface-level relationship with Ling and a mild closeness with her dad, she had no one.

"But just tell me. What do you think will happen if we get together now?"

"I told you. I think it will be great at first, but too much. I think we'll kill each other and break each other's hearts. I think I'll get lost in you and fail my classes."

She was right, but instead of agreeing with her, which I should have done, I lashed out. I was hurt . . . so I hurt her back. "You're not my Carissa, Penny. Not even close."

She pulled away and glared at me. "I didn't say—"

"I mean, it's not like I'm in love with you."

"What?" Tears sprang from her eyes.

"I just thought we should sleep together. I mean, we're obviously attracted to each other." *Oh God, what the hell was I saying?*

"Let me rephrase it then, Gavin." She squared her

shoulders and frantically wiped tears from her face. "What I should have said was that I'm afraid I wouldn't be good enough for you, and that you'd break my heart. Is that better? Do you feel good about yourself now?"

I nodded and shrugged like I didn't give a shit.

"I know my gift was silly, but at least I got you one. You can leave now."

"Fine. Bye. Merry Christmas," I said as I walked out. Penny didn't break like a little girl. She was strong.

When I got into my car, I grabbed the gift I had gotten for her and left it on the doorstep before peeling out of her driveway and screeching down the street.

14. Fourteen Years Ago

PENNY

Sitting on my bed alone, I opened the gift-wrapped box from Gavin that he had left on my porch. It was a home-made CD and a leather-bound journal. I popped the CD into my player and immediately recognized the first song, "Just Like a Woman," sung beautifully by Gavin.

When I opened the journal, I noticed Gavin's sloppy handwriting on the inside cover.

For you, Little P, to write down all those thoughts you keep from me. I hope it takes our entire lives to fill this thing up because I want to know everything on you mind . . . every day. There are no Carissas or Kimbers that have ever made me feel the way you do. Now start writing away. I'll leave a little quote here to inspire you . . .

"It's not what you look at that matters. It's what you see."
—Henry David Thoreau

I was crying then. I wasn't his Carissa. He said he wasn't in love with me. Why would he be? But why would he write this. Why would he say *every day*?

WE KEPT OUR distance for the rest of the winter holiday break. I got a cell phone for Christmas and called him, but he didn't pick up. I left a message so he could have my number. He didn't return my call.

Once I got back to school, I was busy preparing all day, almost every day for our big spring dance recital. I got coffee at Java Hut with Ling every Wednesday afternoon. I always hoped I'd run into Gavin, just to say *hello*, but I never saw him. I even went to fill up my car at Pete's gas station, but he wasn't working that day. Pete said Gavin had cut back on hours to take an extra course he needed, so I assumed he was busy, too.

One particularly freezing Wednesday, Ling and I huddled together on a bench outside the packed Java Hut and were drinking tea when Lance came walking up. "What's up, ladies?"

"Lance," Ling said.

They seemed more familiar with each other than the last time we'd all been together, and I wondered if maybe they'd had a fling after the party. They lived in the same building after all.

In exactly the next moment, the universe decided to take a shit right in my lap: Gavin was walking toward Java Hut, only he wasn't coming over to say hi to me; he was with some redhead, completely oblivious to me, Ling, and Lance. They were laughing and he was holding her hand as they approached the door to the café. I watched them as if they were moving in slow motion in a movie—slow enough for me to catch the joy in their expressions. I could practically fucking smell their joy, it was so visceral. Lance's back was to Gavin, but Ling saw the whole scene play out. When I dry heaved, she turned to me and started rubbing my back. I was like every other girl to him, and it was all my fault. He hadn't even noticed I was sitting there.

"Ahem!" Ling said loudly right before he swung the door open. He glanced over, looking as equally shocked as I was.

He walked up to me, still holding Raspberryhead's hand. "What are you doing here, Penny?"

I held up my cup. "Drinking tea. Remember? I practically own stock in this place."

"Right." He looked nervous.

"Hi, Gavin," Ling said.

"Hi, um, how are you?"

"Who's this?" she said, pointing to Raspberryhead.

"Oh sorry." Gavin ran his hand through his messy hair. "This is Lottie."

The fuck kind of name is Lottie? Guess not much worse than Penny Piper.

I pointed to Lance. "That's Lance," I said.

Understanding spread across Gavin's face. "Hey man. You're Penny's friend, the microbiology major, right?" I had pointed Lance out to Gavin once on our way to the library. Still, I was impressed with his recall.

"Yeah, we're friends," Lance replied, uncertainly.

Oh, that word.

Gavin gave me a pointed look. "Penny, can I talk to you for a sec?"

"What about?"

"Privately?"

I huffed but got up anyway and walked a few feet with him. He left Lottie with Ling the Wolf. I almost actually felt sorry for Gavin's new arm candy.

"What's up?" I said.

"I thought you had conditioning on Wednesdays and Fridays?"

"Nope, my schedule changed." I shivered, and he instinctively reached out to rub his hands up and down my arms, something he always did. I jerked away.

"I don't think Lottie would appreciate that, do you?"

I took him in. God, he was handsome. Why had I turned him down? I'd lost both the possibility of friendship and the dream of something more. The outcome was totally predictable but I had deluded myself into believing I could control our fate. Our "friendship" had started with a life-changing kiss. Why had I thought it would lead anywhere but here?

"I'm sorry for what I said." He swallowed. "On Christmas Eve."

"Water under your bridge."

"I believe the correct saying is 'water under *the* bridge.'"

"I was just making a statement on how you're clearly over it, so you can consider it water under *your* bridge. As far as I'm concerned, my valley's still flooded."

He laughed. "You're funny."

"I wasn't trying to be."

"Will you stop this?" He took a step toward me again but I backed away.

"No. You hurt me and then ten minutes later I was

reading the inscription in that damn journal. Man, you got over that sentiment *really* fast."

"Can we go back to the way things were?"

"Are you going to address what I just said?"

It was bright out but freezing. His lime-green Wayfarer sunglasses were sitting crookedly on top of his head. He had a thick flannel jacket over a white T-shirt that read "Chubby, Single, and Ready for a Pringle." The sun was making his pleading and beautiful eyes look impossibly green. He was perfect. I had told him to date other girls and now he was, and I was feeling exactly how he predicted I would.

"Are you gonna answer *me*?" he said.

"You didn't answer *me*."

"Can we please go back to the way things were?"

"You mean with or without Lottie?"

He shook his head. "I thought we were keeping it platonic instead of atomic. Isn't that what you meant?"

He was right. I had meant it at the time because I was scared. *Did I still mean it?* "She's pretty," I said.

"She is."

I wanted to crumble into a ball and freeze to death in the snow right at his feet. "I have to get to practice," I told him.

"Do you want to study tomorrow?" he asked. Studying with Gavin usually involved lying around listening to music.

"I have conditioning until three."

He looked away, somewhat frustrated. When he looked back, his expression was sincere. "I have to work at five but I can come over for an hour or whatever before . . . if you want. Just to talk."

"Okay," I said with little emotion. We would work things out tomorrow.

I turned around and noticed Ling talking animatedly to Lottie and Lance. She was keeping them occupied.

"Ling's a good friend," I said.

"Not your best friend, though."

"No. I guess not. Though she doesn't try to make moves on me, so that makes things easier." I smirked.

"You liked it, but consider that part over." He put out his fist like we were going to fist-bump. I hugged him instead, and he held me long enough for it to count.

I pulled away. "See you tomorrow."

He nodded.

"Lots," he called out.

Ew, he calls her Lots?

When I walked back over to Ling, she had her arms crossed over her chest. Lance looked oblivious.

"Hey, Lance, Ling and I are gonna walk to the studio now."

"I'll join you," he said.

"That's okay, Penny and I need to talk," Ling said.

I felt my stomach sinking, wondering what she had to say. I waved to Lance, even though he looked like he was going to try to hug me. Instead he froze where he stood and waved back.

Afterward, as we walked up the pathway toward the dance hall, Ling finally said, "So are you sad?"

Fully expecting her to berate me, I was surprised she was sympathetic. "I'm not sad. We're gonna hang out tomorrow."

"But things are going to change between you and Gavin now that Lots is in the picture." She shot me a wry smile.

"Ha. That won't last long. He'll get her name tattooed on his forehead and then be sitting in my driveway a week later."

"You're pretty confident about that."

"We have something. I don't what it is, but it's something different."

When we got to the dance hall, Ling gave me a stiff hug. That was just Ling. She wasn't warm and fuzzy, but she cared.

Joey was more on top of things that day at practice. I guess Doug had made a serious threat. There were other potential dancers Joey could have been partnered with besides me. I knew Joey hated all the other girls in the program. He wasn't particularly fond of me either, but I didn't think he hated me. Even though he was able to pull off the lift he had been struggling with, he still wasn't getting the timing on the *grand jeté* move. We had a few months to work on it before our spring finals performance on May 3. He knew we had to nail it. Our futures depended on it.

THE NEXT DAY, when Gavin showed up at my house, my mother immediately commandeered his attention by having him look at an oil leak under her car.

"It's like the day after I got the oil changed, all of a sudden it started leaking," she told him.

Gavin was on his back on his skateboard, looking underneath her car. "It's not from the oil change," he said. "Where'd you have it done?"

"I don't know, one of those quickie places."

"You should have asked me."

I wanted to kick him. He didn't need to be doing favors for my mom when she spent hundreds of dollars a month on Kiki's pageants.

"Well, if it's not from that, what's it from? I mean, don't

you find it coincidental? I've never seen a drop of oil on the garage floor. I get the oil changed and then take it for a smog check and they say there's an oil leak. Now there's oil on the garage floor."

"Anne, if you want to get under here with me, I can show you what it might be." He rolled out from underneath the car, hands and arms covered in grease, and smirked at her. He was flirting. So shameless.

"Just tell me, Gavin."

He stood and walked over to the open hood of her car. Looking in, he said, "There was no oil in the pan. I unscrewed everything, took out the filter, looked at it. I knew it wasn't the oil change because the oil was pooling underneath where the engine meets the transmission, which is nowhere near the filter. So it could be a broken seal—"

"What, like a rubber band?" my mother said.

"Like a gasket," Gavin replied. "Or . . ." He scratched his chin, wiping grease on it. "Maybe the smog guys dumped some oil down there to make it look like you had an oil leak. Did they offer to repair it?"

"Yeah, and they told me I needed new struts, breaks, and tires."

Gavin started laughing. "I'm going to wash this out thoroughly, and then check your struts and breaks. I can tell you right now, you don't need new tires, but I'll look at everything else."

An hour later, a very greasy Gavin dropped the hood and said triumphantly, "Anne, nothing is wrong with your car. This baby has many more pageant trips in its future."

She smiled ecstatically. Jumping up and down, she said, "I'd hug you but you're a mess, kid!"

He shook his head. "It's okay. I have to go to work anyway."

My mother thanked him endlessly before going into the house to start dinner.

After she left, Gavin and I stood there staring at each other from opposite ends of the garage.

"You didn't have to do that," I said.

"I know."

I walked toward him wearing a pale-pink, long-sleeved leotard and gray sweats. "I don't care about the grease." I jumped up and hugged him, throwing my arms around his neck. Near his ear, I said. "But next time we hang out . . . *we* hang out."

He put me down and smiled. "Deal, Monkey," he said, poking my nose and leaving a black grease smudge on it.

15. Six Months Ago

GAVIN

Penny kept needling me to go out with Briel, but I wouldn't bite. My dad was getting sicker and sicker, and Penny wanted me to go on dates? She was out of her mind, but that was nothing new.

"I think it's in your best interest," she said.

"Best interest? Are we in a parent-teacher conference? I'm not Milo, P. It's me."

"I know, but you've been hanging around the house so much and you know . . . it's just a little weird."

"And what? Is Dickhead getting jealous?"

"Don't do that."

We were standing outside Milo's school selling tickets to some stupid PTA thing. Everyone was giving me dirty looks. Some lady who Penny referred to as "The Ice Queen" walked up.

"Who's this, Penelope?" she asked as she looked me up and down.

"Milo's uncle," Penny said indifferently.

"The incarcerated uncle?"

Penny laughed. "Not anymore."

There was never an incarcerated uncle. I didn't know what the hell this Ice Queen was talking about—or why Penny was rolling with it.

What a piece of work this woman was. Weirdly enough, I still would have fucked her. She was cute, in an impish way. She had a three-year-old on her hip who was clearly outgrowing her, and she was dressed absurdly for school drop-off in spiky high heels and a tight, red spandex dress.

"I like your aviators, Teresa," Penny said in a sincere tone, even though I knew she was being sarcastic.

"Sooo, do you want one ticket for six dollars or two for ten?" I asked. "We also have raffle tickets for a dollar. The grand prize is one week at bitch rehab."

Penny gasped. Teresa turned her skinny nose up at me, turned on her heel, and walked away.

"Really, Gavin? This is Milo's school. I know you wanted to get out of the house today but you can't go around sending snotty women to bitch rehab."

"I was thinking we could go to a strip club or something. Not sell fundraiser tickets to smug moms."

"It's eight thirty in the morning—and I'm a mom!" Even though she hated labels, she always put a lot of emphasis on the word mom.

"Who was that woman anyway?"

"Her kid's in Milo's class. She's nice sometimes but when she's with her little cronies, she acts like she doesn't know who I am. She's just insecure."

I was making eyes at another woman in line and only

partially listening to Penny. "What was the deal with the incarcerated uncle thing?"

"Blame *that* one." She pointed to a Spanish-looking dark-haired bombshell in the back of the line—the mom I'd been checking out. "She asked about you when you came to the performing arts showcase last year. I told her you went to jail."

The hot mom was still checking me out as she got closer to the front of the line. "Are you trying to sabotage everything for me, P? I could have fun with someone like her."

"She's married. Kind of a hussy, though. She probably has hep C."

"You're so judgmental. No wonder why you have no friends here."

"I have friends. Ling's my friend."

"Ling lives in another state."

"And I like Crystal, my neighbor. You'll meet her in a bit. We've been to a couple of happy hours together."

"What does 'been to a happy hour' mean?" The hot mom came up to the table and I turned my full attention to her. "Hellooooo," I said, smiling wide.

"I need two tickets to parents night." She looked me up and down but I couldn't tell if she liked what she saw, or if she was intimidated by the prison thing.

"Do you need a date for it?" I asked.

She giggled. She was still into me despite my fake criminal record. Handing over a wad of cash, she let her hand linger in mine for a few seconds longer than necessary. Penny fake-sneezed on our connected hands. The woman pulled out of my grasp and scowled at Penny.

"Oh, sorry. Better wash up; I've had an icky cold for a month now. Thanks for supporting the PTA. See you soon!"

As the hot mom walked away, I turned to Penny. "You have no shame."

"Always playing with fire, Gavin. I told you, she's married."

"So are you. It's more fun to play with fire."

"Don't be that guy." She elbowed me in the side. "Here comes Crystal." A thin, slightly disheveled woman in her forties walked up and hugged Penny.

"Morning, lovely. I haven't seen you in a while," Crystal said.

"Crystal, this is Gavin." Penny jutted a thumb at me.

"Oh, hey. Penny's told me a lot about you."

I can't imagine what Penny would say about me. Probably nothing nice. I smiled. "Really? Huh. Well, nice to meet you." I shook her hand. Immediately, I knew Crystal wasn't the type to be intimidated easily, or be jealous. That's exactly the kind of friend Penny needed.

"Let's get a drink soon," she said to Penny.

"Yes, soon," Penny replied.

IN THE CAR on the way home I said, "Why didn't you make a concrete plan with Crystal? That's what you have to do to maintain friendships."

"Don't worry about me. Crystal's divorced with four kids. She's really cool but she's got a lot going on. I'll see her when I see her."

It started to snow and the roads were slick with ice. "Slow down," I told her. "Nice way to drop in that detail about her being divorced, by the way. But you know she's not my type."

"Why? Because she doesn't look like a supermodel or a tatted-up emo chick?"

"Slow the fuck down, Penny, you're scaring me. Pull over, please, and let me drive."

She huffed and puffed as she pulled into a parking lot. "Why do you think I'm such a bad driver?"

"Because you *are* a bad driver. You've been in four car accidents in the last two years."

"Fender benders."

"Just get out and let me drive."

She did but seemed annoyed about it. I always felt weird driving her car, but I was more concerned for my life than her ego at the moment.

Pulling into the driveway of her house, I noticed her husband's Lexus was parked at the curb. "What's he doing here?" I asked.

"He lives here. I guess he got off work early. Don't freak out. I texted him and told him you were with me."

I felt like if he walked into the garage and saw me getting out of the driver's side, things would get very awkward.

He opened the inner garage door leading to the kitchen just as Penny and I reached it. He hadn't seen me coming out of the car, which was a relief. "Hey Gavin, thanks for helping Penny out with the PTA stuff. I really wish that I had more time for that kind of thing."

Penny and I just blinked up at him on the other side of the threshold.

"No problem," I said.

"Yeah, you know, my job doesn't really give me that much time off. Gotta provide for the family and all."

He was so smug sometimes. It was fucking obnoxious.

I glanced over at Penny, who looked bored. Her mind was somewhere else. I threw my hands up. "Well, I better be going. I'll head out this way." I pointed at the still-open garage door leading to the driveway.

"Yeah, I came home for lunch and thought Penny and I could sneak in some husband-and-wife time before our son gets home."

I already said I was leaving, you fucker. Always pouring salt in the wound.

"See you, P," I said without looking at her. "Peace, man," I said to her smug-ass husband. *I know you won, asshole. No need to rub it in.* I walked quickly out of the garage and as soon as my foot hit the driveway, the automatic garage door began closing.

Two hours later, I got a text from Penny.

Penny: Sorry about earlier.
That was weird.

> **Me: Whatever. It's fine. I threw up**
> **a little in my mouth when he said**
> **"husband and wife time" though.**
> **Please tell me he doesn't call it**
> **a marriage bed.**

Penny: LOL

Pennyloyalty . . .

16. Fourteen Years Ago

PENNY

I could feel and smell spring coming on. The snow was melting, my feet didn't ache as much anymore, and my muscles weren't as sore. Joey and I had three weeks until our finals performance but we were ready.

After practice I met Ling for a drink and then stopped at Pete's on my way home to see if Gavin was working. We studied together often but he was still seeing Lottie . . . so there was that.

"Hey," he said, walking toward my car. "What's up? Where've you been lately?"

I rolled the window down and stuck my head out. "Just practicing a lot."

"I'm off in ten. You want to get a bite?"

"I just stopped by to say hi."

He rolled his eyes. "Hi, okay. Now let's go eat." He waved to Pete. "Hey man, are we good?" Pete nodded, letting Gavin know he could leave. Reaching for my driver-side door handle he said, "Scoot over, let me drive."

I crawled over the center console into the passenger seat. He glanced at my body and down to my bare feet, wrapped in tape. "What?" I said.

"Aren't your feet cold?"

"No, they're burning up. I had a gross infection on my big toe."

"You look banged up and a little too thin, P."

I looked out the window, avoiding eye contact. "No such thing in dance. Just drive."

"But you have to be strong."

I turned and glared at him. "Drop it, please."

"We're going to get burgers. One burger is not going to make you fat."

He had a bandage on his lower neck, peeking from the neckband of his sweatshirt. "Please tell me you didn't get a neck tattoo." He unzipped his hoodie, lifted his white T-shirt, and pulled a bandage from the left side of his chest, revealing a tattoo of the exact "L" that Laverne wore on her sweaters in Laverne and Shirley.

He smiled. "For Lottie."

I shook my head. "That is Laverne's 'L.'"

"I know. Isn't it funny?"

"No." I shook my head. "Just drive."

Pulling his shirt down and laughing, he put the car in gear and drove onto the main road. "You jealous?"

"Not at all."

WE WENT TO a place that had a million different kinds of burgers and beers; it was mostly famous for the buffalo burgers. The mere thought made me nauseous but it was one of Gavin's favorite places. I ordered a turkey burger, no bun, with a side salad and a light beer.

"A French fry is not going to kill you." He tried feeding me one but I waved his hand away.

"So what's new?" I asked.

"Nothing much. I just found out that I'm three units short of having an English degree, too."

"So you're getting your engineering degree and then you'll take one class over the summer and get an English degree as well?"

"Yup." He took a bite of his burger and talked through a mouth full of food. "Crazy, huh?"

"Wow, Gavin, that's so impressive. I had no idea."

"Me neither. I don't know what I'm going to do with it. Maybe go track down Carissa and write a book with her, or do some stupid performance art in Denver."

"What about Lottie?"

"What about her?" he said nonchalantly.

"Well, you got a fucking 'L' tattooed on your chest."

It wasn't always easy to pry things out of Gavin; sometimes he would catch me completely off guard with a gut-spilling confession. Other times he would be totally enigmatic and evasive. "I like her. A lot. She likes to fight, though." He drank the rest of his beer and smiled serenely. He was staring into my eyes. I was chewing my burger slowly, wondering what he was thinking. "Not like you, Little P. You're a lover."

I swallowed hard.

He looked down at his lap to check his phone. "Speak of

the devil. Lottie's off work. I should probably get home and take a shower. I'm meeting her later."

"Where does she work?" We rarely talked about Lottie if we could help it. I never even asked him how she felt about our friendship.

"Jamba Juice." He laughed.

"Why's that funny?"

"I don't know. I'm convinced all the blender noise makes her a little agro."

"That's a stupid theory." We paid the check. "Come on, I'll take you back to your car," I said.

He grabbed my hands from across the table. "P, don't fall apart over this, okay?"

Like a little girl? I thought. "I'm not going to. You sure think a lot of yourself."

"I just mean don't read into this too much." He pointed to the tattoo bandage.

I breezed past his comment. "Are you coming to my finals performance in three weeks? I think my parents and Keeks are actually gonna be there."

"I wouldn't miss it for the world."

We were staring into each other's eyes. I thought about our blind kiss and how his lips felt on mine. I sighed. "You can bring Lottie if you want. We should all be friends, you know? So you and I can see each other more outside of our one-off study sessions."

"I agree, but I think she's jealous of you."

"Why?"

"I love you for not knowing why." *Did he just say I love you?* It wasn't quite the real thing but it was something.

Several moments of silence passed between us. He was

the only person I could unselfconsciously look at in silence for that length of time.

"I love you, Gavin."

His mouth dropped open like he was going to say something, and then he shut it. My eyes filled with tears.

We were still clutching hands over the table, staring. "I love you too, Penny." He smiled, a small, tight, humble, and loving smile. An expression I'll never forget.

"All right, let's go, dork." I pulled him out of the booth while simultaneously wiping tears from my eyes.

THREE WEEKS CAME and went, just like the snow had come and gone. It was the end of college for me. I had passed my written finals and only had my dance recital left, which would officially allow me to get my degree. Everything was looking up, and the future seemed promising. Ling was going to med school in California in the fall, but we still had the summer in Fort Collins. Gavin was going to take one more class over the summer for his English degree and then he would be on the job hunt, like me.

I saw him a lot in those three weeks; I actually spent a few nights out with him, Ling, and Lottie, like we were on a freaking double date. Lottie was pretty dull, in my opinion, but then again, maybe I was just jealous.

On the night of my performance, I saw Joey outside the auditorium arguing with Doug. "What's going on?"

Joey turned to me, fuming. "I failed the fucking written."

"What?"

"Calm down," Doug said. "I'm going to let him retake it."

"He's the best dancer in this program," I argued, though it wasn't totally true.

Joey was just shaking his head.

"Come on, let's go warm up," I said to him.

He followed me to the backstage door. I stopped on the sidewalk when I saw my family walking up. Kiki had the biggest grin on her face. I think she was relieved not to be the center of attention, for once.

"I'll be there in a minute, Joey. Don't sweat it, man. We'll show him onstage."

He didn't respond. Instead he shot me a pouty look. I hugged my dad, who was practically jumping out of his shoes. "Hey guys!" I patted Kiki's head. "You should be able to get great seats. You're pretty early."

"Your dad insisted on getting here an hour early, even though Kiki had to miss a piano lesson," my mom said.

Jesus. *Can't I have just one night?*

"I'm just excited to see my girl dance," my dad chimed in, breaking the awkward moment. "Your mother is, too."

"Awh, thanks, Dad." I gave him another hug and then hugged my mom awkwardly and thanked her for coming. I was still annoyed by her comment but she was here. That was all that mattered.

I saw Ling and Lance walking up to the auditorium. Lance gave me a squeeze and then immediately went up to my dad and started talking shop with him as they walked inside. Ling and I remained on the sidewalk outside the auditorium.

"I didn't know you were coming with Lance. Are you guys . . . together?"

She scoffed. "Are you kidding? He's obsessed with you.

We drove here together and he wouldn't stop talking about you the entire way over."

"Wait. No. Really?"

She rolled her eyes. "How have you not noticed? By the way, I saw Gavin and Lottie in the parking lot. They're on their way in. It looked like they were fighting or something, though."

"I think they're always fighting."

"Gavin's not exactly easy to get along with."

I furrowed my brow. "What do you mean?"

"I don't know. He's dramatic and all over the place."

"Yeah, but I like that about him." I checked the time. "Sorry, I gotta get in there and warm up."

"Aight, break a leg, sister." We fist-bumped. I smiled as she walked away and I headed to the backstage area to warm up. All of my favorite people were there, and they were about to see me do my favorite thing in the world.

Everything up to the performance was a blur. I was so nervous but before I knew it, Joey and I were next to go on. I peeked from behind the curtain and saw my family, Lance, and Ling in the front row. I searched for Gavin and noticed him and Lottie in the back row, standing in the aisle. They were whispering animatedly and waving their hands around angrily. Suddenly, she stormed out the back auditorium door and he spun around toward the stage, shaking his head as if to send me some subliminal apology. He turned and took off after Lottie, letting the heavy door slam as he left. Luckily, the dancers on stage weren't fazed by it.

But I was.

He was gone.

"Ready?" Joey asked, taking my hand. He seemed to have calmed down.

"Yeah," I squeaked.

Gavin was gone.

I wouldn't miss it for the world. Isn't that what he had said?

17. Five Months Ago

PENNY

Frank got much worse very quickly. One night, Gavin called me to tell me Frank had been unconscious for twelve hours.

I felt helpless as I rocked Gavin on his dad's couch. He sobbed into my shirt. It was three a.m. and he was totally exhausted. "He doesn't feel any pain," I whispered.

Gavin couldn't even speak. He was in my arms, letting loose guttural noises from his chest, like he was trying to push out all the feelings from his body. I always thought about how hard it would be to watch your spouse lose a parent, but Gavin wasn't my husband. I would eventually have to leave him there . . . all alone, in that house, neither one of us knowing when Frank would take his last breath.

There was a hospice worker and a nurse who were constantly in and out, but it didn't matter. Those people didn't exist. It was just Frank and Gavin and me, and the little bit of comfort I could give to both of them.

"I just want him to go," he said before breaking down again.

"Go to him and tell him it's okay."

Gavin stood on wobbly legs, his hands shaking. I wrapped my arm around his waist and walked side by side with him to his father's hospital bed.

Gavin knelt, taking his father's hand in his. He laid his head on Frank's chest. "Dad." He could barely get the words out. "I wish I was around for you more. I wish I was a better son. I wish I went to the Rockies games with you." Each word seemed more painful than the last.

"Shhh, Gavin, you were a good son," I told him as I rubbed his back.

"I love you, Dad. I'll be all right. You can let go and be at peace."

I leaned over and kissed Frank's cheek. "I love you, too, Frank," I said, and then I was crying as hard as Gavin. "You were like another father to me. Thank you."

Gavin and I both cried for what felt like forever. We held each other and then collapsed onto the couch near Frank's bed. At four thirty a.m., I got a text from my husband asking if I would be able to take Milo to school. I couldn't believe he had the nerve to ask. Why couldn't he call in late for work or ask his parents, who lived nearby? I told him no, and that I would call my mom and have her come and get Milo. My mother agreed without complaint. She still had a soft spot for Gavin.

At six thirty-three a.m., the nurse shook us awake. Frank Berninger had just taken his last breath. Almost immediately, I could see relief wash over Gavin's face.

"He's gone," he said.

"Yes," I said. It was the only response I could muster.

The hospice workers prepared for the removal of the body while Gavin and I sat around in an exhausted daze the whole morning. Around noon, they took Frank's body away. My mother showed up a couple of hours later with a bag of groceries.

She didn't say much; she just hugged us both, went into Gavin's kitchen, did the dishes, and started warming up homemade chicken soup on the stove. She brought us each a bowl on the couch.

Standing in the doorway to the kitchen, my mother said, "I'll get Milo from school and take him home. You both look like you need some rest."

I never really talked to my mother about my relationship with Gavin. She had grown to accept the fact that he would be in my life, and that he and I could be close without having a sexual relationship. One time she accused me of having an emotional affair with him, but I had shut her down by saying, "Leave it alone. You don't understand. No one understands." She never uttered a word about it after that. She loved him, too, and I didn't think she could imagine our lives without Gavin.

After she left, Gavin set the soup on the table. "I can't eat, P."

"I know." I set my bowl down, too. He kicked his shoes off. We lay down. I let him cry into my chest until, eventually, we both fell asleep, wrapped up in each other, the way we had always been.

18. Fourteen Years Ago

PENNY

The auditorium was full, our music was playing, and Joey was dancing well. But inside, I was a wreck. I had to get my mind off of Gavin. On the first Cheshire Cat lift, Joey dug his nails into my thigh, making my leg tremble as he held me. "Get it together," I seethed behind my big, bright smile. He maintained his own smiling mask as he held me up.

At one point, as I was facing the audience, I caught a glimpse of my father and Kiki smiling widely, their faces full of pride. It gave me a surge of confidence to know that my family was rooting for me, even if Gavin wasn't there.

A moment later, I was about to perform the *grand jeté*. I distinctly remember being in the air and feeling my back leg touch my head. I was in slow motion. I'd never gotten that kind of extension. I remember smiling, knowing that I was executing the move flawlessly. I was in the air with my arms outstretched and my head back when I felt Joey grab my front ankle. Then everything went black.

A few seconds later, I could feel myself on the ground writhing in pain. It felt like someone had taken a sledge-hammer to both my knee and my head. I didn't know ex-actly what had happened—all I could see was Joey standing over me, looking penitent. The music was still playing but I could hear the audience murmuring and stirring.

"Cut the music!" I heard Doug yell.

The music went out. A moment later, my father was at my side, on his knees, my mother hovering over him in shock. Doug came to my other side. "Don't move," he said.

"What happened?" I said in a weak voice.

Doug pointed at Joey and yelled, "Get the hell out of here!"

I looked up and saw Lance, Ling, and Kiki standing qui-etly behind my mother. Their eyes were wide, their expres-sions pained. "Where's Gavin?" I asked.

"You hit your head, Sweet Pea," my father told me.

"Where's Gavin?" I repeated.

"He's not here," Ling choked out. I didn't understand.

"What happened, Doug?" I asked.

"You've been hurt, Penny. An ambulance is coming. Don't move." He stared into my eyes, looking sorry and sad.

"How?" was all I could say. I was moving in and out of consciousness. My knee was throbbing.

"Please just stay still," Doug said.

I looked at my dad. "My knee. It's bad."

"We don't know that yet," he said.

But I knew.

My dad rode in the ambulance with me. Once we arrived at the hospital, they couldn't give me pain medication until they were able to do a CAT scan to make sure my head was okay. Once that was out of the way, they gave me morphine and did an MRI on my knee. Lance stayed at the hospital with my dad all night. My mom took Kiki home and Ling left for an early-morning flight to her parents' house in California. She had finished finals early as well and wanted to take advantage of the downtime before graduation. She asked me if I wanted her to cancel, but I just shook my head. What could anyone really do?

I tried to call Gavin, but his phone went straight to voicemail. Throughout the night, I went in and out of sleep. Lance stayed, refilled my water cup every hour, and tried to comfort me as my dad slept in the waiting room.

"You don't have to stay," I told him.

"I want to," he said.

IN THE MORNING, the orthopedic surgeon came in. He was thin and absurdly tall, at least six foot six, but his face was kind as he hovered over my hospital bed. Lance was slouching in a chair across from me, and my dad was standing next to my bed as I lay there helpless, my strong body just a broken pile of bones.

"Hello, Penny. How are you feeling this morning?"

"I'm in a lot of pain."

He nodded. "We'll get you something for that right away." He walked out and talked to a nurse, then returned a moment later. "Let's look at your MRI and X-ray results." He put scans up on a light board and then turned to me. "You had a mild concussion, but otherwise you're fine—"

"What about my knee?"

"I'm getting to that."

"Cut to the chase, doc," I said. A moment later a nurse was pushing morphine through my IV. I felt my chest tighten up and the wooziness of the drug settle in.

"You have some torn cartilage—"

"That doesn't sound too bad, Penny!" Lance chimed in excitedly.

"Let me finish," the doctor said. "There's a piece of cartilage between your femur and tibia that gives your knee stability."

"The meniscus," I mumbled, thinking about Doug.

"Yes," he confirmed. "There's a significant tear in your meniscus, as well as a tear in your ACL."

"You can repair them both with surgery, though, right?" my father asked.

"Both tears are very severe, I'm afraid. We'll do the best we can. We have a great team here, but there are no guarantees that your knee will fully recover. It'll take time."

"Will I be able to dance again?" I could hear myself talking but I was starting to fade from the morphine.

"All I can say is that you'll need surgery and several months of physical therapy before you'll be able to walk properly. Every patient recovers differently, and I've seen star athletes make remarkable recoveries. But that's the exception, not the rule. Recovering from two severe injuries at the same time . . . perhaps it's best to adjust your expectations now."

My eyes were starting to close. *I'll never dance again, I'll never dance again, I'll never dance again.*

Lance stood up, smoothing the hair out of my face and holding my hand.

The doctor was looking at me strangely. "Are you okay?" he asked.

"Can I have morphine?"

"The nurse just administered a dose. You should close your eyes and get some rest. We need the swelling to go down around your knee before we can get to work."

I looked at my father. His eyes were watering. The room started to go dark. The doctor was still talking, but I couldn't hear what he was saying. Lance was asking him questions. I didn't even know why Lance was still here.

"Dad?" I mumbled. He grabbed my hand and squeezed it.

"What is it, Sweet Pea?"

"Where's Gavin?"

He shook his head. "Get some sleep, baby girl."

AFTER A SOLID day in the hospital, my phone went dead. I hadn't heard from Gavin. If he needed to find me, it wouldn't be that hard—after all, my parents' phone number was tattooed on his hand.

Three days passed. The swelling went down in my knee and I was scheduled for surgery. My dad seemed to be taking my injury worse than me, though I was looped up on so many drugs I don't think I really knew what was going on. My mom and Kiki were there a lot, Ling seemed to call every hour on the hour, and I literally couldn't get rid of Lance.

An hour before my surgery, my family went to the hospital cafeteria to get some breakfast while Lance sat in a chair in my hospital room, studying. He looked up when he noticed me stirring after a short nap.

"Are you ready for this?" he asked.

"Lance Stone, you are a dead ringer for Tobey Maguire. Have I told you that?"

"Yeah, like nine hundred times in the last three days." We laughed. I was on so many drugs, I couldn't even remember what day of the week it was. "Do you like Tobey Maguire?" he asked.

"He seems nice, and he's cute." That made Lance smile.

"I can't be here when you get out of surgery but your family will be. I'm pretty sure I'm the only person who still has a final left."

I shook my head. "Don't worry about it. You've done enough."

He looked at me tentatively. "I know there's nothing between us, Penny, but I'd like there to be."

"Oh yeah?"

"Yeah."

He stood and came toward me. Taking my hand in his, he said, "I know this isn't the first thing on your mind, but I want to see you through this thing. I'll be here for you, and then you can decide if you want there to be something more between us, too."

I nodded. "Okay."

Moments later, my family was back and the nurses were prepping me for surgery. My dad held my hand as they wheeled my bed down the hallway.

"Everything's gonna be okay. I love you."

My mom mouthed the words, *I love you, too.*

"Count backwards from twenty, Penny," someone said.

"Twenty, nineteen, eighteen —"

"PENNY." A SHORT brown-haired nurse I had never seen before was hovering over me. "You've just had surgery and you're in recovery. You're coming out of the anesthesia. How are you feeling?"

"Gonna throw up." They sat me up and gave me a little tub to throw up into.

My parents came in and stood on either side of my bed. "The doctor said the surgery went well," my father said. "You have a long road ahead of you, but this was the first step and it was a success."

I don't think I even cared at that point, I was so exhausted and depressed. "Oh. Good. Where's Keeks?"

"She's at a friend's," my mother said.

They wheeled me back to my regular hospital room and tried to get me to eat some broth, which I threw up immediately afterward.

At around six p.m., my mother was getting ready to leave.

"You should go too, Dad. You need a shower. Your pits are stinking up this entire hospital floor."

"Our funny little Sweet Pea is back," my dad said.

"Just go, I'll be fine. I'm gonna take a nap."

"Come on, Liam," my mom said. They held hands and started to leave the room together. Were things getting better between them? Had my injury brought them closer? *Hopefully something good comes out of this.*

My dad stopped in the doorway and turned around. "Please try to eat something, Penny."

"I will, Dad. Don't worry."

Doug came to see me shortly after my parents left. He told me the dean at CSU had questioned Joey about the accident, and that the dance department was withholding his degree. He told me my life wasn't over, that I'd get better, that I'd find satisfaction as a teacher. None of this brought me any relief.

He hugged me and told me to hang in there, then he left. Once he was gone, I flipped on the TV and dozed off to the opening jingle of *The Golden Girls*.

WHEN I WOKE up, the room was dark and the TV was off. My knee was aching so intensely I thought I was going to die. I went to press the button on the remote to call the nurse but was startled by a figure in the corner, leaning up against the wall. He stepped into the light.

"Gavin?"

His expression was one of deep sorrow. There were tears in his eyes.

"I'm so sorry, P," he choked out.

"I need morphine," I said.

He went to the door and peeked into the hallway. "She's in a lot of pain," he told someone before coming to my bed-side. He collapsed onto my chest, tucking his head under my chin. I felt his body shaking. He was really crying.

"I'm sorry," he said again. I didn't hold him. I couldn't bring myself to show him any affection. My arms stayed at their sides.

"Where have you been?"

He stood and wiped tears from his face. "Lottie threw my phone into a lake. I called your parents' house the day after your performance but no one answered. I thought everything went well. You had that routine down. When I called your cell, it went straight to voicemail."

"You got into a fight with Lottie and left the auditorium. I saw you."

"I'm sorry, Penny. I fucked up." The nurse came in and pushed morphine into my IV. "I finally got ahold of your mom this morning and she told me what happened," Gavin said. "I went looking for Joey. I was gonna break his legs."

"Please don't do that. He's going to be punished. Believe me."

"How do you feel?" He was searching my eyes.

"Fucking fantastic. Did you and Lottie break up?"

He studied me closely. "No, we just had a fight."

"You missed my performance because you got into a fight with your girlfriend. You weren't there for me like you said you would be. You should leave. I don't know why you're here."

"I'm trying to be here for you now. I told you I'm sorry. It was a miscommunication, Penny. A badly timed fight. That's all."

I started feeling groggy from the meds. "You said you wouldn't miss it for the world," I slurred. "What a lie."

"Penny, I love you. You're my best friend. I fucked up and I'm sorry." He was squeezing my hand. "Please forgive me."

"It doesn't matter. I'm dating Lance now," I lied.

He swallowed hard. "What? I thought you didn't date."

"I never said that. I said that I wasn't ready to date when we met. I said I would see where our friendship took us, and I asked you to wait. You didn't. And when I needed you most, you weren't there. I hardly knew Lance before this accident but he's been here every day—unlike you. The only reason he's not here now is because he's taking his last final. In fact, he'll be here soon."

Gavin was shaking his head.

"You should leave before he gets back."

"You're overreacting," he said. "Don't go jumping into some bio-nerd's arms."

"I resent that. My father is a microbiologist. A very intelligent, kind, loving, loyal, and reliable man."

"How many times am I going to have to say I'm sorry?"

"Until I feel like forgiving you, I guess. Look at me!" I pointed to my knee, wrapped in a wad of bandages and elevated in a sling.

"I'm looking at you. I always see you, Penny." His eyes were intense.

"No, *look* at me." I started to cry. "I'll never dance again."

"Shhh, don't cry, please. Your mother said the surgery was a success."

"I'll never dance again. Not like before."

The nurse came in. Gavin and I went quiet. She saw the tears and said, "I'll ask the doctor to up your dosage. We brought it down before you went into surgery, but clearly you're in a lot of pain."

"Thank you," I mumbled, though I wasn't in the kind of pain she thought I was.

Gavin was staring—no, more like *glaring*—at me. The nurse came back a moment later and pushed more morphine through my IV.

That heavy-chested feeling hit me again and my vision got fuzzy. Gavin's expression turned sympathetic. "I'm sorry," he whispered.

I shook my head.

"Don't date that guy. Please, P."

"Go."

"I love you."

"Go be with Lottie." I was fading from the meds. "Go," I slurred, and then I was out.

19. Three Months Ago

GAVIN

"Ahh!" Penny was screaming with delight as she turned the go-cart swiftly and spun out into the guardrail. When I bumped into her, Milo flew by us in his cart.

Some worker kid yelled, "No bumping!"

Penny was laughing hysterically. "I'm gonna pee my pants," she squeaked.

"Don't do that!" I shouted. She was as red as a tomato.

"You're smiling, Berninger."

"Am I?"

"I love your smile. I'm glad it's back." Penny pointed to Milo in his go-cart, way ahead of us. "Come on," she said, "he's kicking our ass. We can't let him win."

She took off. I followed behind her, smiling again as I listened to her scream and squeal. She flew from one side of the track to the other with total abandon. Penny was a bad driver, even in a go-cart. Milo crashed in front of us right before the finish line and got stuck. Penny flew by him, yelling, "Ha ha, sucker!" She threw her arms up and grabbed the checkered flag from the worker's hand.

"Hey!" he yelled, but she couldn't hear him over her own hysterical laughter.

After she took off her helmet, her hair was flying everywhere. The worker kid came and grabbed the flag out of her hand. "You're not supposed to do that," he said.

"I won, though. Don't I get to keep that thing?"

"No," he said as he walked away.

She looked at me and smirked. "Twenty bucks for five minutes—in the off-season, no less! I win and I don't even get to keep the checkered flag."

"Your hair looks really good right now."

She socked me in the arm. "Come on, I have to get home and help Milo with some stupid project."

"Okay."

I tried to hold her hand on the way to the car, but she pulled out of my grasp.

"Not in front of Milo."

"That stuff doesn't even faze him."

"Yes, it does."

She drove home like a maniac and I had to remind her we weren't in go-carts anymore.

Leaving me in the driveway of my dad's house, she pulled away and then stopped and rolled down the passenger-side window.

"Good day today, huh?"

"Yep," I said, nodding. "Thanks, you guys."

I threw up a peace sign at her and she cruised down the street to her house.

My dad's house was dark and deafeningly quiet. I grabbed a thicker jacket, a beer from the fridge, and my guitar and went out onto the porch. I messed around on the guitar all night, drinking to hopefully pass out later. On my fourth beer, I heard the unmistakable sound of Penny's ankles cracking and Buckley's leash jingling.

"Hey," she said from the curb as Buckley took a shit on my dad's front lawn.

"Really, Buckley? You fucker!"

"He likes this lawn," Penny said, laughing. "He shits on it every morning."

I huffed. "I know. I can't believe you leave it."

"I thought it would give you something to do."

"You're helping your grieving friend by making him pick up moist dog poop every day?"

"Well, does it make you mad?"

"Yeah, it does." She came walking up to the porch and sat down next to me while Buckley stayed on the icy lawn.

"Perfect, then I have successfully redirected your anger. Now, tell me why you're sitting out here in the cold." It was the end of February so it was still pretty chilly.

"It's hard to be in there sometimes."

"I can understand that. But it will go away, trust me."

"I'm not staying here, Penny. I'll rent it out or sell it, but I'm not staying—it's too hard. We've already talked about this. As soon as I go through all my dad's stuff, I'm going back to Denver."

"Okay, okay. I won't bug you about it anymore. Let's talk about something less loaded. How was your date with Briel?" She grinned devilishly.

"Ha! As if she didn't tell you herself. It was two dates,

actually. We got coffee the first time and then I saw her band play the other night. She's a great singer."

Penny was nodding. "She is. But do you like her?"

I shrugged. "It's hard to know how I feel. I know it's already been two months, but Dad's death is still so fresh in my mind. I'll say this: Briel's nice, I enjoy her company, and she's decent looking."

She elbowed me in the ribs. "You're so shallow. She's beautiful."

"She *is* beautiful. Not like you, though."

"So you're gonna go out with her again?"

"Yeah, I guess. I like her accent. The way she says my name, *Gaveen*. And her visa expires in three months."

"What's that supposed to mean? Is that a plus because you know you won't have to commit?"

"Yeah, kind of."

She elbowed me again.

"No, we had fun. She came back to my apartment after the show and I played her some songs and she sang along. But they don't mean anything."

"The songs?"

"Yeah."

"Did you sleep with her?"

"Penny," I warned. The fact was that I *had* slept with Briel, but it was awkward as hell. Not passionate. It felt like she was fawning over me. She told me tall American men were like unicorns in her country. I guess it did make me feel good, but the feeling was short-lived. I'd take go-carts, celibacy, and Penny over Briel any day.

Penny and I still had a spark that couldn't be snuffed out. All the plans I'd drawn for the life I thought we'd have together were playing out in some parallel universe. Even if I was stuck in this stupid version of us, where she was encouraging me to go out with other women, I knew there was a Penny and Gavin living as a couple out there, right along beside us.

Penny shivered, and I put my arm around her. "Wait, did you say *your* apartment? When did you go back to Denver? I didn't even notice you'd left."

"I just went for the day last Saturday. I don't tell you everything, you know? Anyway, you're the one who pushed her on me. Now I think she's in love with me. I guess her mom's coming to visit and she wants me to meet her."

"Wow, that was fast." She stared straight ahead. "And for the record, I didn't push her on you. I just suggested you date her to take your mind off things." She huffed. "I should get going before you-know-who sends a search party out for me."

"Wait, let me play you something. Have you ever heard the song 'Joy' by Iron and Wine?"

"I don't know that I have," she said.

"Let me play it for you. I've been listening to it a lot, and it reminds me of you. I appreciate what you've done for me and I want you to know it."

"I'm sold. Play it."

I started strumming and singing:

Born bitter as a lemon, but you must understand
That you've been bringin' me joy

"Stop!" She cut me off. She was crying. "Stop, please."

I put down the guitar and took her in my arms. "It's true,

Penny. If it wasn't for you, I don't know how I would have gotten through these last two months."

She sniffled and we held each other for a long time.

"Penny!" I heard her husband yell from their lawn. "Are you out here?"

She jumped up and grabbed Buckley. "Shit, I have to go."

She walked briskly down the street, ankles cracking, knees popping. I stood on the sidewalk and watched. I heard Penny yelling but knew I shouldn't get involved. I loved her, after all. What was I supposed to do?

20. Fourteen Years Ago

PENNY

Lance came to almost every single one of my physical therapy sessions in between finals and graduation. I was trying to rehab my knee but progress was slow. Almost every session ended in frustration, but Lance had the patience of a saint.

On Commencement Day, Doug wheeled me up the ramp to the stage to receive my diploma. Although I technically hadn't completed my final's performance, Doug had given me an A and some good news: Joey wouldn't be graduating.

I didn't press charges against Joey. The university basically rejected all his pleas to transfer his dance credits to another college after Doug filed a report about the incident and the months leading up to it. I don't know where he went, but I never saw him or heard from him again.

As we all hung out after Commencement, I could tell Gavin was no longer standoffish toward Lance. He had no right to be. He was swept up in Lottie, and Lance was there for me in ways Gavin couldn't be. I had forgiven him, and we had fallen back into our friendly routine of hanging out once a week or so, but something had changed between us. I think we could both sense it.

"Congrats, P," he said as he bent to kiss my cheek.

"Thanks. Congrats to you, too. I'm sorry I couldn't make it to your engineering department ceremony yesterday. You know I can't miss a single PT session, right?"

"Don't sweat it," he said. "My mom and dad were there. Lottie, too."

Gavin, Lottie, Ling, Lance, my family, and I were all by a tree waiting for the parking lot to clear out after the ceremony. My dad was getting over a nasty bout of pneumonia and was hacking pretty badly, but he still had dragged himself out of bed to see his baby girl graduate.

"Liam," Gavin said, "why don't you guys take off so you can go home and get some rest? We'll take Penny out to celebrate."

I noticed Lottie's shoulders sag. She whispered something to Gavin. "We'll do that tomorrow," he whispered back. She pouted but we all ignored her.

My parents and Kiki hugged me good-bye and headed toward the car, leaving me with Lance, Ling, and the two lovebirds.

Lance was checking his voicemail and smiling. "Yes! I have an interview tomorrow at a huge pharma company. I'm stoked—it's already starting!"

I high-fived him. "We all have so much to celebrate. Let's get outta here."

"Ugh, I really feel like a fifth wheel," Ling said.

"We'll get my crutches and go to a bar. This isn't a double date—just a casual hang." Ling rolled her eyes at me.

Gavin and Lottie rode in his car, and Ling and I went with Lance in his pristine vehicle. When Lance helped me into the front seat, he pulled my seatbelt around for me and then pecked me on the lips. It was our first kiss.

I grabbed his neck and pulled him in for a more intimate kiss, but the sparks just weren't flying. He was trying, but strangely it felt awkward on his end as well. Too forced and rigid. When he pulled away, he was smiling, so I smiled back.

"That was nice," he said before shutting my door and walking around to the driver's side.

Ling leaned forward from the backseat. "What was that? I thought you didn't like him?"

"He's growing on me."

"Sounds like a freakin' fairy tale."

"Shh, he's coming." I swatted at her and gave Lance a big smile as he opened the driver-side door.

ONCE WE GOT to the bar, I used my crutches to propel myself to a barstool. All my friends made way for me and basically kicked some guy out of his seat so I could sit at the end of the bar. They gathered around me, menus in hand.

"I'll get your first drink," Gavin said. "Wait, are you allowed to mix pain meds with alcohol?"

"I'm not on that stuff anymore, so I'm drinking, yo! Tequila shots!"

Lance shook his head. "I'll get Penny's," he said to Gavin.

Gavin raised a brow. "I was just gonna buy her one celebratory drink, man."

Thankfully Lottie was busy talking to Ling and wasn't watching this lame macho face-off unfold.

"Actually," Gavin said, "how about I get this round, then you get the next?"

Lance nodded. Gavin could be extremely hard to deal with, but when it came to me, there was a gentleness in him. This was his version of backing off.

I hadn't drunk in a while so the alcohol hit me pretty hard. Before I knew it I was swaying on the stool. Gavin wouldn't leave my side and Lottie wouldn't leave him, so I had at least two bodies to break my fall if I fell to the ground. Around eleven, Lance said, "I gotta get going to prepare for my interview tomorrow. Ready, Penny?"

Gavin had his arm around Lottie, and Ling was talking to some guy at the end of the bar.

"I guess," I said. Though I didn't really want to leave.

"We can drop her off if you have to get going, Lance. You want to stay a little longer, P?"

"Well, I just want to wait for Ling. I told her I'd wait," I lied.

"I'll take them," Gavin said.

"Seems kind of senseless since Ling and I live in the same building," Lance argued.

"Why not let the girls decide?" Gavin countered.

"Ling!" Lance called down the bar, waving at her.

She stood up and stalked toward us. "You trying to cock block me, Lance? I'm pretty into that guy—can't you tell?"

"Jeez, I was just checking to see if you wanted a ride. I have to get going."

"I can take care of myself, but thank you." She turned to Gavin. "You staying for a while?"

He nodded.

"Great. You can give me a ride if things don't go well with the hot guy."

"No problem."

She looked back at Lance. "I think we're covered, Lance. Penny has the okay from her doctor to drink, and I think she wants to celebrate a little longer—that is, of course, unless Penny wants to go home with you."

They all turned and looked at me. "Sorry, Lance. I just want to hang out for a bit. Do you mind?"

"It's fine," he said before leaning down and kissing me on the cheek.

"Please don't be mad. Good luck tomorrow. I know you'll get the job."

He shrugged and walked away. "We'll see."

Gavin pretended like Lance wasn't annoying because, honestly, what could Gavin really say when Loonie Lottie was on his arm?

"You're just gonna play Mr. Cabdriver to these girls?" Lottie said.

"Yes, I am," he shot back. I think he was past the point of taking her shit. Lottie was a year behind us at Colorado State, so she wasn't in celebration mode. Still, she could've been a little less whiny and clingy and let the rest of us bask in the glory of our achievements, if you ask me.

I continued to drink from my perch on the stool with my leg propped on a chair. After Gavin triple-checked to make sure I wasn't going to take a plunge face-first onto the floor, he and Lottie went out onto the dance floor. He was a good dancer even though he swore he wasn't. Meanwhile, Ling sucked face with Romeo at the other end of the bar for about five minutes and then eventually came over to hang out with me.

"What happened? I thought you were into that guy?"

"He was supersmart and great to talk to . . . and then he kissed me. Ick. He practically stuck his whole tongue down my throat. I was like, 'Dude, it's not a race to Tonsil Town.' Just a total turnoff, you know?" She looked out onto the dance floor. "Figures that Gavin's a good dancer."

"Most guys who are good kissers are good dancers. Have you noticed that? Not that I have that much experience. It's just a rhythm thing, and an understanding of the way another person moves." I started to feel sad.

I was pretty out of it by the time we left. As we headed for Ling's, I was surprised when Lottie asked to be dropped off first. "Why?" Gavin asked. "You don't want to come back to my place?"

"No, I have to work early." She lived in a complex on the way to Ling's, and I lived closer to Gavin, so it actually made more sense to drop her off first. I didn't think Lottie thought of me—The Gimp—or even Ling as much of a threat anymore.

When we got to her building, Gavin got out and walked her to her door. When he returned, he quietly drove the rest of the way to Ling's. She hopped out, shot us a peace sign, and said, "Thanks, G."

"No problem."

"Penny, I'll see you tomorrow."

"See you," I said.

Once we were back on the road, Gavin looked over

at me and said, "I like her. You were right; she is a good friend."

"I don't want to go home, Gavin."

He threw his head back and laughed. "Okay then. You want to stay at my place? Sleep with Jackie Chan?"

"I thought we could spoon. I'm just cold and lonely."

The honesty wasn't hard under the influence.

"I'm pretty sure Lance would be willing to solve that." There was an edge to his voice.

"You can take me home then."

"No, we'll go back to my apartment. Mike's at his girlfriend's place. But don't you need meds from home?"

"You have Advil, right?"

"Yeah."

"That should be fine."

"Okay."

We drove the rest of the way in silence. He carried me up the stairs but seemed so far away.

"What's wrong?" I asked.

"Nothing."

"Tell me."

"Nothing at all."

He laid me on his bed and very carefully took off my shoes. "I'm not going to break," I said.

"It's only been a few weeks since your surgery."

"I know but I'm tough and drunk and I'll be okay. I just need to call my parents."

I dialed them from my cell phone, but oddly no one answered. I left a message on the machine saying I was staying at Ling's. I didn't want to explain why I was staying at Gavin's.

Lying down, fully clothed, I turned on my good side and curled up. Gavin left his clothes on, too, and curled up behind me. I dozed off in his arms, with his face nuzzled in my hair. Nothing was awkward and nothing hurt. It felt exactly right to have him there, but he wasn't mine; he was Lottie's.

At four in the morning, I woke to the sound of my phone vibrating on the bedside table. I didn't recognize the number so I didn't answer. Ten seconds later, I had a voicemail. I pushed the voicemail button and instantly recognized my aunt's voice—my mother's sister. My heart started racing. It was unusual for her to call me at all, let alone at four in the morning. As I went to call her back, I noticed that I had several missed calls.

"Penny, sweetie," she sounded choked up, "you need to come to the hospital downtown as soon as possible." I was wiping sleep from my eyes, trying to process what I was hearing. That was her entire message. No details whatsoever.

Gavin sat up behind me, rubbing my back. "What is it?" he asked.

I hung up. "I don't know. I have to go to the hospital, though. Something's wrong. I think it might be my mom. I feel sick." I tried dialing everyone. My mother, my father, my grandparents. No one answered.

Gavin got up and started rushing around, collecting my shoes and sweater. He helped me put them on and then carried me very carefully down the stairs and put me into his car.

At the hospital, he hoisted my wheelchair from the trunk and brought it around to the passenger side, helping me in. He rushed me through the front sliding doors and yelled something at the receptionist. She pointed to the elevator and said, "Third floor."

We were greeted by a swarm of crying family members standing just outside the elevators on the intensive care floor. Kiki was hysterical, sitting in a chair, hunched over and sobbing into her knees. My mother was on the other side of the room, near the waiting room, looking shocked, tears streaming down her face. When we made eye contact, she collapsed into my grandfather's arms.

"What's going on?!" I yelled. "Where's Dad?"

My aunt Marla came to me and knelt in front of my wheelchair. "Penny, your dad had a heart attack brought on by the pneumonia. They brought him here and he coded three times. They did everything they could." She could barely speak. "He's gone."

Gone? Where? Where did he go?

I stared at her, uncomprehendingly. "He fought hard, but they couldn't save him. I'm so sorry. We're all going to miss him so much."

The earth shifted on its axis then. When someone says the words *he's gone* to you, it's hard to get your bearings. Your brain is fighting to process the information and protect you from it at the same time. In the immediate aftermath, the finality of death is impossible to accept.

"Where?" I didn't shed a tear. "Where is he?" I said, blank faced. My insides felt cavernous; all I could feel was my aunt's voice echoing *he's gone*, over and over again.

She took my hand as Gavin pushed my chair down the hall toward the ICU bay. Inside the room, my grandmother was sitting next to a bed, holding someone's hand. There were no beeping machines, no monitors . . . just my father's lifeless body.

I was in shock. My grandmother looked at me, crying, and said, "It's not natural."

"What do you mean, Gram?" My voice was weak.

"For a mother to bury her child."

I looked at my father again.

He was her child.

Gavin pushed me close to the opposite side of the bed so I could take my father's other hand in mine. That's when I knew . . . when the reality finally hit me. He *was* gone. I couldn't feel him anymore. His body was lifeless . . . soulless.

The moon, the sky, the stars, all the planets in the universe—they all crashed into me with one single, heavy thud. There was nowhere to go but sink into myself and try not to be crushed by the weight of it all. My head involuntarily dropped into my lap and I sobbed.

"Please God, no. Not you, Daddy."

21. Fourteen Years Ago

GAVIN

You can't feel anything but helpless when you see someone you love suffer such a momentous loss. What could I do?

Penny stayed in the hospital room, sobbing into her lap until they finally came in to wheel away Liam's body. No one else was there; Penny was the only one who wouldn't leave his side.

"What are you doing with him?" she asked the orderlies.

"We have to take him now," one of the men said. At the same moment, a grief counselor and a priest came into the room.

"You can bless him," Penny said, "but he wasn't religious. I don't even know if he believed in God." She looked up at me as more tears fell from her eyes. "There was still so much I didn't know about him, and I'll never get to ask." She broke down again. The priest said a prayer and knelt beside Penny's chair. He tried to comfort her.

"Your father is at peace, my child. He's not in pain."

Penny continued sobbing.

I lifted her out of her wheelchair, her knee brace clinking against the side of a small couch. She didn't flinch. I sat down, holding her on my lap. Her arms were around my shoulders, her face in my neck. Tears and snot were soaking the collar of my T-shirt. She was hyperventilating.

Rubbing her back up and down, I repeated, "Breathe. Take a breath. Breathe, Penny."

She cried and cried until I finally felt her body resign. The tension was gone and it was like I had a sleeping child in my arms. "You need water, baby."

Nodding into my shoulder, she said, "I want to see my mom."

I put her back in her wheelchair and rolled her into the ICU waiting room, which had cleared out significantly since we had gotten there. The only people left were Penny's mom, Kiki, her aunt, and her grandmother.

Anne stood on shaking legs and walked toward Penny's chair. She knelt next to it. I had never seen Penny's mom be affectionate toward her, but deep down I knew she cared about her because of how loving Penny was. Maybe once Kiki was born, Anne had transferred all her energy to her youngest. But now Penny was like a baby, mourning her dad like no one else.

Penny rested her head on her mother's shoulder. "Mama," she cried.

"I know, Penny, I know."

Kiki was crying quietly in the corner. I suddenly felt out of place. Still rubbing her back, I bent near Penny's ear and whispered, "I'm so sorry. Should I go and leave you with your family?"

"Don't leave, Gavin."

ANNE WAS STRONG that day. She held Liam's mother up, comforted Penny and Kiki, and held both their hands as we walked to the parking lot.

I asked quietly, "Anne, why don't you let me drive you all home? I can come back and get my car later." Liam's sister, Penny's aunt Jane, had finally arrived from Boulder. She and her husband both looked wrecked. They took Penny's grandma in their car, and Anne told everyone to meet back at the house.

I drove the station wagon with Penny in front because she still couldn't bend her knee. In the rearview mirror I could see Kiki's and Anne's stunned faces. Penny was making quiet mewling sounds, as if her body was so depleted she could no longer cry properly. I hadn't known that kind of grief before.

Inside the house, everyone sat in the living room in silence. I offered to pick up food for them, but no one was hungry. At four in the afternoon, there was a knock on the door. I answered. It was Lance.

"Penny texted Ling," he said from the other side of the threshold. "I didn't know if it was too early . . . but *you're* here."

"Penny's my best friend."

He shook his head and looked away down the street.

"Can I talk to her?"

"She just lost her dad. I don't think she feels like talking."

Penny hobbled into the hallway on her crutches.

Standing behind me, she said, "Lance, I'll call you later, okay? Right now I need to be with my family."

Lance looked from Penny to me and back again as if to say, *Is this guy family?* But to his credit, he caught himself. "I'm so sorry, Penny," he said. "I'll call you tomorrow and check in."

That rest of the night was surreal. Anne asked me to stay with Penny in her room, while she and Kiki slept in Kiki's room. I don't think anyone could bear to go into the master bedroom yet.

The rest of the family members left. Lottie was blowing up my phone while I was peeling Penny's clothes off. I had plied Penny, Kiki, and Anne with water and crackers for hours, until they were finally so exhausted they crawled into bed.

Penny was shivering, her body still shuddering every thirty seconds from hyperventilating for so long. I curled up behind her and tried to soothe her. "How's your knee, Penny?"

"What knee?" She fell asleep a moment later. Her body still spasmed periodically throughout the night. It was hard for me to sleep, knowing that she was so physically strung out.

Around two a.m., I heard Anne crying in the bathroom. I went into the hallway and knocked on the door. "Are you okay, Anne?"

She opened the door, her face red and puffy, no makeup on, her hair a mess. There's no vanity in that kind of grief. "I wish I had been a better wife," she said.

I rubbed her back as we stood there in the doorway. "He loved you. You loved him. That's all that matters."

"I neglected him," she said. "He took care of us . . . and I neglected him."

"It's just life. I think it happens when you've been married for so long. But I saw the way he looked at you. He adored you, Anne." She fell into my arms and cried.

"Penny loves you," she said when she was finally able to catch her breath. "Penny's afraid she loves you too much. She'd never loved anything as much as her father and dancing until you came along. She can't dance anymore . . . and now her dad's gone. She's lost so much, all at once. You're all she has left, Gavin."

"She has you and Kiki and Ling . . . and Lance." I hated saying his name.

"Pfft, Lance, please. Lance is a distraction. She loves *you*. Oh Gavin, what am I going to do? How am I going to take care of these girls?"

"You just will. You have to."

She wiped the tears from her eyes and squared her shoulders. "I just have to. You're right. I need to give Penny more. I've neglected her, too. I've poured everything into Kiki."

"Stop beating yourself up, Anne. No one could have predicted this. He was so young."

"He was our rock."

"You'll be the rock now."

She nodded, and I could sense her resolve.

THE NEXT MORNING I took a cab to get my car and bring back chicken soup from a deli near Penny's house. Penny, Anne, and Kiki thanked me endlessly. I told them I had to get home and feed Jackie Chan, but I promised to come back later.

The truth was that I hadn't spoken to Lottie since I'd dropped her off at her apartment. I had thirteen voicemails from her. I did text her to tell her I was okay, and that I had a family emergency, but I waited until I was in my apartment to call her back.

"What the fuck, Gavin?" she said the minute she answered the phone.

"I'm sorry, Lottie. Penny's dad died right after commencement."

The phone went quiet for several moments. "You said family emergency." She didn't bother asking what happened. That should have been a red flag, but in the moment, I was too exhausted to notice.

"They're like family," I told her.

"Hmm, well, okay . . . Tell her I'm very sorry." She huffed into the phone. "But I need you too, Gavin. Can I come over?"

Maybe she's going to break up with me.

"Okay."

I rushed around, making sure there was no evidence of Penny. When the doorbell rang, I opened it and said, "If you're going to start a fight with me, can you let me shower first? I've been running around the whole day."

She started untying her long black coat to reveal nothing but a matching lace bra and panty set underneath. "Why don't we shower together?"

She walked past me into the living room. I closed the door and followed her toward the bathroom.

22. Fourteen Years Ago

PENNY

In the days following my father's death, my mother flip-flopped between crying and getting shit done. She had my father cremated, planned his service, cried, went through all of their finances, cried, called the lab, cried, went to Home Depot to buy a gallon of paint, cried, painted her bedroom like a crazy person, and cried some more. Kiki and I helped.

When we were done, she stepped back to admire our work. "Shall we paint the whole house?" she asked.

That's exactly what we did. It was my mother's own brand of bereavement therapy, and Kiki and I were happy to go along with it. I hobbled around, filling up pans, while she and Kiki painted. Gavin popped in periodically, and Lance came over to help for a few days, too. I was amazed by how patient Lance was with me. He never pushed me for anything more, even after I had surprised him with a kiss on graduation day. Even though I still didn't feel a spark between us, I was comforted by his solid presence. I was even coming to rely on him.

WE HELD MY father's service on a beautiful lakeshore just outside of Fort Collins. Gavin played my dad's favorite song, "Hey Jude," on his Telecaster. Everyone cried.

Kiki spoke for all of us. After all, she was the best public speaker in the family, even at her young age. My mom helped her write the eulogy. I don't know who added it, but there was a line in there that said, "My dad loved us all, and he loved his job. But his favorite thing in the whole world was watching my sister dance. She's such a beautiful dancer, and my dad was so proud of her." My stupid knee ached at the words. *My dad was so proud of her.* I broke down.

This time, Lance was there to comfort me. Gavin and Lottie were there, too, but in the back row. My mother, stoic, sat on the other side of me. Ten days of huffing paint and crying had made her zombielike. How the hell Kiki pulled that eulogy off without falling apart, I'll never know. I guess all of her pageant training was paying off in ways I hadn't expected. I certainly wouldn't have been able to stand in front of a crowd and speak about my father without crumbling into a ball and turning to dust myself.

A MONTH BLURRED by. My father had a great life insurance policy, thank God, enough for Kiki to go to college and my mom to pay off the house—but not enough to set them up long-term. My mom would have to get a job. The lab, fortunately, adored my father and offered my mother a well-paying secretarial position. She'd never had a job in her life, but she was grateful.

I'd never realized how brave my mother was, and my respect for her grew with each day after my father's passing. She funneled all of her pageant energy into being a strong woman and mother. She refused to be defined by her grief and widowhood.

I, on the other hand, fell apart on the daily: at physical therapy, in my room alone, and especially when I was with Gavin.

One night after dinner, Kiki came into my room, closed my door, and sat at the end of my bed. "Do you think it would kill Mom if I told her I didn't want to do the pageants anymore?"

I shook my head. I knew this was coming. "No, Keeks. I know I haven't always been the best big sister, and I've never really given you any advice worth taking, but this I know for sure: You have to tell her. She can take it now. She's different. Hell, she might even be happy about it. But you also have to find something to focus on. Maybe not right now, but eventually, when you're in high school and stuff. Stick with the piano or play a sport or something."

"No, I know. Cara Keller plays softball. I think I want to try that."

I cringed inwardly at the thought of Kiki telling my mother she was swapping pageantry for softball, but at least my sister would learn teamwork, not superficial competition with, and hatred toward, other girls. "I think that's a great idea. But give Mom another couple of months. Didn't she cancel the upcoming pageants anyway?"

"Yeah."

"Wait until she brings it up."

"Yeah, that's what I'll do. Thanks, Penny." She left my room and went to bed.

Later that night I went into my mom's room, where I found her in the walk-in closet, sitting on the floor. She was clutching one of my dad's shirts to her face, crying into it. I sat beside her and cried with her.

She started laughing and crying at the same time. "Remember when I was pregnant with Kiki and I made your dad drive all the way to Denver to that chocolatier I loved?"

"I remember. I went with him."

"I was convinced it was the only thing that could make me happy."

"Did it?"

"Yes, for about three hours." We laughed. "You were an easygoing baby. Kiki gave me such a hard time. I never felt well while I was pregnant with her."

"Well, you were older."

"After I had her, I had postpartum depression. And I never told you. You were too young, anyway." She was blinking up at the ceiling. "Kiki cried so much as a baby. I just couldn't bond with her."

I looked up at the ceiling, too. "I remember her crying."

"I wanted to throw her in a trash can. I had visions of it." Shocked by her candor, I was speechless as she went on. "I was in a very dark place, and your dad helped me out of it. He would have done anything for me."

"I know, Mom."

Minutes were strung on a clothesline of memories until she spoke again.

"That's how Gavin is with you. He'd do anything for you."

"Gavin has a girlfriend. He and I are just friends."

"Lottie won't last," she mumbled.

Trying to change the subject, I said, "Is that why you gave Kiki so much attention?"

She paused, contemplative. "Yes. I'm sure part of it was guilt—later, relief that I had finally bonded with her."

I put my arm around her awkwardly. My knee brace got in the way of everything. She held me back for a long time. I hadn't realized how much I'd missed her affection.

"Mom, Kiki doesn't want to do the pageants anymore. I told her to hold off on telling you, but she came to me tonight. I just thought you should know."

She wasn't the least bit surprised. "I know. I was going to talk to her about it and let her know it's all right with me. I'm still proud of her."

"Me too."

"And, Penny, I'm proud of you, too. You're a college graduate and you're a beautiful dancer. Your knee will heal. And you'll get your chance again. I believe it."

"I hope so."

TWO WEEKS LATER, Gavin called and asked what I had planned for the day. I told him my mom was taking me to physical therapy at ten that morning.

"Want me to pick you up afterward? We can go grab a bite."

"Yeah, that sounds good. I'll be done at eleven thirty."

"See you then."

"Peace."

On our way to physical therapy I asked my mom what she was doing for the rest of the day.

"Kiki and I are going to see a therapist as well, but a different kind. I just thought it would be good if we both had someone to talk to. Let me know when you're ready, Penny. I can set up an appointment with Dr. Rush for you, too." She was still on an impressive proactive streak, hoping my father's sudden death wouldn't fuck us up too horribly.

"Thanks for the offer, Mom. I just wanted to let you know that Gavin's picking me up, so I'll see you guys back at home. Good luck at therapy today." I hobbled into PT.

Stephanie, my physical therapist, worked my knee hard that day. I was finally doing weight-bearing exercises for the first time, and it hurt like hell.

At eleven thirty, I made my way out to the bench in front of the clinic and waited for Gavin. Even though it was summer, there was a chill in the air. I had on a tank top and shorts.

At eleven forty-five, I texted him.

Me: Where are you?

No response.

At noon, I tried calling my mom but her phone was turned off. She must've been in her therapy session with Kiki.

At twelve thirty, Gavin still wasn't answering. I was worried that he had gotten into a car wreck and started to panic. I called Lance. He was there in just ten minutes.

"What happened?" he said after I got in the car.

"Gavin was supposed to get me, but he's an hour late and not answering his phone."

"What were your plans?"

"We were just going to get some lunch," I said, irritated.

"I was just asking, Penny."

I looked at him and felt guilty. It wasn't his fault Gavin flaked. He was there to get me in ten minutes flat. I noticed he had on suit pants, a dress shirt, and a tie. He must've come straight from his new job.

Finally, I got a text from Gavin.

> Gavin: Fuck, P. I just drove by your PT and you were gone. I'm so sorry. Fucking Lottie locked me out of the house and threatened to kill herself. I almost called the police. She finally let me in to get my keys. She's at work now. Where are you? I'll come get you?

> Me: GO. FUCK. YOURSELF. I waited an hour. I was cold and my fucking knee is killing me. I'm done with Lottie's shit and you should be too. You thrive on having a psychopath for a girlfriend. I got a ride. Thanks anyway.

> Gavin: Please don't do this.

I didn't respond.

"Getting a lot of texts?" Lance remarked.

"It's Gavin. He got into a fight with Lottie. Shocker."

"She's kind of a nut, huh?"

"Yes, but people like Gavin like that sort of thing. Makes

him feel cool, you know?" I wasn't in the mood to psycho-analyze Gavin. "So, are you working right now?"

"Yeah, I was on my lunch. I'll drop you at home—I have to get back. Sorry, I wish I could take you for that bite but I'm out of time."

Lance had already landed a job as a pharmaceutical sales rep for a large company in Fort Collins selling a diabetes drug. Something about the fact that he had a job immediately after graduation made me like him more.

"What about tonight? Let's go out. I need to get my mind off my dad." *And Gavin.*

"Yeah, for sure, I'd love to. Dinner at seven?"

We were pulling into my driveway. "Perfect. See you then." I got out and did a backward wave to Lance as he pulled away.

As soon as I got to the door, I heard the familiar, rumbling engine of Gavin's car coming down the street. I walked into the house to the kitchen and calmly collected a dozen eggs from the refrigerator.

When he pulled into the driveway, I walked out and started chucking eggs at his car one at a time. "You want crazy?" I yelled. "I'll give you crazy!" He got out, trying to dodge the flying ova, but one got him in the hip.

"Ouch! Stop, Penny!"

"You call yourself my best friend?"

"It wasn't my fault, Penny!"

"Leave!" I screamed. "My dad just died and you leave me on the side of the street in the cold with a fucked-up knee?"

I almost fell over, trying to balance on one crutch, holding the carton of eggs in the other hand.

He held his hands out, palms up. "Just let me explain."

"Don't use your martyr act on me." I had to stop throwing eggs or I was going to fall over. "And don't come any closer." We were at least ten feet apart. His eyes were searching mine. "You hurt me every time I'm already in pain. You claim you're my best friend but I can't ever count on you to be there."

"I'm sorry, Penny!"

"I don't want to see you right now, Gavin! You need to figure things out with Lottie. I don't even know if we can be friends anymore. I don't know if I'm getting in the way of your relationship with her, or if she's getting in the way of my relationship with you, but it's not working."

"She's in love with me, Penny. And she's jealous of you. She knows you're going to be in my life . . ." He paused and swallowed. "Forever."

"We'll see. I'm going out with Lance tonight."

He let a frustrated breath. "Okay. I get it. You can't stay mad at me for long, though. I know you."

"Go home, Gavin."

"Fine," he said through gritted teeth as he walked back to his car.

"Lottie doesn't know what love is," I shouted.

He turned. "Do you?"

"Yeah, Gavin. I do. I know it's not fucking with someone all the time. Locking them out, throwing their phone in lakes, starting fights . . . leaving them out in the cold."

Silence. He was staring right at me when he whispered, "I'm so sorry. Please forgive me."

Don't cry, Penny.

"Go. Now."

I went into the house, locked the door, turned off my

phone, and slept until my alarm went off at six p.m. I could smell dinner scents emanating from the kitchen. My mother hadn't cooked since my dad died, so this was progress.

I cleaned myself up and went into the dining room where Kiki was sitting at the table, waiting. "Finally! No takeout," she said.

I sat down next to her. When my mom turned, she noticed I had gotten dressed in jeans and a blouse and put on makeup. I no longer had to wear my knee brace 24/7 but I still could only wear flats.

"You look nice! I made fettuccine Alfredo." The moment "Alfredo" came out of her mouth, she started to cry a little. It was my dad's favorite.

I went to her, took the pan out of her hand, and set it down. "Why did you make this?"

Breathing hard, she said, "I'm okay, Penny. Dr. Rush told me to make it."

"Dr. Rush sounds like a quack."

She laughed through tears. "Your dad would have said the same thing. Why do you look so pretty? Why do you look so much like him?"

"Do you think Dad was pretty?" I smiled.

Kiki got up and joined our hug. My mom rocked us back and forth. "I'm so lucky to have you girls."

"Are you going somewhere, Penny?" Kiki asked.

"I'm going to have dinner with Lance. Will you save me some of this, Mom?"

"Of course, darling."

Lance rang the doorbell at six fifty-two. Always punctual . . . and sometimes a little too early. I opened the door and kissed him. A full, openmouthed kiss.

"Wow, Penny. I didn't expect that."

"Well, you know me, full of surprises. Where are we headed?"

"I know a nice little Italian place I think you'd like. Do you need your brace or your crutches?"

"Nope, I'm on a high dose of Advil and the doc said I should walk around a bit. No dancing yet, though."

He opened the passenger door like a true gentleman. For once, I appreciated how clean his car was. When we pulled out of the driveway, it was dusk. I turned to look through the window and could just see Gavin, dressed in his typical head-to-toe black, leaning against his car across the street, watching us drive away.

I texted him.

Me: Creeper.

He didn't respond. That's when I realized he'd seen the kiss on my doorstep.

"Was that Gavin?" Lance asked as we drove by.

"No," I lied. "Just my neighbor."

23. Fourteen Years Ago

GAVIN

Penny: I need you.

Me: Where are you?

Penny: On the bench across the
street from the Stop and Shop.

I drove like a bat out of hell. Penny and I hadn't been good
for two months, but she needed me now. We talked daily in
some form, but things had been strained. She hadn't gotten
over that day I left her at the PT clinic, and I was furious
and jealous that she was dating Douche-face. She was also
grieving about her dad still . . . and grieving about dance,
which made her a loose cannon, a raw nerve . . . all the
time. The prognosis on her knee wasn't great. Her ligaments
were healing, but it would be months before she'd be able to
walk properly, let alone dance with that effortless grace she

once had. It made her depressed. Without dancing, she was also gaining weight, which made her even more depressed.

When I pulled over to the side of the street, she stood from the bus bench and limped to my car. She was wearing jeans, a tank top, a short black leather jacket, and black combat boots. She looked mean.

"Where's your car?" I asked.

"Broke down over on West Mountain."

"What do you think it is?" I pulled over and texted Pete at the garage about getting a tow truck.

"I don't know what it is. It stalled in the intersection and some lady helped me push it to the side."

I drove toward West Mountain, where I spotted her car on the edge of the road. "Give me the keys." She obliged and stayed in the car.

When I got back a few minutes later, she was looking out the window like a lost little girl. "I put the keys under the mat. Pete will send someone to tow it to the shop."

"Thanks," she said quietly.

I headed toward her house as we sat in silence. Finally, I spoke up. "What's going on, Penny? Why did you call me instead of Lance?"

"Actually, can we go to your place? I don't want to go home right now."

"Sure, but I need to stop by my dad's place and drop off a part for his car first." I studied her out of the corner of my eye. A minute later, she was crying. *What the hell's going on?*

"Hold on, hold on." I parked the car in a nearby lot and scooted across the bench seat. Taking her in my arms, I said, "What is it, P? Tell me."

"I'm . . . pregnant," she squeaked.

My heart dropped. "What?"

"I'm pregnant. With a baby." I pulled back and looked at her face. She was puffy and red.

"Lance?"

She nodded.

"Does he know?" I asked.

"No."

"You told me first?"

She nodded again.

"Have an abortion. I'll pay for it." *Oh my God, I can't let this happen.*

She was speechless. She shook her head.

"You don't even believe in God, so you don't have to keep it for religious reasons," I said.

"Yes, I do." Her sobs got louder and fuller. She tried to say more but couldn't.

"My dad will know what to do." I told her. "We'll go to his place and talk to him."

She shook her head again. "Listen, Gavin—"

"Look, I've been meaning to tell you something. I just broke up with Lottie two days ago. It's over. Okay?" It was true; I'd been waiting for the right time to tell Penny the news, to tell her how I felt about her . . . how I'd always felt about her. I never expected her to drop a bomb before I got the chance.

Don't worry. She'll have an abortion and dump that idiot and then we can be together. Finally. Was I horrible for thinking that?

"Why'd you two break up all of a sudden? I mean, you were the picture of romantic bliss and enduring love."

"Don't be a smartass. We were getting along but she's

been sick for a long time. She just found out that she's bipolar, and she's been struggling with her medication. To be totally honest, it was mutual. She needs time to focus on herself."

"Well, are you sad?"

"I'm relieved."

"Gavin, the bleeding heart."

"Look, I don't want to make this about Lottie. The point is that we did what was best for both of us. Now we're going to do what's best for you: you're going to call Planned Parenthood, make an appointment, and call Lance to break up with him."

Her hands tightened into fists. "Enough! Gavin, listen to me. They told me when the baby's due, based on how far along I am."

"What are you saying? It's too late for an abortion?"

"No!" She stopped crying. "No, it's not too late. But stop and listen to yourself. How can you be so cold? How can you say, 'Get an abortion, Penny'? Just like that? Huh?"

"No, you listen. You're not in love with Lance, and I'm not being cavalier about abortion. This isn't like you. You're resolute about your future. The Penny I know would get an abortion. This is a mistake. Bad timing. The result of irresponsible sex." I stopped. The thought of her having sex with Lance made me physically ill.

"It doesn't matter what you say because I'm not getting an abortion. The due date is my father's birthday." Her face drained of all color as she stared at me, expressionless. "And we used a condom."

Suddenly, I felt frantic. Panicky, like the conversation was slipping out of my control. "P, don't tell me you think this is the second coming of your dad?"

She shook her head. "No. I don't. I just think it's a sign. I know, in my heart, that I shouldn't have an abortion."

"You don't believe in signs."

"I do now."

"We're going to my dad's." My father adored Penny, and I knew he'd be able to talk some sense into her.

When we got to my dad's, I opened the door and walked in, with Penny trailing behind me. He was at the kitchen counter, eating smoked oysters from the can.

"Hey kids."

"Dad, Penny's pregnant with Limpdick's baby and she won't have an abortion because the due date is her dad's birthday and she thinks it's a sign and she's being irrational and she can't have this baby, it will ruin her life and Lance will always have to be around forever and this whole situation is fucked." I was practically crying as Penny stood quietly behind me. My dad just stared at me with an open mouth full of smoked oysters. "And . . . and Penny is pregnant with Limpdick's baby . . ."

"You said that already, son," my dad said. He was a large, formidable man with a thick beard, but inside, he was gentle, kind, and smart. "Slow down," he said as he chewed and swallowed the oysters in his mouth. He looked from me to Penny and back before focusing his eyes on the barstools. "Sit."

Penny reached for an oyster and my dad pushed the can toward her. "Ew, how can you eat those right now?" I said.

She shrugged. "I love these. And I'm hungry."

"No one born after 1967 loves those."

She shrugged again and popped one in her mouth.

My dad took a deep breath.

"Is it true, Penny?" he asked.

"Yes, Frank. It's all true."

"You want to keep the baby, you keep the baby. It's a blessing. Your mom and I will help, but you don't have to marry Limpdi—" He turned and looked at me. "Son, I have to tell you, that's not an appropriate nickname." I scowled. He looked back at Penny. "Lance, is it?"

"Yeah."

"You don't have to marry Lance, dear. Gavin's mother and I got married and it only lasted a year before she ran off to Hollywood. If the love isn't there . . ."

"I know," Penny said. "I know."

I studied her face intently as she ate smoked oysters in silence. *But does she know?*

AFTER SITTING THROUGH my dad's advice, which was the opposite of everything I wanted him to say, I drove Penny home, pulled into the driveway, and turned off Charlize.

"I wouldn't even know if Lance wants to marry me anyway," she said, not looking at me.

"Of course he will. But you don't have to, like my dad said," I told her.

"Why are you so sure Lance will be happy about it?"

"Because he's in love with you." I turned and caught her eye for longer than a beat. She looked away.

"I can't believe you stayed with Lottie as long as you did. Everyone knew there was something off about her. It wasn't a news flash when you told me she was bipolar. I actually have more sympathy for her now, poor thing. She'll have to battle a life-changing mental disorder forever. Maybe you should actually try to be there for her instead of trying to run my life."

"Penny, I don't need to hear it. I told you, it was mutual." Depression was sinking in now. She was trying to push me away, eliminate an obstacle. Penny was going to have a baby and it wasn't mine. I had never even touched her. Would I ever?

Would she ever be mine?

24. Three Months Ago

PENNY

My husband was practically screaming and crying in our front yard.

"What the hell's going on, Lance?"

"Milo said you had a great time with Gavin today. The three of you. How do you think that makes me feel, Penny?"

"We've been married for fourteen years. Why do you need me to reassure you all the time?"

"I can't take this anymore. I've always been second fiddle to him."

"Then why don't you leave?" I started to cry.

"Is it that easy for you?"

"No, it's not. It's never been easy, Lance. Never. I'm sick of being caught between you two."

"You want to teach your son that it's okay for his wife to cavort with other men?"

"*Cavort*? Are you kidding me?" I was almost speechless. "I'm not cavorting with Gavin!"

The unmistakable roar of Gavin's car coming to life echoed down the street. Lance and I stood there frozen, glaring at each other.

"He'll never be out of our lives, will he?"

"Why would you want him to be?"

"Because you're *my* wife. The mother of *my* child."

The labels killed me. "You don't own me and you don't own Milo. And Gavin has nothing to do with the fact that you and I are married and have a child."

I was seething. I hated that he was trying to control me with guilt and shame. He'd been doing this off and on for our entire marriage, but lately, it had been getting worse.

Lance started doing fitness competitions ten years ago. He called it a hobby, but I knew it was some misguided attempt to seem more macho—especially after our many fruitless attempts to have another kid. I think he needed a testosterone boost just to prove to himself that he wasn't the reason we couldn't get pregnant, but this came with a major downside: he was always moody, and sometimes his temper was completely out of control.

I had asked Lance once if he was unhappy because we were basically kids, with a kid, when we got married. He'd said, "No. It's because you weren't ready." No matter how much I tried to convince him that this marriage, and Milo, was my choice, I knew a part of him didn't believe me—and never would. And because of that, Lance's own happiness waxed and waned over the years.

We were still glaring at each other as Gavin drove slowly toward our house.

"And here he comes. The fucking interloper. Tell him to get his own wife and kid."

"I'm not just your wife, Lance. And I'm not just Milo's mother. I'm Penny. I'm a fucking *person*."

Gavin pulled up to the curb, turned the engine off, and stepped out of the car.

"Lance?" He didn't dare look at me as he calmly approached Lance.

"Mind your own business, Gavin. I don't know why you're here. On my property."

"Technically I'm on the sidewalk, so I believe this is city property—"

"Oh fuck off," Lance said. I never really heard him talk that way to Gavin, but Gavin *was* being a smartass.

Milo came to the open front door. He must have heard the commotion.

"What's up, Milo?" Gavin said.

"'sup, G?"

"Go inside, Milo," I said.

"What's going on out here? It's so late."

"Did you hear your mother?" Lance yelled. "Get back in the house."

Milo gave me a scared look before retreating. "Please don't make a scene on the street, Lance," I pleaded.

Lance looked at Gavin, who had his hands shoved deep in his pockets, his arms pressed to his sides. "What are you doing here? I'm trying to have a conversation with my wife."

"Come grab a drink with me in town, man," Gavin said. We could all sense the tension coming off Lance in waves. Gavin was trying to get him away from me . . . trying to protect me. Trying to smooth things over. Trying to help me.

"Oh, we're buds now? After all these years of you trying to steal my wife, we're just gonna grab a friendly beer?"

Gavin shook his head. "I never wanted to steal your wife. I never wanted Penny in that way."

It stung to hear those words. I felt my throat tighten.

"Really? You expect me to believe that?" Lance said.

"It's true," I told him, though I was barely able to speak. Noticing once again that Gavin and I were on one side of the curb, and Lance on the other, I shook my head at the absurdity. "If I wanted to be with Gavin, I would have been with Gavin fourteen years ago. And vice versa. We were always just friends."

I never told Lance about the Blind Kiss study, about me and Gavin sleeping like spoons, tangled up in each other. I never told him how we spilled our guts to each other regularly, how we laughed, how we cried together without judgment or expectation. Was I supposed to destroy a bond I had built with another human to stroke and soothe Lance's ego? All because Lance and I had sex with an old condom from his wallet in the backseat of his car?

I never told Gavin the truth about that condom. How my whole life had been decided by one moment of desperation and insecurity. How I didn't have the courage to be a single mom. How I was too heartbroken and grief-stricken to see through those hazy months after graduation. How I married a man I didn't love.

Because it's true. Though I learned to love Lance in my own way over the years, I didn't love him while we had awkward and painful sex in the back of his car, my injured knee bumping against the back door. A part of me knew we were being reckless, that an old condom was as good as no condom, but I wanted to be close to someone . . . I *needed* to be close to someone. And the someone I wanted to be with was with someone else. That grave mistake, that inability to go after the person I really wanted, led to my beautiful child . . . but the guilt haunted me for fourteen years. Guilt that I had never been 100 percent truthful with Lance, with Gavin, or myself. Now life without Milo seemed like death, and after he left for college, I would be caught in purgatory with Lance and Gavin.

A decade's worth of secrets and half-truths were crashing down on me as I stood in the cold, facing my husband of fourteen years and standing next to the love of my life. Who was I willing to hurt *for* more? Who was I willing to *hurt* more?

"Why are you here, Gavin? Really?" Lance asked.

"Because we're family. All of us."

Lance scoffed and looked away.

"Because I've always cared deeply about Penny and her family," Gavin added, correcting himself. He was not family in Lance's eyes, and he knew it.

"What do you want now?" Lance asked.

"Everyone is hurting. I just want to defuse the situation."

"You are the fuse and the fuel, Gavin. Don't you see that?" Lance said.

He nodded and then glanced over at me in defeat. I said nothing. I didn't even look up from the ground. I. Said. Nothing. Gavin was quiet as he got into his car and drove half a block down the road to his father's house.

I pushed past Lance, went inside, and headed to Milo's room. He was pretending to be asleep in his bed.

"I'm sorry you had to see that, Milo. Trust me, it was just stupid adult crap. Your dad and I are fine," I told him.

"What about Uncle G?" he whispered.

"He's fine, too." No one acknowledged the fact that Milo was grieving for Frank as well. We were all too busy being selfish adults.

"What about you?" he asked.

The question lingered in the air as I tidied up and closed the blinds. How could he have empathy at such a young age? I went to his bed and kissed his forehead. "I'm always fine. You don't have to worry about me."

He nodded. "I know."

My phone buzzed in my pocket as I closed Milo's bedroom door. I looked at it in the dark hallway.

Gavin: Are you safe?

Me: Yes.

25. Fourteen Years Ago

GAVIN

She was glowing. A visible light radiated from her thin shoulders and flushed her cheeks with color. Pregnant Penny was such a beautiful sight. Indescribable.

We were in her mother's house, in the basement dance studio. Penny had cranked the heater up and was wearing only a thin pink nightgown as she stretched her leg up on the barre spanning the mirrored wall. I could see everything. Her white panties, her belly, plump with life. She had never been shy around me but she was even less self-conscious now that she was carrying life.

"I'm showing so early. Isn't it weird that I feel the healthiest I've ever felt? And my knee is like bionic now."

Sitting on the basement steps, I could do nothing but watch her.

"Are you gonna talk or just sit there and stare?"

"Sit here and stare," I said, blank faced.

"Stop, Gavin."

"I'm just trippin' on you being pregnant."

"Well, I am. Six months and I look nine months, huh?"

I shook my head. "You look great."

"That's because I eat now. It's impossible not to."

"Good. You're so much stronger looking." I liked her with a little meat on her bones. I wanted so badly to reach out and touch her lush skin. "You never told me how it went with Lance. Why'd you wait so long to tell him?"

"Don't know." She was dancing to "Plainsong" by The Cure.

"I love this song," I told her.

"I know, that's why I'm dancing to it," she said breathlessly as she twirled.

Don't do that to me. Don't tease me. She jumped and did a pirouette. "Be careful," I told her.

She had some grace back but still looked unsure on her feet. It could have been her knee or the pregnancy. I knew she needed to dance, though. She would always need to dance.

"What did he say? Was he mad?"

She turned the music down a little. "Who, Lance?"

"No, the pope. Yes, Lance."

Dancing away with her back to me, she said, "He asked me to marry him."

Something exploded in my brain. I held my head, thinking I had just had an aneurysm. I stood up shaking, as if I was no longer in control of my body. As I slowly walked toward her, she stopped dancing. Grabbing her hands, I scanned her ring finger but there was nothing. "You said no?" My voice was not my own.

She was staring up at me, the chocolate pools of her

eyes swirling with confusion. We were inches apart. I could have bent and kissed her slightly parted lips.

"Why are you looking at me like that?" she asked.

I placed my hand flush on her belly and she didn't flinch. "Have you felt the baby kick yet?" I asked.

"Flutters." She was still scanning my face with intensity. "What's going on in that big brain of yours, Gav?" She put her palm to my cheek.

"Don't touch me like that."

Shaking her head and pulling her hand back, she said, "Yes, you're right. Sorry."

"You said no, right?" I asked again.

She swallowed.

"Tell me you said no." I grabbed her hand and ran my thumb down her ring finger. "No ring."

Her eyes filled with tears. "I can't live with my mom, Gavin. My mother can't support a baby and me. She can barely support herself and Kiki on a secretary's wage."

"Get a job then. I can help. My dad can help."

"I'm not taking handouts."

"It wouldn't be a handout. Tell me you said no."

I pulled her to me as she started to cry. I held her tightly against my body. *This is how it feels to have your heart broken.* She felt guilty because she knew she was breaking me apart.

"What did you think?" she sniffled. "That you and I . . . what? You just graduated from college."

"I have two degrees now. I'll get a better job than Pete's garage. Tell me you said no."

Pulling away with resolve, she wiped the tears from her face. "But I love him."

I shook my head vehemently. "No! You don't."

"Yes, Gavin. He's going to be the father of my child."

"That doesn't mean you love him."

"I said yes. I said yes. We're going to get married."

The crushing ache in my chest was getting stronger. "Why were you waiting to tell me? Why?" My voice was frantic.

She walked over to get her long sweater, insecurity showing in her movements for the first time since I'd met her. "Because I knew you'd have this reaction. Lance is ready to be a husband and a father. He cares so much for me."

"Yes!" I shouted. "He's in love with you. I get it! I know how he feels!"

"Oh, don't come at me with your declarations now. You said I wasn't your Carissa, remember? I'm probably not even your Lottie or Kimber, either."

How far would I go to convince her? *No, Penny, you're not my Carissa or Lottie or Kimber. You're my everything.*

I was too weak to fight anymore. "That's right. What we have is different," I said, resigned.

She put her tiny hands on my shoulders to calm me. "Friendship," she said. "A deep, meaningful friendship."

"A deep, meaningful friendship," I repeated. But I had to try one last time. "I can take care of you, Penny."

Still staring up at me, she silently shook her head for several moments. Was she contemplating it? "It's too late," she whispered, before pushing past me and running up the stairs.

I left Fort Collins that day. I ran from Penny and her growing belly, my dad's worldly advice, Pete's garage, and all the reminders that I was in love with a girl I couldn't have.

26. Three Months Ago

GAVIN

Sitting in the shadow of my father's porch, I stared at Penny's house the next morning. Had I done the right thing by intervening? Was I muddying the waters for her? Had I always been?

Lance left for work first, and then Penny took Milo to school. When she returned, I got into my car and sped down the street.

"Get in," I yelled from the window as she was heading into the house.

Startled, she turned and stared at me for a few moments before walking toward my car. There were dark circles under her beautiful eyes, and she was wearing sweats and a hoodie, and her hair pulled back into a bun. She looked tormented.

"What do you want, Gavin?"

"I want you to get in the car and go for a drive with me so we can talk."

She took a deep breath and got in, reluctantly. She shoved her large purse between us, creating a physical barrier.

We drove to Grandview Cemetery, where both of our fathers were buried: mine in the ground, hers in an urn behind a little glass window in the mausoleum. I never understood why her mom chose to do that.

"I always wondered, why didn't your mom let you guys spread the ashes somewhere special for your dad?"

"I don't know why my mom does half the things she does. Is that what you wanted to talk to me about?" She stared out the car window impassively.

"How often do you guys fight over me? Am I making things harder for you?"

"What do you want to do, Gavin? Run away to make my life easier and happier? Do you think that'll solve everything?"

"I don't know."

She turned to me. "When you're on your little treks around the world with your latest fling, do you think Lance and I are hunky-dory?"

"I don't know, Penny. But what was this latest fight over?"

"Milo told him we had a fun day together. It was enough to push him over the edge."

"I thought you told Lance everything?"

"I tell him when I'm with you. I don't tell him I'm having the best time of my life." Her voice cracked. She looked out the window again.

I threw her purse on the floor and pulled her into my arms. "We're close now," I whispered near her ear. "Aren't we?"

"I don't know what to do. Why are we going to the cemetery?"

"Because I haven't been here since I buried him and I need you. I need you with me. I also need to tell you that I can't sit by and watch you be miserable anymore. Last night was the last straw for me. You need to ask for a separation."

"What are you going to do, fight him?"

"No. I'm going to get out of your life so he won't have anything to be jealous of. So you can go on and not feel conflicted. I'm not helping you by being in Fort Collins."

"I told him you have a girlfriend."

"I've always had a girlfriend. You know that doesn't matter to him. He'll always be jealous as long as I'm around. Listen, why don't you have Ling come out? You guys can stay in my apartment in Denver and put some space between you and Lance."

"And you?"

"And me what?"

"Put some space between you and me?" she said.

I didn't answer even though she was right. "Let's go see my dad."

We walked slowly toward my father's grave. The grass hadn't grown in yet, reminding me of how recent his death was. I kissed the top of his tombstone. "Hi, Dad." My throat was tight but I tried not to cry. Penny stood behind me, rubbing my back.

She kissed her hand and touched his tombstone. "Hi, Frank." We stood there in silence for several moments. "What are you thinking about, Gavin?"

"I'm thinking about the day he came to see me after I moved to Denver. He told me you were marrying Lance, but I already knew. He said you'd been over a lot recently, pregnant and shooting arrows in three feet of snow in his backyard. He wondered why you were always there . . . if it was because you missed your dad—"

"It was because I missed you." Her voice broke.

"I know. That's what he said. He told me to grow up, to come back, to go to your wedding, and to be a good friend." My voice was shaking now, too. "He said it would be worth it to have you in my life forever."

"Has it been, Gavin?"

"Well, you're here with me now, rubbing my back. You've always been there for me. So yes. But how much can we fuck with what's right? I can't watch you and Lance fight anymore."

"It's complicated."

I looked down at the tombstone. "You gave my dad something he never got from me. When you asked him to walk you down the aisle, when you brought Milo to his house . . . all the things he wanted so badly from me . . . a semblance of family . . . he got all that from you." I turned and looked at her. "Thank you for what you did for him."

She nodded, unwavering, stoic.

"But, Penny, you and Lance . . . it's not real, it's just comfortable. And now I'm not sure you can even say that anymore, can you?"

"No, I can't."

"What are you going to do?"

"Take you up on your offer. I'll have Milo stay with my mom for a few weeks until I can figure things out with Lance. I'll put some space between us."

"You need to demand that you guys go to counseling at least."

"I can't divorce him, though, Gavin."

"What? Why?"

"He's all I've ever known."

"You're conditioned to feel that way but it's just inertia. You're a capable and intelligent woman, Penny. You don't have to accept these imagined limitations. You could finally start your career and get a job."

"Doing what? I've never worked a day in my life."

"Teaching dance." She cocked her head to the side and smiled softly, as if she were touched by my words, but she didn't say anything.

After a moment, I took her hand and pulled her toward the car.

"Do you want to go up to see your father?"

"Okay," she said.

I drove my car to the mausoleum. "Just tell me this. What else has he done to you? Has he ever hit you?"

"No. He's just controlling."

"Yeah, that's the understatement of the century."

"I don't think he would be that way if it weren't for . . ."

"Say it, Penny. Go ahead."

I turned my whole body toward her and looked at her intently, waiting for her to say the words.

"He's jealous of my relationship with you."

There it was. "Penny, he's kept you at home, doting over your child, but Milo's a fucking genius, for God's sake. He'll be off to college in the fall, and then what? What will you do, Penny? Make pie for Lance? Let him tell you who you should hang out with, and when and how often?"

She started crying into her hands. I had finally broken her down. I gave her a T-shirt from the backseat, and she blew her nose into it. "Thanks."

"I'm sorry, Penny. I don't want to make you cry. I just want you to confront the truth. I want you to be happy." She blew her nose again. "Let's go inside."

We went into the mausoleum, where we immediately came upon her father's urn behind the glass. It was a beautiful copper vessel engraved with the words *Liam Charles Piper. Husband, Father, Brother, Son. Brilliant Loving Soul*.

"Penny!" We heard Kiki's voice before we saw her. "I didn't know you were coming to visit Dad today."

"Oh fuck," Penny said under her breath. Her eyes were still puffy from crying. She turned toward her sister and tried to muster her biggest smile. "Hey, Keeks."

Kiki's big blue eyes shot open wider than I thought possible. She looked up at me. "Gavin, what's going on?"

"Hey, Keeks," I said. "Long time, no see." A part of me still couldn't believe that the former, beribboned beauty queen was now a tomboyish microbiologist with a platinum-blond pixie cut. Even more amazing: she worked at the same pharmaceutical company that Liam had worked at for most of his adult life.

"Is something going on, Penny?" she said.

"Penny," I coaxed her.

Penny just stood there, shaking her head. Kiki pulled her in for a hug. "Is this about Dad?"

Penny shook her head.

"Is it about Milo or Lance? Are they okay?" Kiki asked.

I looked at her and mouthed, *Lance*.

Kiki hated Lance. To be fair, she didn't approve of most men, or traditional values of marriage and motherhood. After she left the pageant circuit and Liam passed away, she grew into one of the fiercest, strongest feminists I knew. She was dead set against Penny marrying Lance, believing she was doing it out of a warped sense of obligation. She was very vocal about her feelings for Lance, which meant that Kiki didn't come over to Penny's very often.

"What did he do this time?" Kiki pressed. "Don't tell me. I already know. He's an ass. He's been an ass since you married him."

Penny shook her head. "He's a good dad. And no, he hasn't been an ass since I married him."

Kiki gripped Penny by the shoulders. "Don't lie in front of Dad's ashes, P. What happened?" Kiki was getting angrier by the second.

"He's fed up with my relationship with Gavin and . . . I don't know, lots of other things."

"Gavin is your best friend." People always said that but it never helped the situation. Even Kiki knew it.

"Keeks," Penny warned, "he doesn't understand."

"Let's go outside," I said. "We'll fill you in on everything." Kiki let go of Penny and touched the glass in front of the urn. "Dad, sorry you had to see this."

Penny touched the glass, too. Emotional, she managed a weak, "Daddy."

ONCE OUTSIDE, WE shared our plan with Kiki to send Penny to my apartment in Denver while I stayed at my dad's house in Fort Collins, which seemed to quell some of her anger.

Kiki took out her keys and handed them to me. "Take her to my apartment for now. I'll go to her house, pack up some of her things, pick up Milo from school, and drop him off at my mom's."

Penny merely nodded and handed over her own keys. Her lips were dry and the cold air was not helping. She looked sick. She *was* sick, and tortured. She gave Kiki her keys and Kiki gave me hers. Penny attempted a smile, but her swollen lips cracked and began to bleed. I wiped the blood away with my thumb and rubbed it on my jeans.

I walked Penny to the passenger door of my car and helped her in. "My fucking knee," she said, but I knew that wasn't why she was weak.

She looked out the window the whole time during the short drive to Kiki's apartment.

"You know Kiki would let you stay here instead of my place?" I told her as I unlocked the front door.

She wandered into the living room and curled up on the couch. "No, it's too close. I want to get away."

I draped a throw blanket over her and squeezed her shoulder.

"Thank you, Gavin."

I nodded. "I'm going to talk to him. I want you to know that."

"He won't listen to you. He's too hurt. *I* hurt him. I've been hurting him for our whole marriage." She started to cry again.

"Just let me talk to him. I won't start a fight with him, I swear. I won't let it get to that. You just focus on getting some rest. I'll be back later and we'll figure things out."

She waved me off, turned over, and fell asleep.

27. Fourteen Years Ago

GAVIN

Why am I in Carissa's bed? Fuck. I was naked and alone. Blurry memories from the night before came flooding back to me.

We had gone out and I had gotten drunk. I started spilling my guts about Penny. Carissa told me she could make me forget about everything for a little while.

Liar.

Carissa stood in the doorway, wearing a kimono.

"Did we . . . ?"

"That has to be the most insulting morning-after statement ever, Gavin." She looked pissed.

"So . . . we did?"

"No, we didn't. You wouldn't shut up about Penny. Total turnoff."

The doorbell rang and Carissa left the room to answer it.

"Gavin!" she yelled. "Your daddy's here!"

What the hell?

I threw on a pair of jeans and stumbled over to the door, glancing at the clock on the way. It was eleven a.m. "You look like shit, kid," my dad said when I opened the door.

"Thanks." I gave him a quick side-hug.

"You smell like shit, too."

"How'd you find me? You could have called."

He smiled sympathetically. "I know you better than you think. You would have pretended everything was fine, but I can see that it's not. You'd just keep running, like you always do."

"I'm not running."

"Listen, I need to talk to you. Throw on a pair of shoes and a shirt and let's get brunch."

My dad didn't do brunch. He meant a burger and a beer. I sighed. "Tell me how you knew I was here."

"Penny thought you might be."

Of course she did. "Fucking Penny," I said. When I turned around, Carissa rolled her eyes at me and sashayed into the bathroom, shutting the door behind her.

I walked over and whispered through the door, "I'll be back in a bit."

"No, you won't," she said in a muffled voice. "Get your stuff and leave."

My dad laughed from the doorway. "Nice." I walked into Carissa's bedroom, grabbed my bag, threw on a T-shirt and shoes, and met my dad in the stairwell.

"Where are you staying, son?" my dad asked as we walked toward the car. "Not here, I hope? Looks like you've been evicted by the little lady."

I shrugged. "Just couch-surfing. Mike already got a roommate."

"You planning on staying in Denver and looking for a job?"

"Yeah, that's the plan."

We got into his truck and he started the engine. Without looking at me, he said, "I'll float you. Get you set up here until you find work."

Relief washed over me. "Seriously, Dad, that would help me out so much—"

"On one condition . . ."

Oh shit.

"Penny wants you to be in her wedding. And I told her I would walk her down the aisle."

"What?"

It had been two months since I'd walked out of Penny's basement after she told me she was going to marry Lance. We hadn't spoken since then.

"She's been coming over a lot. Hanging around, shooting arrows in my backyard. She misses you. She wants you to be in the wedding. It's in a month."

"She feels so close to you that she'd ask you to give her away?"

He pulled up at a stoplight and turned to look at me. "Her exact words were, 'Gavin told me you were sad you didn't have a daughter to walk down the aisle.' So this was actually *your* doing."

It was true. I remember him telling me that once, and me telling Penny. He wished he would've had more children, for both of us, so I would've had a sibling.

"And then . . . ?" I asked.

"And then she said she missed you like crazy and wanted you to be in the wedding. Lance is okay with it." He paused and looked over at me. "You better be there, son."

"Dad—"

"You better be there, son." He wouldn't take no for an answer.

"Fine, I'll be there."

After "brunch," my dad and I looked through the local listings for apartment rentals and put down a full month's rent on a little studio that afternoon.

I slept on the floor for a week until my dad was able to haul my stuff from Fort Collins in his truck. "Don't forget the terms of our agreement," he said to me before leaving.

How could I forget?

A week later, I finally called Penny.

"Hey."

I could hear her breath catch in her throat before she uttered a single word. "Hi."

"So you want me to be in your wedding? I'll only accept officiant or ring bearer."

She laughed. It had been too long since I'd heard her laugh. "I want you to be a groomsman. Will you do that for me? Lance's sister is going to be a bridesmaid, so we have to even out the two sides."

"I want to be on your side."

"Gavin, I want you to be in the wedding. This is what I'm asking, and it would mean a lot to me if you said yes, okay?"

"Okay." I'd do anything for her. "I'm wearing Converse, though. I'll do the suit, but I'm wearing Converse. Okay? No arguments."

"Come barefoot if you want. I just want you there."

"Aren't you ready to pop?"

"I'll be very close on the big day. Don't laugh at how I look."

"I would never." I was lying. I planned to devote the entire day to making jokes about Penny wearing white over her gargantuan belly.

PENNY'S WEDDING WAS in a cheap hall where they held senior dances and Bar Mitzvahs. The centerpieces were decorated with fake flowers and the whole scene just screamed "shotgun wedding."

I showed up with my dad an hour before the ceremony and found Penny sitting in a backroom on a couch: legs spread, giant belly making her already-huge dress look silly. "My mom picked everything out. Can you tell?" she said, laughing.

She tried to sit up to hug me, but I reached my hand out and said, "No, you stay there. How's your knee?"

"Hurts like a motherfucker."

I looked around the backroom, with makeup and curling irons strewn about. "Where are the bridesmaids, and who'd you partner me with? Please say Ling."

"Don't kill me. We just did it based on size. You're so tall, and Ling and Kiki are so short."

"Well, who the hell is left, Penny?"

"Lance's sister, Isabelle. She seems nice. Really pretty. Looks like Christina Ricci, but taller."

For I moment I thought it didn't sound so bad. All I had to do was walk down the aisle with her arm linked through mine, and if she was cute . . . but then I remembered she was Lance's sister.

"Whatever." I plopped down next to Penny on the old floral couch. "Where are they anyway? Aren't they supposed to be back here, giving you moral support or primping you or something?"

"They're on a far more important mission: buying me ice cream." She smiled wide and then turned her body toward me and rested her bare feet on my lap.

I laughed. "Okay, so what's up with the dress? It's not Penny-like at all. Why all the taffeta and tulle?"

"Because I was lazy, and I told you, I let my mom do everything." She shivered. "Ahh, he's rolling." She put my hand on her belly.

"What's this?" I said, feeling a hard spot.

"It's a foot or something." I felt a forceful movement in her belly. It was freaky but magical.

Why can't this be our baby?

"So it's a boy?" I asked.

"Yes. We're naming him Milo Liam Stone. What do you think?"

Sadness overwhelmed me but I wouldn't let myself cry in front of her. "It's a great name." I held her swollen feet in my hands and massaged them.

She let her head fall back, took a deep breath, and closed her eyes.

When the girls came back, no one batted an eye at me on the couch, rubbing Penny's feet, except for Isabelle, who raised an eyebrow.

Penny's mom spoke up first. "Isabelle, have you met Gavin?"

"No." She looked right at me. She *was* cute-ish.

I stood up and shook her hand. "I'm Gavin. I'm—"

"—a family friend," Anne interjected.

"Right," Isabelle said. "Nice to meet you."

"Eat fast, Penny, it's almost time," Ling said, passing a pint of ice cream to her before turning to me and hugging me. "Hey kid," she said. "Aren't you supposed to be with the groomsmen?"

"Do I have to?"

"I think you do in this case. Your dad's already over there."

I left the girls and walked through the ceremony space where most of the guests were already seated. An event coordinator directed me to the room where Lance, his groomsmen, my dad, and his dad were waiting. I walked directly up to him and smiled. "Congratulations, Lance." We shook hands.

"Thanks, man. How's she doing?"

It was strange how he knew that I went to see her first. "The girls just brought her some ice cream so she seems happy. Not nervous. Stunning. You're a lucky man."

"I am."

My dad patted me on the back as I tried to swallow the lump in my throat.

"Hey, Gavin, I don't mean to put you on the spot, but Penny hoped you'd give a little speech since you're close to her family. You know, in lieu of her dad," Lance said.

A wave of nausea hit me. Why hadn't she asked me something so important herself?

"You can do it," my dad said behind me.

"Okay," I said, though my mind was racing. What was I supposed to say, *Congratulations, you got the girl, dick*?

When the event coordinator came to get us, we filed out of the room and took our places in the processional line next to the bridesmaids. Isabelle flirted with me the entire time as we waited our turn.

We walked down the aisle to Pachelbel's Canon in D emanating from a speaker overhead—definitely Anne's choice. I wondered why Penny hadn't asked me to play something for the ceremony. I had my guitar in my trunk and I'd planned a song for her, but I was hoping to play it only for her.

Once we reached the altar, I went to the right to stand with the groomsmen and Isabelle went to the left to stand with the bridesmaids. We waited a beat before Penny emerged at the end of the aisle and wobbled toward us on the arm of my very own dad. I couldn't take my eyes off her.

My father kissed her on the cheek and handed her off to a smiling Lance. Penny looked yellow. She was beautiful but not the radiant, blushing bride I imagined if she and I were getting married that day. A judge officiated the ceremony, and when it was over, Penny and Lance gave each other an awkward kiss before turning toward the crowd and bowing. I thought that was weird, but maybe it was in Penny's nature as a dancer.

Afterward, everyone scattered from the ceremony area to the reception space for the cocktail hour. My father and Anne chatted each other up easily. I knew there was no attraction there, but they were friendly. After Liam's death, our families had become intertwined—and would remain that way for the rest of my dad's life.

Isabelle clung to me near the bar while I did shot after shot. If I could have put the whiskey in an IV right then and there, I would have. I needed liquid courage for the speech.

Lance's best man, Roger, gave some stupid speech he

had copied off the internet, and implied that Lance had been some kind of player before he met Penny and settled down. I laughed at the absurdity of it.

Lance got on the microphone next and said, "That'll be a tough act to follow. Thanks so much, Roger. We also have a family friend of Penny's here to say a few words on behalf of Penny's family and her recently deceased father, Liam, who we all wish were here right now. But before that, let's have a moment of silence to say a little prayer for Liam." *God, he lays it on thick. Fucking Eddie Haskell.*

I put my head down and looked up a moment later to see Lance gesturing for me to come up. There's nothing more sobering than giving a speech, especially at a wedding for the girl of your dreams.

"Good luck," I heard Isabelle say behind me.

Penny was smiling at me as I took the microphone. "Hi, I'm Gavin, Penny's friend from college. On behalf of the Pipers, thank you all for coming. Though I haven't known Penny for long, her family has welcomed me with open arms, and I know they'll do the same for Lance." I heard Kiki snort behind me. "Penny and her dad were very close, and I know that if he were here, he'd tell Lance how lucky he is, and he'd probably say something like, 'Take care of my Sweet Pea.' Liam loved to watch Penny dance, and he was her biggest fan. We all wish he were here."

I looked over to a tear-soaked Penny and smiled. She smiled back, though she looked crushed. I tried to change the subject. "She's a good friend and a good person. And from my family and hers, we wish you both many years of happiness. Congratulations! Please raise your glasses and toast this beautiful couple and the little one on the way. Cheers!"

I knew it was a pathetic speech, but I think I did what Anne and Kiki couldn't. Everyone clapped and then the dancing began.

I danced with Anne and Kiki first. Kiki was in full rebellious preteen mode and had chopped off her hair, as well as part of her bridesmaid dress; it looked like a miniskirt in the front, with a long train in the back. Her mother wasn't amused but she'd been giving Kiki more freedom since Liam had passed. Truth be told, Penny probably would have done the same thing if she weren't eight and a half months pregnant.

Isabelle came to dance with me during all the fast songs. "You're a good dancer," she told me, so I turned goofy on her and did The Running Man, The Sprinkler, and The Bus Driver. I threw an imaginary fishing line out to reel her in and she played along, giggling. It's not like I had anything better to do. I definitely didn't want to count the number of times Lance rubbed Penny's belly while posing for the photographer.

During the money dance, my father got into Penny's line so I stood behind him. I watched carefully as he danced with her. They talked and smiled and laughed as though it were *our* wedding, and he was her new father-in-law. When I asked to cut in, he happily offered her hand to me. I tried to shove a twenty down the front of her dress, but she swatted at me, laughing and pointing to a little bag around her wrist.

"We'll have to do some special maneuvering around your massive belly," I said.

She punched me in the shoulder. "Thanks for the speech, by the way. It was really nice. Maybe a little *too* nice."

"You're welcome" was all I said. She nuzzled up to my neck. "You shouldn't do that. It looks too intimate," I told her. She pulled back a little.

As she looked up at me, I saw worry in her eyes. "I'm sorry, Gavin."

"For what?"

She shook her head and looked away. "I don't know."

"Hey, after the garter toss, meet me in that little room. I wrote you a song, but it's just for you."

"Are you going to try to make me cry myself into labor?"

I smiled. "Wouldn't that be funny if your water broke right now and you had to go to the hospital in your wedding dress? Amniotic fluid all over it? How would you explain that one to Milo?" She laughed. "Are you going to tell him the truth when he's older?" I asked abruptly.

She pulled back for a second. "I don't know, Gavin. That's a weird question on my wedding day." She flicked a glance behind us. "I'll meet you in that room, but you have to move on. I have many gentlemen waiting to dance with me." She wiggled her eyebrows.

I looked back at the long line. "Yeah, no surprise there."

AFTER THE MONEY line dances and the garter toss, Penny met me on the dusty floral couch in the side room where I was already poised with my acoustic guitar.

"So this is an original?" she asked.

"Yes, just for you, Little P."

I strummed a few chords and then went into the regular rhythm of the song. It was slow and easy to play.

> Tonight as I watch you from afar,
> I sit outside and pray,
> Seeing all the things that made me love you
> All the things that made me stay.
>
> A minute turned to forever,
> A kiss left on your lips to remember.
> I'm your lover, I'm your friend.
> You're mine.
> You were always my lover, for a lifetime in my mind.
>
> It's all within our grasp,
> No more longing, angst or anger.
> Because you're too afraid to ask,
> We'll let go, come back, imagine.
> Our present becomes our past.
>
> Growing old like this . . . letting go, coming back again.
> Telling tales like this . . . of how it all began.
>
> I'll hold your hand and your babies, I'll watch your
>   children grow,
> And one day you'll say, "Howdy, old chum."
> And I'll say, "No, I'm your lover . . . remember?
>   And you're mine."
>
> It's been this way forever. I've always been your
>   lover . . . for a lifetime in my mind.

Penny was a blubbering fool by the time I was finished singing.

"Did I make you sad?" I asked. It was hard to tell because she was smiling and crying hysterically.

"Is that a song about longing?"

"No, it's a song about lifetime friendship."

"I loved it. It's our song," she whispered. Reaching up and hugging me she said, "So you forgive me? You're still my best friend?"

"Always. Now let's go get our groove on."

"Deal." She wiped away the tears.

I led her onto the dance floor just as the Talking Heads song "This Must Be the Place" came on. She wasn't dancing goofily and neither was I. We were just kind of swaying to the music, bobbing our heads, circling each other and smiling at one another, thinking about the word *home* in the song, and what it meant. True to the lyrics, we would have to make up our story as we went along because we refused to let go.

Twirling her, I said, "Isabelle is shooting me googly eyes."

"You gonna tap that?"

"You're so ladylike."

"You love that about me," she said.

"One of the many things, P."

Moments later, Lance showed up. He looked a little sauced and had no rhythm at all. He was trying to dance seriously, but Penny was just laughing at him, poor schmuck. Moments after that, I was fucking his sister in a bathroom stall. I had to find some way to cope.

28. Three Months Ago

GAVIN

After meeting up with my aunt and letting her have whatever she wanted from my dad's house, I headed over to see Lance. It was dusk and I could see lights on inside the house, so I knew he was home.

When I knocked on the door, I noticed it was slightly ajar. I could see him sitting on the couch in the living room at the end of the hall. I walked into the foyer slowly, trying to gauge his mood.

"Gavin," he said when I reached the living room.

"Lance."

He was wearing suit pants and a dress shirt, sans tie, the top two buttons open. There were dark circles under his eyes. He looked wrecked. Holding up his glass, he said, "Drink?"

"No, thanks."

"So, you gonna tell me where the fuck my wife and son are?"

"Can I sit down and talk to you first, man to man?"

He gestured toward a chair opposite the couch.

I sat down and was silent for a moment before saying, "Kiki took Milo to Anne's for a few days. He doesn't know anything, just that Penny's taking a trip. She's going to stay at my apartment in Denver."

His eyebrows shot up and his hand curled into a fist on his knee.

"Not with me," I said in a hurry. "I'm staying at my dad's . . . with my girlfriend." That last part wasn't entirely true.

"So this mystery girlfriend—"

"Briel."

I knew he wasn't interested in hearing about Briel so we sat in silence until he spoke again. "What does Penny need to go to Denver for?"

"She's going to get away for a few days to think. I can't say more than that. You guys should probably talk."

He tilted his cup back, swallowed the rest of the brown liquid, walked over to the counter, and poured more whiskey. When he sat back down, he said, "Some time, huh? To think?"

"She loves you, Lance."

"Does she?"

"You know she does. And she's always been loyal to you."

He smiled as if he thought what I said was so horribly funny. "You call your 'friendship' evidence of Penny being loyal to me?"

I blinked.

"She and I are friends. We've always been friends."

"Friends that fall asleep on each other. I saw you two—"

"You mean the night my dad died?"

He shrugged.

I never got a single word of sympathy from Lance over my father's death. His damn ego had gotten in the way.

"Yeah, we fell asleep on the couch together. We were exhausted."

"I don't want to hear anymore, Gavin. Get out of my house."

I stood up and then sat back down. "No. I came here to say one thing. It's not me, no matter what you think. It's not me. But if that's the way you feel, if you think Penny will be happier . . . that your marriage will be better, I'll get out of her life. You'll never see me again."

He tensed up but didn't argue.

"She and I are friends. But I'm willing to throw it all away for her happiness and safety, because that's how much I fucking love her, okay? But are you willing to make some sacrifices, too?"

"Maybe."

"Because I think if you were, you'd get your happy wife back. She's the most loving and forgiving person I've ever known."

"I know," he said, his voice cracking. "The problem is that she doesn't leave much for me. She spreads herself too thin."

"I know that's not true because outside of caring for you and Milo, there's not much else going on in her life. And even if that were a little bit true, I'd take anything she was willing to give to me, if I were you. I've always wished for that myself."

"I know. That's the problem. She probably wishes for the same."

"I don't know, Lance. She's a mess right now. You guys have to work your stuff out first."

He didn't respond. I got up without saying anything more.

THE NEXT DAY, I met Briel in Denver for lunch and told her what was going on with Penny.

"Why is it your business?" she asked.

"It just is. She's my best friend."

Briel frowned over her glass of wine. "Wow. I always thought Penny and Lance had perfect love," she said in her thick French accent.

"Far from it."

"Do you have love for her?"

"Don't be like that. Penny is like family to me." Briel was quiet after that. I think she didn't want to come across as jealous. It was still early enough in our relationship that every word mattered, and every date was a tone-setter. We had both agreed that we would keep things casual, but I could already see her straining against that.

After lunch, I told her I had to run by my apartment to pick up more clothes, although a part of me just wanted to check in on Penny to see how she was holding up. Afterward, Briel and I would head back to my dad's house in Fort Collins and make dinner together.

Briel waited in the car as I jogged up the stairs. When I walked into my apartment, I noticed all the blinds were closed and it was quiet and cold. Where was Ling, or Penny for that matter? I went into my room and saw the lump of her body in my bed, covered from head to toe.

I stood there, thinking about what I should do.

29. Three Months Ago

PENNY

I could hear him in the room. He was quiet at first, and then I heard him shuffling through drawers. It sounded like he was packing. Was he just going to ignore me? Maybe he was trying to let me sleep.

All of a sudden the blankets whooshed up, and he slid in and covered us again from head to toe. We were under the blankets, lying face-to-face on our sides.

"What are you doing, P?"

"Lying here."

"Where's Ling?"

"I told her not to come."

He shook his head. "So you're gonna mope here all alone? Have you even brushed your teeth?"

"I think you know the answer to that."

"Talk to me. It's three p.m., and judging by the looks of things, you haven't gotten out of bed." He reached his hands out to hold mine and I let him take them.

"I'm depressed. I talked to Milo and he asked a million questions. All of which I had to skirt around. Lance called and left three voicemails, asking to talk, but I don't think I'm ready."

"Tell him that."

"What are you doing here?"

"Just picking up a few things. Briel's downstairs, waiting in the car. We just grabbed some lunch."

I tried to kick him but he grabbed my foot. "Get out of my bed and go be with your girlfriend," I said.

"This is my bed, dork."

"Well, get out of your bed and let me sulk."

"No." Gavin blinked and swallowed. This was Gavin's tell for *I'm about to say something you're not going to like.* "I told Lance I would leave you alone if he got help."

I felt a stabbing ache in my chest. "Leave me alone? As in what?"

"You know."

"You can't do that." Tears started forming in my eyes. "You can't do that."

"I didn't know what else to say. I need to protect you." He wiped a tear from my cheek and whispered, "I'm sorry. I hate to see you break like this."

"Don't do that. I'm not breaking. You think you're protecting me by never talking to me again?" I scowled.

Closing his eyes, he said. "I'll figure it out."

"Tell me something, Gavin. When will this happen?"

"When will what happen?"

"When will we stop talking forever? When will we stop being there for each other? When have you agreed to stop being my best friend? Huh, fucker? Answer me. When will we never talk again?"

He didn't say anything for a long time. His eyes remained closed until he finally spoke. "When one of us dies, I guess."

"Exactly, and you know it's true."

He gave me a bow. One I needed so desperately. A second later, he sat up abruptly and moved to straddle me.

"Ouch, get off me!"

"No." He pinned my arms above my head and ran his gaze down my body. "You're a mess and you've had that T-shirt and those underwear since we were in college. I know you can afford underwear, P. Go shopping. Call Ling and have dinner with her. Eat something, for the love of God. You look like a waif."

I was still pinned. Turning my head to look away from him, I said, "No!"

He ran his tongue up the side of my face. I wiggled and squirmed. "Ahh, gross! Get off me!"

"So very cute," came a French accent from the doorway.

Gavin jumped off me onto the floor, still smiling. Apparently, he didn't care what Briel thought. I pulled the covers up to my neck. "Hi, Briel. Gavin was just leaving."

"And Penny was just rolling her depressed ass out of bed and into the shower."

"Fine," I grumbled.

LING FLEW IN that evening. "I was going to come anyway, so good thing you actually want me there," she said over the phone. I was so glad she knew what I needed before I did.

We stayed up late eating junk food and watching reruns of *Who's Line Is It Anyway?* She didn't press me on anything, but she already knew the whole story from Gavin, Kiki, and the little fragments I had given to her.

The next day, Ling took me to the mall. I got three new outfits, five pairs of fancy underwear, and a bikini wax, which I had never had and never will again. Ling said I needed to feel good and confident when I eventually faced Lance. All I felt was pain.

I had a drink at six on the dot, and at seven Ling and I sat down at a fancy restaurant, where I ordered a margarita.

"There's no answers in the bottle, Penny," Ling said.

"Are you shrinking me, Ling?"

"God, no. I'm just saying getting drunk is not going to make you feel any better."

"Isn't that what you're here for . . . to watch me get drunk? I'm going through shit, my friend."

"It's a phase. And no that's not why I'm here." She shook her head and looked away, seemingly disappointed. "Tell me this: did you stay with Lance because of the money and security?"

I rolled my eyes. "You know that's not true. I stayed with Lance because I thought it was the right thing to do for Milo."

"Was it?"

"You *are* shrinking me."

"No, I'm just talking to you."

I downed the last of my margarita. "It was the right thing to do for Milo. Gavin was unstable, fickle, all over the place for so long."

"Is he now?"

"I don't know."

"Besides college and his one fuckup, hasn't he always

been there for you?" She raised her eyebrows. She already knew the answer.

"I'm just tired of fighting that fight. I'm tired of fighting for Gavin and justifying myself to Lance."

"I'm just tired of watching you make your life decisions based on the men in your life," she replied coolly. That stung, but it made sense coming from her. Ling was eternally single by choice, and she said what she felt. Having no significant other allowed her to roam through life without a filter. To be herself. I envied her. She was a great friend to me, but we had vastly different outlooks on life.

I thought she would lecture me more or say I told you so, but she said nothing after that. Finally, I asked, "Ling, do you think I should leave Lance?"

"Honestly, yes. I don't think you'll ever be happy with him and I think it's selfish what you're doing." I knew she'd say that.

"I know." I paused, looking around the restaurant. "Let's get outta here. How 'bout the Tipsy Hat?"

"That dive with the cover bands?"

"Yeah! C'mon, it'll be fun. We'll dance."

Little did I know, Ling was already calling in reinforcements.

30. Three Months Ago

GAVIN

Ling: Tiny Dancer still can't hold
her liquor.

Me: On my way. I had a feeling.
What's she doing?

Ling: Don't text and drive. She's
hanging on the bartender at
the Tipsy Hat.

Me: Masen? The guy with the
piercings?

Ling: The very same. Quit texting
and driving. I have a 6 a.m. flight.
I'm a freaking doctor and can't
stay out at all hours of the night
like this. Just get your ass over

here. I'm catching an Uber to the
Marriott by the airport. You can
take over from here.

> Me: Don't leave. Wait until I
> get there.

Ling: I'm not an asshole. Stop
texting and driving.

> Me: I'm doing voice to text
> so shut up.

Ling *was* kind of an asshole. I would never say it to her face; she was a good friend, but not at all willing to put up with Penny's dramatics. She probably told Penny to get a divorce and get laid. She believed in work and casual relationships . . . and that's about it. I think because she was a psychiatrist she tried to avoid shrinking anyone in her real life. Like Ling, I believed in work and casual relationships, too . . . but when it came to Penny . . . well, Penny was home for me.

Ling was standing near the door of the Tipsy Hat when I walked in. I spotted Penny near the bar.

"Finally. I need to get out of here."

"Nice to see you, too, Ling. It's been a while."

She gave me a rough hug and said, "I already told her bye, so I'm taking off."

"Did you tell her I was coming?"

"No. She said she'd be fine getting back to your place."

I glanced over at Penny. She was wearing a short, black, semibackless dress, leaning over the bar, and talking to Masen.

"That guy is a walking STD. Why is she flirting with him? She doesn't even seem that drunk."

"She's only had three or four drinks, but she hasn't eaten all day."

"Nothing at all?"

"No. She got weird about pigging out last night. She went into food-guilt mode. You know her."

Penny was five-six and probably weighed a hundred and twenty pounds. She was thin already, but now looking at her in a backless dress, braless, it seemed like she had dropped another ten pounds overnight.

"I'm gonna run out and get her a sandwich."

She huffed. "Fine, I'll wait."

Penny still didn't know I was there, and I wasn't sure how she was going to react. I got her a turkey sandwich from the deli across the street, which was kitty-corner to my apartment.

When I returned, Ling was still at the door. "So Penny's been flirting with the bartender?" I asked.

"I don't know, kinda."

"I guess that's all I'm getting out of you."

"You guessed right. I gotta get some sleep before my flight tomorrow. Good luck," she said as she walked out. I gave her a salute and finally headed into the bar.

I plopped onto the barstool next to Penny and held the turkey sandwich out to her.

She looked at me, shocked. "Ling, did you shape-shift into Gavin?"

"Eat the sandwich, Penny."

"Oh, just what I need, another controlling husband."

"You look gaunt."

"I assure you, I'm not starving to death."

"Please eat it."

I looked up and caught Masen looking down Penny's cleavage. Glaring, I said, "'Sup, Masen? How's the hep C?"

"Cut the shit, Gavin. You wanna drink or you wanna get the fuck outta here? I'll make sure Penny finds a warm bed."

I rolled my eyes. "I'll take an Alpine Duet, and she'll have a water."

"Make that a vodka soda with lime, please," Penny said with a flirty smile.

"Eat the sandwich, Penny, and I'll stay here as long as you want while you drown your sorrows."

She took five reluctant bites and said, "I'm full."

"Two more bites."

"Quit treating me like a child. Why are you here anyway? Ling obviously called you."

"She was just looking out for you. She wanted you to be able to cut loose, but she has an early flight."

Penny stood up and clapped her hands. "Well, in that case, cutting loose is exactly what I'm gonna do."

I sat at the bar and watched Penny dance to every funky eighties song the cover band knew over the next hour. She tried several times to lure me out on the dance floor, but honestly, I enjoyed watching her more. Even after all these years, she still danced with the raw abandon and utter grace she always had.

What if Joey hadn't dropped her that day? Would Penny's life be different? Would we be together? After her injury, any variation of the name Joey was like a bad word. If Penny got into a checkout line and the cashier's name was Joseph, Joe,

Joey, Josephine, even Jodie, she'd switch lines. I told her including Jodie was ridiculous but she said it sounded too similar. That was how she dealt with it.

Finally Penny got bored dancing alone, so she grabbed Masen, who kept looking over at me, probably worried I was going to kick his ass. Lilly, the other bartender, started serving me a small shot of whiskey with each beer I drank.

"Lilly, are you trying to get me drunk so you can take advantage of me?"

She pointed to Penny. "Is that the girl you always talk about?"

"That's her."

"I thought she was married? She's not wearing a ring."

"I don't know. She's out of her mind."

When Penny came back to the bar to get another drink, I said, "How come you're not wearing your ring?"

"I called Lance today and told him I wanted to separate. You're the first person I'm telling."

For the first time in my entire life, I was speechless. Penny just separated from her husband, something I thought would never happen.

"Earth to Gavin. Aren't you going to say anything?"

"Does this mean you're gonna run around fucking a bunch of guys?"

She narrowed her eyes. "Don't be a jerk. I told him I wouldn't cheat on him. I just need to get out and have some *me* time."

"I see."

"I see? What's up with you?"

Lilly was eavesdropping. When I looked up, she walked away. "Nothing. I think it's good. You could use the space."

"I'm only staying out here for a week. I need to get back to Milo."

"Milo's fine."

"He's still my son, and he's confused. Lance told him Mommy and Daddy had a fight."

"Mommy and Daddy? You guys baby Milo so much, but the kid is smart as fuck. When you're not around he acts totally different."

"How do you mean?"

I gestured to the stool. "Sit."

"No, I'm going back out there with Masen. Just tell me how Milo's different."

"He's into girls and stuff. I bought him condoms."

"What?" She looked furious. "How dare you. You're not his father."

"Well, apparently neither of you gave him 'the talk' because he came to my place and asked *me* about it. Like . . . how to do certain things."

"Oh God, I'm so pissed right now. You better not have said anything weird."

"I told him to be kind and respectful and to make sure he cares a lot for the girl. I didn't give him any specific pointers, Penny. Are you kidding? I told him he should wait as long as possible, and once he was ready, he should wrap it up."

"You did?"

"Yeah, I said it's a lot better when you're in love."

She was staring at me, blinking impassively, but her bottom lip was quivering.

"Penny?"

A tear sprang from her eye and ran down her cheek. "Thank you," she said in a low voice.

"So I did good?"

"Yes, Gavin. That's exactly what I would've said to him. I just wish he would've come to me."

"Trust me, P, boys want to hear this stuff from another man—not their mom." I stood from the stool. "We should go now."

She shook her head. "No, I want to dance more."

Watching her saunter back out onto the dance floor, I thought about how badly I wanted to lick her back. I shook the thought away—I had to. It felt like hours had gone by, all while she continued flirting with Masen. I finally got fed up.

Walking up to them, I noticed Masen froze while she kept dancing with her arms slung around his neck.

"Penny, let's go," I said.

"No." She didn't look at me when she said it.

"Penny, come on, I have something to show you."

She stopped and turned with her hand on her hip. "Are you joking?"

"No, come outside with me."

She rolled her eyes. "Fine."

We walked out of the bar and then I yanked her around the corner into a little alleyway. "Let's go home. You've had a lot to drink."

"I'm fine. I thought you had something to show me?"

"Yeah, that wall. Isn't that mural cool?"

She turned to look. "I guess. What is it?"

"It's a Will Ryan Band album cover." The cover is a painting of his wife, Mia, I think." It's her back as she's walking into a lake wearing a long flowing white dress. Some fan must have re-created it here.

"I love the Will Ryan Band."

"I know." I was staring at her as she looked up at me, questioningly. She still intrigued me so much. Her dark-chocolate eyes and chocolate hair. Beautiful.

"So is that it? That's what you wanted to show me?"

"Just be quiet." I gripped the back of her neck and kissed her. She opened to me immediately, like we kissed every day. I pulled away. Her eyes were open wide. We were both breathing hard.

"Again," she said breathlessly. I pushed her against the wall and kissed her harder. Everything came back. All the youthful feelings, the blind kiss. It was happening all over again.

"You taste so good . . . you *feel* so good," I said.

"Again," she begged. I kissed her with even more force, our tongues twisting. One hand went to her bare back and the other moved from her neck to cup her breast over the sheer material of her dress. I felt her hardened nipple. "God," she moaned, and crashed her lips back into mine.

I moved her hand over my beating heart and pulled her toward me, her body completely flush with mine.

Suddenly, she pushed my chest away, forcing me to stumble back. "What are you doing?!" she shouted.

"What?" I said.

"I'm still married, Gavin. What are you doing?"

I looked around, confused. "You kept saying *again*."

She started crying.

"I'm sorry," I said. I felt horrible. She looked so confused. "I'm sorry, P. Come here."

"No. Why'd you do it?"

My chest started to hurt. "I . . . I did it because you were flirting with Masen. I hate-kissed you for being a flirt."

"Hate-kissed? You're insane. I feel so guilty now."

"So do I. I'm still with Briel, too, you know."

"Really?" she said, like it was the most preposterous thing she'd ever heard. Shaking her head, she turned and started to walk away. I grabbed her by the elbow, swung her around, and threw her over my shoulder.

"Stop! I have a dress on. Put me down!"

"No one's looking! It's after midnight. I'm taking you home."

ONCE WE GOT to my apartment, I tossed her on the bed. "You can sleep here, you little tease. I'll go torture myself on the tiny couch."

"You can sleep in here, Gavin," she said, without hesitation.

"Trust me, you'll hate the couch; you can feel the springs poking you in the back while you sleep. I don't want to listen to you bitch about it in the morning."

Pulling her dress over her head and slipping under the covers in just her underwear, she said, "I mean, you can sleep in here with me. But we can't fool around."

I had seen her naked a million times, but never after I had just made out with her. The blood from my brain was traveling southbound.

Even after giving birth to a nine-pound baby, and the years she'd spent out of practice, Penny still had a dancer's body, long and lean.

"Sleeping next to your mostly naked body wouldn't be torture at all."

"Suit yourself," she mumbled. "Just grab me a T-shirt, please."

I threw her a Pixies T-shirt from my closet and she pulled it on, jumped out of bed, and went to the bathroom.

When she was done, she announced, "It's all yours. I used your toothbrush for old times' sake."

"Penny?"

"What?"

"I'm sorry. I shouldn't have done what I did. I don't want it to change anything. I fucked up by confusing you even more. I know you were just in the moment. You never would've wanted that if you weren't all mixed up over Lance."

"Gavin . . ." She reached up and put her hands on my stubbly jaw, running them up and down. Her eyes searched mine. "I was in the moment because I've never been kissed like that by anyone but you." Her eyes welled up. "It's too soon, and yes, too confusing. I don't want anything to change between us, either. I'm afraid of what could happen to us. I love you, you're my best friend, and I don't want you to let this go to your already-giant head, but you know I've always been attracted to you. But I can't do this right now."

I nodded. I understood. There were at least ten funny, sarcastic, and mean retorts I could have said, but I didn't because the truth was, her kindness, her loving nature, her smell, and her touch were so intoxicating, I was incapable of forming coherent sentences. And I didn't want to ruin the moment. She might have felt guilty about Lance but I was positive she liked every second we were kissing.

"You gonna say anything?"

"I want so badly to sleep with you, Penny. But you're right. It's better this way. I'll be back in a minute."

I took a shower. A long shower.

You do the math.

Afterward, I slid into bed and fell asleep smelling her hair.

31. Three Months Ago

PENNY

When I woke up, Gavin was spooning me, sound asleep, with his hand on my hip under my T-shirt. I stirred. It felt like he was still half-asleep as he slowly caressed my side. I didn't want to stop him but I knew it was wrong.

He buried his face in my neck and pulled my back flush to his front. I could feel him hard behind me. I tensed. "It's nothing," he whispered. "Just the morning. Relax, go back to sleep."

We slept for a few more hours and then he got up, took a shower, and got ready to leave.

"Stay as long as you want. I'm going back to my dad's. I'm really sorry about last night. I hope nothing has changed between us." He was looking right at me, into my eyes, with honesty and penitence.

From the bed, I threw my arms out. "Come here." He leaned over and hugged me. I held him to my chest and said, "Nothing's changed."

He pulled away. "I support any decision you make, P. I understand if you go back to him. He loves you. How can he not?" And there it was. Gavin believed there was no way a person couldn't love me.

Gavin nodded. If Gavin had urged me to get a divorce, or if he had tried to make me feel bad about going back to Lance, it would have been much harder for me to confide in him. I needed my friend—and he knew it.

THREE DAYS LATER, while I was running errands in Denver, I got a call from Lance. "I know you said you needed your space, but I wanted to let you know that I canceled my next fitness competition. I told my boss I needed to cut back on my hours, and I'm seeing a psychologist now. She actually suggested that we go to marriage counseling and already referred me to someone. Would you be willing to go with me this Friday?"

He was trying. "Yes. I will."

It sounded like he was going to cry. "Thank you."

DR. LAKE, OUR marriage counselor, was a petite woman in her fifties with short black hair, a wide nose, and a no-nonsense attitude. She walked with a limp and a cane.

Gavin's name came up more than once, but each time Dr. Lake tried to put the focus back on our relationship. What was missing in our marriage? Why were we unhappy?

"Penny, when you say that Lance seems unhappy, distant, and emotionally and physically unavailable, be specific. In what ways?" Dr. Lake said.

"Well, he works more than most people—"

"So I can buy you the things you like," Lance interrupted.

"Let Penny finish talking, Lance. Then it will be your turn."

"When he's home, he works out in our home gym two or three hours a night. He claims to be too busy to make it to Milo's school functions, like PTA fundraisers, and when we're intimate, it feels one-sided, like he's rushing things."

"Do you agree with Penny, Lance?"

"I guess. But it seems like we weren't really connecting even before Gavin came back to town."

"Tell me, Penny, what is your understanding of your relationship since Gavin came back?"

I thought carefully before giving my answer. "Gavin's father, Frank, was dying. That's why Gavin came back to town. Gavin is a very good friend of mine, and he's been a very good friend to our family, but I admit that we were spending a lot more time together than usual. Death makes people vulnerable, Dr. Lake. I was close to Frank—he was like a father to me after my own father passed away—and after he died, Gavin and I lived in a bubble of grief together. I think Lance felt threatened by that."

Lance made a grumbling noise.

"Let's not speculate about Lance's feelings, Penny," Dr. Lake said firmly.

"I don't think he would disagree with me," I said.

"They're too close," Lance added.

"And that makes you angry, Lance?"

"Well, yeah. I mean, she spent almost the entire week before Frank died at his house."

I shook my head. "I was trying to be there for both my friend *and* his dying father."

"Okay, Penny," Lance said. "Call it what you want."

"Penny, why have you stayed with Lance when it sounds like you have so much resentment toward him."

I sighed. "I don't *resent* Lance. I think he's a good father and husband. But I do feel like he can be self-absorbed and controlling. And that frustrates me."

"Lance, what do you think about that?" Dr. Lake said.

"Gavin," Lance said curtly. "He's the source of everything. I saw them through the window once, sleeping on the couch together, and then the next night he was singing to her on his porch. He was fucking spooning and serenading my wife, Dr. Lake. How's a man supposed to feel about that? There's no boundaries to their friendship. And I got tired of coming home to an empty house and a plate of food I had to reheat while she was down the street with Gavin."

"You've always had to reheat your dinner because I never know when you're going to be home, Lance. That's nothing new."

"Yeah, except you're usually there when I'm reheating it. We don't even have that little bit of family time anymore, Penny."

Dr. Lake cut us off just as we were getting to the meat of things. "I can tell the two of you have love for each other, otherwise you wouldn't be here trying to work things out. But our time is almost up—"

"—I've heard separation leads to divorce eighty percent of the time, Dr. Lake. What do you think? I mean, Penny is insisting on a separation so she can go do whatever she wants. Do you think it's fair to me?" Lance interrupted.

"In my experience, separations can help couples get the space they need to evaluate their relationships. Penny might feel smothered. She might be having a hard time working out how things got to this point, but she's here. Penny, perhaps you can speak directly to Lance and tell him why you think separation is a good idea."

I nodded and turned to him. "Because I'm in a fog. I want to say, yeah, let's just sweep this under the rug, but clearly both of us are unhappy. Gavin isn't going anywhere. He'll go back to Denver and be with his girlfriend, but he and I will always be friends, the way we were before you and I even started dating. That has to become a nonissue or else we can't move forward."

He nodded. "Okay, I hear you. I'll agree to one month. That's all I can handle, Penny. I want a decision in a month. Until then, I'll go stay with a friend. You can move back in and stay with Milo."

AFTER WE LEFT the counselor's office, Lance followed me to my car and opened the driver-side door for me. "I love you so much, Penny. I'm sad that our marriage has come to this. Please promise me that you'll be faithful to me during this separation. I can't bear the idea of another man putting his hands on you."

I nodded. "I'll keep my distance from Gavin for now. I just have to go back to his place and pick up my stuff first. Okay?" Without another word, I got into the car. Lance closed my door, gave me a sad little wave, and headed for his own car.

Looking down at my phone I saw a text from Gavin.

Gavin: How are you?

Me: Just got out of couples
counseling.

Gavin: And . . .

Me: It went well. I asked for a
monthlong separation and
Lance agreed.

Gavin: Good. Don't do anything
crazy.

Me: How's Briel?

Gavin: Fine. We're out right now,
let me call you later.

Me: That's okay. I'll be at my
house with Milo. Lance is
staying with a friend.

Gavin: Copy.

Copy? There was something so distant in that sign-off. Maybe he was pulling back, knowing that I needed it—or maybe he needed it in order to focus on Briel? I should have been relieved—it was exactly what I needed at the time— but something in his tone made me unsettled.

32. Thirteen Years Ago

PENNY

I went into labor a little after ten on a Monday morning, twelve days before my due date. Lance had gone to Phoenix for a quick business trip the night before. He wasn't scheduled to be back until the next day.

The first person I called was my doctor, who told me to keep track of the contractions and to call someone immediately to come stay with me. The next two hours were a blur. The doctor told me, on average, first labors could last as long as twelve hours, which would give Lance plenty of time to get home and be present for Milo's birth.

I frantically dialed Lance's cell but he didn't answer, so I calmly left a message: "Damn it, I'm in labor! You need to come back NOW."

He called back almost immediately. "I'm in a cab, heading back to my hotel! I'll grab my things and get on the first flight back. Hang in there, sweetie."

I called my mother next. "Kiki and I will be there in

twenty minutes!" she said. Lance and I were living in a small house about six miles from my mother's house and twelve miles from the hospital.

Unfortunately, my doctor was completely wrong: my labor was progressing fast and my contractions were coming one on top of the other. There was no way this was going to be a twelve-hour labor.

I called Frank, who lived two miles away.

Gavin answered. "Penny?"

I was breathing hard. "How'd you know?"

"Everyone has caller ID, silly."

"What are you doing there?"

"I came to visit. What's wrong? Why are you breathing hard?"

"I'm in labor and Lance is trying to fly back from Phoenix right now. He won't be back for hours. Ahhh!" I screamed. "Fuck, this hurts!"

"We'll be there in five."

Five words from Gavin could calm me down. But not for long. I was in the throes of labor after all, alone in our little house on Pine Nut Drive. Five minutes felt like three hours.

Gavin and Frank arrived right on time. Gavin ran around frantically, looking for my overnight bag, which Lance had conveniently put on the top shelf of our closet without telling me. Frank helped me to Gavin's car, but I was in so much pain I could barely walk.

"I managed to catch your mom before she left the house," Gavin said behind us. "She's meeting us at the hospital with your sister."

Frank got in the driver's seat while I lay down on

Gavin's lap in the backseat. Frank quickly but cautiously drove us to the hospital as we swerved through Monday-morning traffic.

"Oh god! This hurts."

Gavin rubbed my sweating head. "I know, baby, just breathe in and out."

I was wearing a nightgown and slippers. Gavin had thrown a heavy jacket over my shoulders since it was snowing out. Still, I was sweating bullets.I felt a gush between my legs. Looking down, I could see amniotic fluid spilling across the leather seat and onto the floor. "Oh no."

"It's okay, Penny. Your water just broke."

"Not that. The baby's coming. I can feel it." I put my hand between my legs and felt the baby crowning as we pulled into the emergency entrance of the hospital.

"I'll get a wheelchair!" Frank said.

"Tell them he's crowning. It's happening!" I yelled.

"Oh, Jesus!" Gavin said.

They brought out a stretcher and somehow, between Gavin, a nurse, and an orderly, I managed to get up on it, but I was writhing in pain. My mother and Kiki appeared on the other side of me as I was wheeled in. "Call Lance!" I kept saying. "He's going to miss it!"

Inside the labor and delivery room, there were nurses and doctors moving around with focused speed. Gavin and Frank must have gone to the waiting room because now it was only my mother and Kiki. My sister was rubbing my shoulders and my mom was scurrying around to find a washcloth to wipe my forehead. "I have to push!" I screamed.

"Push!" the unfamiliar male doctor said. I briefly thought I didn't want him looking at my crotch, but modesty quickly disappeared when I realized there was a baby coming out of me.

"Mrs. Stone," the doctor said, "take a breath in, deep and full, bear down, and push; you've almost got the shoulders out."

I reached down and touched Milo's head. It was all real and happening. I sat up with the help of my mom and sister, who were each holding one leg back. Before I could blink, I pushed my nine-pound son out of me with the last bit of energy I could muster—and I did it all without even taking a Tylenol. I was so proud of myself, but sad that Lance had missed a moment in my life that made me feel so much self-worth and pride. Sad for him that he had missed his first son's birth.

The doctor turned Milo upside down and suctioned his mouth, and as soon as Milo starting crying, he rested the slimy, wailing, and amazing little creature on my chest. "Hello," I squeaked. "It's nice to meet you."

My mother was crying, my sister was crying, and all I could think about was how badly I wanted to show Gavin the little miracle I was holding.

After they cleaned Milo, my mom and sister got to hold him for a few minutes, until the nurse said I should try breastfeeding. At first it was painful, but then my mother showed me how to help him latch on properly. It was a moment I'll never forget. There was a new love, warmth, and maternal instinct inside of me, and I could see those same things inside of her for me. Milo finally latched on and was part of me again.

"I wish Dad were here," I whispered. "He'd be so happy."

"Me too," she said. Her face was blank but tears were running down her cheeks in streams.

"Will you go get Gavin and Frank?" I asked Kiki.

"Are you sure?" she asked.

"Of course, Keeks."

When they all came in, Milo was still suckling at my breast. I didn't even attempt to cover up.

Frank came toward me first, but he was apprehensive. "Get over here," I said, waving to him. "Look at my beautiful baby."

He kissed my forehead. "You did good, Mama." Gavin stood behind him near the door. For some reason he didn't come closer.

My mother called Lance, who had managed to buy the last ticket on the next flight to Denver and was getting ready to board his plane. She told him our big baby had come barreling into the world impatiently, and I could hear Lance exclaiming on the other end. I gestured for Kiki to hold the phone to my ear.

"How are you doing, Mommy?" Lance asked.

"Good. He's beautiful, Lance."

Lance wasn't crying but I could tell he was emotional. "I'm so sad I missed it, sweetie."

"Me too, but it happened so fast. How long until you're here?"

"I'm about to board my flight, so I'm hoping to be there in three hours. Who's there right now?"

"Just my mom, Keeks, Gavin, and Frank."

Silenced descended.

"Lance? Are you there?" I said.

"Was Gavin in the room when you delivered the baby?"

"Oh no," I said, like it would have been complete blasphemy, even though I'd wished he'd been there with me. "Of course not. Just my mom and Kiki. But I called Frank because I could feel the baby coming and knew he could get to me sooner. Gavin just happened to be in town."

"Oh. Okay. I'll be there soon, sweetie."

Kiki started complaining about being hungry, so my mom said, "I'm gonna head down to the cafeteria. You okay?"

"Yeah, I'm good." I smiled.

Frank followed them but Gavin stayed in the room, near the door. When the last nurse left the room, he shuffled toward me.

"Come here," I said.

Gavin was silent, standing at the side of my bed, watching Milo nurse. He blinked rapidly, like his mind was on hyperdrive.

"What?" I said.

His mouth opened like he was going to say something, but he shut it and shook his head.

"Say something, Gavin."

With his hands in his pockets, he bent to kiss my forehead. He let his lips linger there. I felt his body jerk a bit and then I felt moisture in my hair. He was crying.

"Gavin. Look at me."

When he pulled back, there was so much pain on his face. It hurt me to look at him. Tears actually fell down his cheeks. He stood there, shaking his head.

"Please, you need to say something."

He took a deep breath. "You're so beautiful right now. Seeing you like this. I'm happy for you, I really am, but I gotta go, Penny. I can't be here when Lance gets here."

"Why?"

His silence was deafening. He took two more deep breaths and said, "Because he has everything I want." He shrugged. "I gotta go."

"Wait, you can't leave. I want you to be the godfather. I already asked Lance if that was okay with him."

He laughed in that hysterical way people do when they've been crying. "You're not religious, Penny."

"You know what I mean."

"I guess I do. I can't believe Lance is okay with it."

"Well, it makes the most sense. Kiki's going to be the godmother."

"Are you saying I'm like a brother to you?" He was stroking Milo's peach-fuzz-covered head.

"No, because it just makes the most sense."

"I'd be honored, Penny," he said, but his face was full of anguish.

"I'm not trying to hurt you. I'm trying to keep you close."

"I know, but it hurts to be this close." He bent and kissed the top of Milo's head.

His face was inches from my breast, but I didn't flinch. When he stood up straight, he wiped his eyes and attempted to collect himself. He laughed again.

"What?" I said.

"At the moment, I think I'm more jealous of Milo than Lance."

I shook my head. "There's my Gavin."

GAVIN AND FRANK left about twenty minutes before Lance showed up. I tried to take a mental picture of Lance's face the moment he laid eyes on Milo. He was so proud and excited to see him; I almost faded into the background once he took Milo into his arms.

"What do you think? Can you believe I did it without any medication?"

Lance didn't look at me. His eyes were glued to Milo. "I'm just glad this little guy came into the world safely."

I wanted the credit, of course, but Lance wasn't getting the hint.

"Well, it was terrifying."

Finally, he looked down at me. "But you seem fine now. Are you in pain?"

"Strangely, no. Just sore." But I was sad. I was sad that he had missed the birth of our child. That he had missed the grueling car ride, and the fear I felt when I thought I was going to give birth on the side of the road. I knew he couldn't help it, that he had arrived as soon as he could, but Milo's birth was the first of many moments when I felt let down by Lance.

33. Two Months Ago

PENNY

Over the fourteen years of my marriage, I learned how easily Lance could distance himself when things got hard for our family.

In the first few weeks after Milo's birth, Lance took on more hours at work and more clients in the name of furthering his career, but I knew it was so he could get out of the house. My mom, Kiki, and even Frank had helped me out, but I needed my husband. Meanwhile, Gavin kept his distance in Denver, looking for the next girl to focus his energy on. We kept in touch by phone, but it took him a long time to adjust to the fact that I was married with a child.

At home, Lance couldn't handle hearing Milo cry all day, which is what he did almost constantly for the first three months of his life. Once, in the middle of the night, I had asked him to go to the nursery to change Milo and rock him back to sleep. I was exhausted from staying up with him all day and night. Instead, Lance brought Milo into our room, laid him next to my head, and changed his diaper. I had asked why he did it and he blew up at me. I had told him I needed to sleep and he had said, "But I have to go to work tomorrow and you don't." He always wanted me to be awake if he had to be. I never asked him to get up with Milo again after that night.

There weren't many options for me in the years after I had Milo. Sure, I could have left Lance and gotten a job, but there was more to it. I did love Lance, and I knew he loved me. He was also extremely levelheaded about our future. He worked hard and made investments and planned vacations—he was so reliable in that way. He was romantic, too. He'd bring me flowers, chocolates, and lingerie for no reason at all. He'd write beautiful messages in greeting cards. After a few years, I got comfortable in my relationship with him. I even became more like him. I took on his sense of humor and his OCD about germs. He insisted that we keep an immaculate house, and I complied. Gavin had predicted I'd change to suit Lance's needs, and he was right.

Every so often, though, Gavin would pop into our lives and disrupt the image Lance was trying to create. Before Gavin found out his father was sick, he was completely untethered. He'd had a slew of girlfriends over the years, the longest relationship being his most recent one, with Jenn. Three years they spent together, never committing to more than a casual relationship, though I know she wanted more, which is why he eventually broke up with her. Before Jenn, every time Gavin broke up with a girlfriend, he'd show up in Fort Collins and want to hang out with me and Milo. This irked Lance. He kept quiet about it out of respect for me, so I tried to return the favor by telling him everything we did together.

But I hid my true feelings. I made Lance believe Gavin was my brother, and not a man I held so dear to my heart.

Gavin had built a successful mechanic's garage from the ground up. Other than his work, he lived like a typical bachelor, traveling with friends all over Europe, taking off to Hollywood to see his mom anytime he felt like it. I called it running. He called it freedom. Either way, it was something I envied fervently. He went to concerts constantly, always inviting me, though he knew I could rarely go. He did what he wanted.

But every now and then, he'd call and say, "Penny, I'm lost. I want what Lance has. I'm tired of my life."

I had tried to convince him that there was nothing to envy about Lance's life. "You want to work sixty hours a week selling pharmaceuticals?"

Gavin would always just reply, "You know what I mean."

Now Lance and I were in counseling.

ON MY WAY to the counselor's office, I knew I had to make a decision. In the month we had spent apart, I danced a lot in my home studio and dove into Milo's activities, but mostly I stayed at home, soul searching. Gavin was swept up in Briel, not atypical for him in the beginning of a relationship. I knew it would end in a month or two when she went back to France, but at least he was giving me the space I needed.

I thought a lot about Lance and our marriage. He had been trying so hard in therapy to prove to me that we could work it out. And I believed him.

In the parking lot after last week's counseling session, I had let Lance kiss me good-bye. It was a passionate kiss. I missed his hands on me, the way he always smelled like the cologne he had worn for years, which had became a source of comfort to me, of marital ease and unselfconsciousness. He had put his strong arms on my hips and in return I had gripped his forearms. He had been wearing a gray dress shirt with the sleeves rolled up. His skin was warm. When I had left the parking lot last week, after our intimate moment, I was sure I knew the decision I was going to make.

Pulling out of my driveway, I waved to Milo, who was playing Ping-Pong in the garage with his friend Kale. Heading down the street, I noticed a For Rent sign in Frank's yard. Gavin had told me he was going to wait awhile, fix up the house, and then sell it. I wondered why he wanted to rent it out now.

A week later in the parking lot of the counselor's office, I texted Gavin.

> **Me: I thought you were selling your dad's house? Why is there a For Rent sign?**

> **Gavin: Change of plans. I'll explain everything to you later. I gotta go.**

That was abrupt.

Once inside Dr. Lake's office, I gave Lance a quick peck on the cheek and sat down next to him.

"Did you meet with her before I got here?" I said to him.

"We had a short talk. I think this session is actually unnecessary, right, Dr. Lake?"

"I do. Penny, if you're up for it, Lance would like to have a private moment with you to discuss things."

My brain was a little fried. I hadn't expected to be alone with him. I turned toward Lance. "What do you mean?"

"Just what Dr. Lake said. I'd like to talk to you in private. Are you okay with that?"

"I'm okay talking in private," I said. He was trying to give me the space I needed to feel comfortable. "Where do you want to go?"

He stood up. "Why don't you follow me to 415?"

It was one of our favorite date-night spots. "Sure . . ."

I looked at Dr. Lake curiously but she simply said, "Good luck, you two."

ON THE WAY to the restaurant, I thought about how I was going to tell Lance I wanted to try again, but that I wanted a lot to change. I *needed* a lot to change in order to move forward with him. I just had to be up front and communicate.

Inside the dimly lit room, we took our seats at a small table for two. He reached for my hands naturally, and I let him take them.

"I love you, Penny."

"I love you, too."

"I did a lot of thinking while we were apart." He studied me closely, and I sensed he was about to drop a bomb on me. The silence hung like a frozen bullet, staring me down.

"Did you meet someone?" I blurted out.

He jerked his head back. "Jesus, no. Let me finish. There are so many things I love about you."

"Thank you," I said, still stunned.

"But I bring none of them out in you anymore."

"That's not—"

"It's true," he said. His eyes welled up. "I realized that if Gavin didn't exist, we would still be right here . . . talking about why our marriage isn't working."

"Why do you think it's not working, Lance?"

"Because we're different." I was waiting for him to cut me down, but he didn't. "I feel like I forced you into this marriage. Like you've changed because of me."

"You didn't. And I didn't. I mean, yes, I've changed, but we both have."

"See, even now you can't stand up for yourself. That wasn't the Penny I married. The Penny I married was spontaneous . . . an artist. I feel like I've robbed you of that."

"I *chose* to be with you," I said. "You know that, right?"

"Penny, I brought you here because I wanted to tell you that I'm filing for divorce."

I held my hand to my head. I was certain I was having a stroke. Lance didn't blink; he just looked at me with sympathy, but I could tell from his eyes that his mind was made up.

What in the hell?

The room started spinning. Suddenly, I started to cry—huge, body-wracking sobs. He brought my hands to his mouth and kissed them. "I'm so sorry," he said. "I never meant to hurt you."

I sobbed for minutes but it felt like hours. I was breathing hard, trying to comprehend it all, trying to see what my future would look like. Weekends swapping Milo. Me, alone in our huge house.

My heart was filled with grief for my failed marriage, for my uncertain future, but there was also an undeniable feeling of relief. He was letting me off the hook. He knew that if it were up to me, I would stay, just to keep our family intact. He was still kissing my hands. *Did I even hear him correctly?*

I finally calmed down enough to speak. "Did you say you're filing for divorce?"

"Yes. I want you to be happy, Penny. And I can't make you happy."

"I don't want to be with Gavin, if that's what you think. I don't want Milo to have divorced parents."

"I know you don't want to be with Gavin. I spoke with him this morning."

"You did?"

"We just made small talk, but I realized he's pretty into his girlfriend, Briel. He encouraged me not to make any rash decisions, but the decision was already made up in my mind."

"Oh" was all I could say.

"For the last month, I've had the same thoughts about Milo at least ten thousand times. About what this would do to him. I also thought about how badly I didn't want to fail. What would it say about us that we couldn't endure? We love each other but we can't make our marriage work? And then I realized Milo is almost off to college. He's smarter and more mature than we give him credit for. We can give him more love this way. I've been terribly selfish, Penny. I want to take advantage of these last few months with him. I want to take him camping, fishing, and hunting. You've been his mother and his father lately, and I've been totally absent—both physically and emotionally. That wasn't fair to him or to you. And as far as failing, I don't give a shit anymore what people think. When I realized my anger came from not being able to make you happy, I only saw one solution. And now my mind's made up. God, you are so precious to me still, but I've turned you into a shell. I don't want to see you this way anymore. We both deserve to be happy, don't you think?"

I nodded. "What will we tell Milo?"

"Your mom is bringing him here in a half hour. We'll figure it out."

Within thirty minutes, I ordered a very stiff margarita and planned out what we would say to Milo. We knew we had to keep it simple.

"You don't seem upset anymore," Lance said to me.

"Of course I'm upset. I'm heartbroken, but these last few years have been hard on me. I've totally given up who I am and I didn't communicate with you like I should have. This is the most we've talked to each other in years. And this is definitely the most we've ever agreed on. I'm so sad about what's happening, Lance—I wanted things to work out between us. But I think you're right. We'll just keep going in circles if we don't end it now."

"You agree we'd be fighting a losing battle?"

"I agree that we need a change, and this seems to be the only solution."

When Milo walked in, I noticed he was looking more and more like his dad every single day. He had big eyes and a face that looked a little sad, even when he was smiling. Today he looked especially worried. He had handled the separation beautifully, and we'd talked enough for me to know that he wasn't oblivious to our problems. He was as emotionally intelligent as he was academically intelligent, but he was my baby boy. How would I explain to him that the life he once knew was over?

The moment Milo pulled up a chair and sat down, I leaned over, kissed his cheek, and started crying.

"Mom, please don't cry. Whatever you guys are about to tell me, I can handle it."

Lance was still holding both of my hands in one of his. He reached out and side-hugged Milo. "We love you, son."

"But you're getting a divorce?" Milo said.

All Lance and I could do was nod.

Milo lowered his head. "Well, I guess that's that."

"You're not upset? You don't have questions?" I said.

"I *am* upset. I'm sad for you guys, but I've been sad for you guys for a while. I just want you to be happy."

I broke down in tears and dropped my head into my hands on the table. Milo rubbed my back. "It's okay, Mom. I'm going to college in the fall, so you don't have to worry about me." The reminder of Milo leaving drove the stake in deeper. He'd applied early to MIT and gotten in. Soon enough he'd be across the country, in Boston.

"I'm going to rent an apartment at that complex down the street until Milo leaves for college," Lance said. "I have an appointment with a broker in the morning."

"And then what?" I asked.

"I think I'm going to transfer to Denver."

I looked up at him in shock. "Why?"

"Fort Collins is too small. We need to put some space between us."

I squeezed his hand, and we all sat in silence as we waited for the check to arrive.

LANCE CAME BACK to the house to pack a few things. I told him he could sleep in the room with me, but he was a gentleman through and through; he crashed on the couch.

After Milo fell asleep, I started going through old photos, wondering what I could've done differently. Instead, I ended up lingering over my old black-and-white dancing photos, which made me both hopeful and sad at the same time. *What might have been?* I thought.

What could still be?

34. One month Ago

PENNY

An entire month went by but I still hadn't told anyone about my divorce—including Gavin. Up until that point, he had been distant. He said he needed to talk, but he avoided making a plan with me. Once Lance moved out and served me with papers, I knew I couldn't put off telling him.

I carried the papers around in a manila envelope for days. All I had to do was sign and it would be over, but something was preventing me from doing it. As I sat in my car in the parking lot at Milo's soccer practice one day, I finally decided to tell Gavin.

Me: Can you talk?

Gavin: What's up?

Me: Can you talk, not text?

Gavin: I'm in the middle of something right now. You okay? Lance being cool?

Me: Yes, I'm fine. Lance is being cool. I just need to talk. I thought you did, too?

Gavin: I do, I do. I'll be in Fort Collins in a month. I'm having some work done on my dad's house next month before the renters move in. We'll get lunch, okay?

I wasn't going to tell him via text. Gavin was probably busy with the garage and Briel. Still, it was unusual for him to be that distant.

Later that night, he called my house phone. "Hey, P, can I talk to Milo?"

"Um, okay."

When Milo opened his bedroom door, I handed him the phone and whispered, "Don't tell Gavin about your dad and me, okay? I need to tell him in person."

He nodded.

Twenty minutes later, Milo was in the kitchen, getting water. "That was it?" I asked. "He didn't ask to talk to me?"

"Nope," he said, taking a gulp of water.

"What did he want?"

"He was just checking up on me, seeing how things were going with school and soccer. He apologized for missing my first few games and said he'd be out here in a month.

He hoped to spend a few days with us, maybe catch one of my games and take me out for a bite."

"How nice of him," I said sarcastically, annoyed he was avoiding me.

Milo shrugged and then turned to leave the kitchen.

"Wait," I said. "Can I have a hug good night?"

"Oh yeah, sorry, Mom."

He came over and gave me a quick hug. "I love you, Milo. Sleep tight."

"Thanks. Love you, too."

Over the next few weeks, I focused on being alone. I hadn't signed the papers yet, and I was still carrying them around with me everywhere. Lance's lawyer called and asked why I hadn't signed them yet. I told him I would very soon.

Lance took Milo for a weekend and when Milo returned Sunday night, he seemed happier.

"What'd you and your dad do?"

"We went camping, roasted marshmallows, the whole bit."

"Just the two of you?" I asked.

My brilliant son knew I was onto something. "He doesn't have a girlfriend, Mom. But even if he did—"

"If he did, it would be a little too soon."

"Well, I guess. But you're always with Gavin."

"No, I'm not. This is practically the longest I've gone without seeing Gavin, and I've barely spoken to him. Plus, Gavin is just a friend. He's your godfather. He's family. And anyway, you've had deeper conversations with him lately than I have."

He looked at me sympathetically. "Okay, I'm sorry. Why

don't you come and volunteer at the school? You can hang out with Crystal; she's there a lot and you two haven't really hung out lately."

"She lives across the street. We have plenty of opportunities. Don't worry about me, Milo."

"You seem lonely, Mom."

"It's okay to be lonely sometimes." It was hard for me to be alone, but I wanted Milo to be more independent than me. To understand there would be seasons in his life when he wouldn't be the center of attention, when he might be alone at night with no one to call but his mom or dad, or maybe not even us. It was something I grappled with from time to time, but in the past, I'd always had Gavin. Now I wasn't so sure.

THE NEXT NIGHT, I took Milo to dinner with my mom and Kiki at The Kitchen, one of my favorite restaurants in Fort Collins. My mother had never been there before. She immediately picked up the menu and began huffing and puffing about the prices.

"Twenty-six dollars for chicken? I can buy five whole chickens for that money."

She'd become very frugal since my father's passing. I wanted to remind her that she used to spend forty dollars to have Kiki spray-tanned before pageants. Instead, I blurted out, "Lance and I are getting divorced."

My mother gasped.

"Mom, it's okay."

I looked at Kiki, who was grinning, but quickly stopped.

"Are you happy about this, Aunt Keeks?" Milo said.

"Not happy. Of course not. I don't want to see you two go through this. But I must say, I didn't think you'd ever go through with it, Penny."

"I didn't. *He's* the one who filed for divorce," I said. "And I haven't signed the papers yet."

"What?" my mother and sister said in unison.

"He's got someone else!" Kiki shouted. "That bastard."

Milo rolled his eyes.

"Stop it, Keeks. He's not a bad guy—and you don't know the whole story."

"He's leaving you," she argued.

"It was mutual."

My mother was still speechless.

"What did Gavin say?" Kiki asked.

I called the waiter over. "Let's get some drinks. And before you ask, Gavin is a nonfactor. He doesn't even know yet." The waiter arrived at our table and I ordered a bottle of champagne for the table.

"You want to celebrate that Lance is leaving you?" my mom said, aghast.

Kiki turned to my mom, "Is she losing it?"

"I think so," my mother said.

"I'm right here," I told them.

"She's not losing it," Milo chimed in. "She's just being herself."

"Listen to Milo. Don't be sad for me. Lance and I are ending a shitty marriage amicably and respectably to give ourselves a chance at happiness. What's wrong with that?"

The waiter popped the cork and poured three glasses. "A toast!" I said, holding up my glass. My mother and Kiki held up theirs as well, though they still looked stunned, and Milo raised his Coke. "To family, to respect, to accepting change, and to new beginnings!"

When we clinked our glasses, something hit me: a brief burst of sadness . . . and a longing for Gavin to be there.

ON THE WAY home, I pulled over into a strip mall and turned toward Milo. "I'm getting my first tattoo, and I want you to come with me."

35. One Hour Before the Lunch Heard 'Round the World

GAVIN

After fixing a little electrical problem in my dad's house, I thanked the renters and referred them to the property management company who'd be handling the house while I was away.

I walked down to Penny's place and Milo answered. Hugging him, I said, "Hey kid. Shouldn't you be at school? Where's your mom?"

"I think she forgot I have a half day at school today for teacher conferences. I have a pretty good idea of where she is, though."

"Where's that?"

"Has Mom ever told you about the old dance studio she used to go to when she was a kid?"

"Sure. But isn't that a Subway now?"

"Yeah, but it's going out of business."

"Seriously? A Subway near a college is going out of business? Huh." I shrugged. "Is she eating lunch there?"

"She said she was gonna go check it out, but I think she just goes down there and sits on the bench outside."

I'd never heard of Penny doing this. "What? Why?"

"I don't know. I think it's nostalgic for her or something."

"Is your dad here?"

"My dad?" Milo looked at me strangely.

"Yeah, your dad."

"No, he's not here. Um, I don't mean to be rude but I have a shit-ton of homework to do and then I'm going to stay at my friend's house tonight. Do you want me to tell Mom you stopped by?"

"Hey, wait a sec. I'm glad I ran into you, Milo, because I have some big news. I'm leaving for a bit. In fact . . . I'm going to France."

He blinked for several seconds, his expression blank. "Why?" he asked.

"My girlfriend, Briel, is from there. She's going back home . . . and I'm going with her."

"Oh . . . that's great, G. Does Mom know?"

"No, I need to tell her. That's why I came by. Do you really think she's down at the Subway?"

"Yeah." He was apprehensive and I had no idea why. "Did she know you were coming down?"

"No."

"Try her there, I guess. If you can't find her, you can always come by tonight. Like I said, I'll be sleeping over at my friend's house."

We hugged and he held on to me longer than usual. "This isn't good-bye just yet. I'll see you at your game tomorrow, okay?" I said.

"Sure. See ya, G. Good luck with Mom." He gave me a long look before he shut the door.

My stomach was churning. I was finally going to tell Penny my news. I'd been avoiding her for a couple of months, but I couldn't put it off any longer.

When I pulled Charlize into the Subway parking lot, I spotted Penny right away. She was staring into the distance blankly, holding a manila envelope and spacing out. When I got closer, she must have recognized the familiar purr of my engine because she turned her head and stared at me as I pulled into the parking space.

I got out and walked up to her. When she stood, she seemed taller. I looked down and noticed she had heeled boots on, tight jeans, and a fitted sweater. Her hair was done and she had makeup on. I hadn't seen this side of Penny in a long time. She looked amazing.

"Hey! Surprise, surprise," she said as she hugged me. She smelled like heaven. I missed her arms around me.

"You look fantastic, P. Do you always get dressed up to hang out in front of Subway?"

"Ha! I was hoping to meet the strip mall owner. I'm thinking about converting this place back into a dance studio once Subway's lease is up, but I'm not sure if I have the funds."

"That would be amazing. Can't you guys sell one of your cars or something? Or maybe a Tag watch?"

She laughed.

"Oh, shut it. Let's grab some lunch. You keep saying you want to catch up, but I haven't seen you in so long. We can walk across the street to that little pub by Bank of America, if you want to?"

"You just read my mind. I'll drive, by the way."

She looked at me suspiciously. "Big news?

I shook my head. "Let's get a drink first."

I DROVE US both over and parked by the bank. I was positively shaking by that point. I didn't know how Penny would react to my news. On our way into the pub, she spotted an outgoing mailbox and dropped in the envelope she was carrying.

At the bar, I ordered a beer and she ordered Chardonnay and some beer-cheese pretzels. I was surprised. Penny usually stuck to salad.

"That's different for you." She looked like she'd lost a lot of weight.

"Don't think you can distract me so easily. Tell me what's going on. Did you break up with Briel?"

I guzzled my beer and took a deep breath. "Don't be mad, okay?"

She looked surprised. "Why the hell would I be mad?" she said before picking up her glass of wine and downing the whole thing.

"Jesus, Penny." She motioned to the bartender for another glass.

"Spill, Gavin."

"Briel is pregnant."

Penny started breathing fast, her nostrils flaring. The bartender refilled her glass. She downed it and slammed it on the counter.

"Shit, Penny! Be careful. You almost shattered your glass!" My voice was getting high and loud.

"You're moving to fucking France?!" Now she was yelling. I had to get her out of the bar.

HALF AN HOUR later, I was exhausted. We had just had our first knock-down, drag-out fight in what seemed like forever, and now we were standing in the Bank of America parking lot, her face covered in tears and Charlize running behind me.

"Is this it?" she asked.

"This is it, P."

She wrapped her arms around me, and I tried to commit the feeling of her, the smell of her, to my memory.

I got into Charlize and revved the engine. "We'll talk on the phone or email or something, okay?"

"Okay," she said.

I nearly choked on my next words. "I wish it were you, Penny."

As I drove away, tears started streaming down my face. I felt my phone vibrate and pulled it out of my pocket.

> Penny: Lance and I are getting
> a divorce. I thought you should
> know.

I nearly drove off the road. The manila envelope she dropped in the mailbox. Her ranting and raving about how alone she was about to be. Suddenly, it all made sense.

Fuck.

36. Present Day

PENNY

After I texted Gavin, I got into my car and drove the speed limit all the way home, listening to the old songs Gavin and I loved, like "Plainsong" by The Cure. I cried and cried until I couldn't cry anymore.

I returned to an empty house. I plopped down on the couch and flipped on the TV. Buckley jumped up to sit next to me, and for the first time, I didn't kick him off.

I texted Milo.

> **Me: Hi Honey. How'd your day go? Did you already head over to Kale's?**

> **Milo: Yeah, I'm here. His mom is gonna drop us off at the movies.**

> **Me: Okay. Be smart.**

Milo: It's kinda hard for me not
to be.

Me: Ha! But don't be a
smartass.

Milo: Did Gavin tell you he's
moving?

Me: Yep, and having a baby too.

Milo: Wow! He didn't mention
that. How'd you take it?

Me: I'm ok. I'm always ok.

Milo: I know. Did you show
him your tattoo?

Me: No, but I'm sure he would
have been shocked.

Milo: I love you, Mom.

Me: Love you too.

I never took naps during the day but TV wasn't appealing to me and I was emotionally exhausted. I fell asleep with
Buckley curled up beside me.

AT SEVEN, I woke up, ate three crackers, and uncorked a
bottle of pinot noir, wishing Kiki or my mom or Ling were
there with me. I had to learn to get used to being alone
more than I ever thought I would. I checked my phone to

see if Gavin had responded and noticed there were two messages from Lance.

> **Lance: Did you sign the
> papers? Please don't forget,
> Penny.**

> > **Me: I dropped them in the
> > mail today. I promise.**

> **Lance: Thank you. See you
> tomorrow at Milo's game.**

> > **Me: K.**

I undressed down to my underwear and threw on a long
T-shirt I had stolen from Gavin years ago that had a graphic
of a cat wearing a police officer's hat above the words *Who's
Laughing Meow?* It made me smile, but the moment was
fleeting. At least I had Buckley.

Plopping back on the couch with my wine, I began flipping through the channels without any luck. Finally, after
several minutes, I decided to switch to music. Out of some
form of self-torture, I drank more red wine and put on Dan
Auerbach's "When the Night Comes" because it was the
saddest song I could think of. But at least it got me off the
couch and onto my toes. I danced for about thirty seconds
when my phone pinged. It was a text from Gavin.

> **Gavin: Got your text from earlier.
> Still processing it. You okay?**

> > **Me: Yeppo.**

Gavin: You alone? What are
you doing?

                    Me: I'm always alone. Just
                    drinking and dancing.

Gavin: Dangerous combination.
Can I watch?

What the hell is his deal?

                    Me: Where are you?

Gavin: In your driveway.

                    Me: Creeper.

Gavin: Yep.

I ran to the door and swung it open. Standing in the doorway like I was twenty-one again, clad in only a T-shirt, I took him in. He was wearing his jeans cuffed at the ankle, Converse, a black T-shirt, two days of growth on his face, and a cocky-ass grin.

"Nice shirt, you little klepto," he said, twirling his keys around his index finger.

"I thought I would never see you again."

"Have I ever been predictable?"

"Come in." He followed me down the hall toward the living room. I poured him a glass of wine and handed it to him.

He sipped his wine delicately. I loved watching him drink wine. He was watching me, too, and there was a little twinkle in his eyes, like he was kissing me with them.

"Well, Tiny Dancer, I came here to see a show."

"Right." I said. I moved our white couch out of the way. Gavin took a seat on the floor near the stone fireplace, crossing his feet at the ankles. Buckley curled up on his lap.

I flipped the same song on from the beginning and made up a little routine to it—a combination of contemporary dance and ballet. I danced with my eyes closed, unselfconsciously. What the hell did it matter anymore?

When the music ended, I stopped and opened my eyes. Gavin stood and walked toward me, never taking his eyes off mine.

He picked up the wireless speaker and my phone, grabbed my hand, and led me down the hall to the guest room. We stood face-to-face a foot apart while he held the small speaker between us. "Put that song on again and tell me you believe there's a God."

I put the song on repeat, set the speaker down, reached up, and placed my hands on his cheeks. The light coming from the hallway was enough to see the blissful look on his face. Leaning up on my toes wordlessly, I told him I believed there was a God. And then I kissed him.

When I pulled away, his eyes were still closed. "Was that like our sweet blind kiss or your mean hate-kiss?" I asked.

"Neither. It was better than both."

"Are you still leaving in two days?" My throat ached.

He nodded, looking more regretful than I had ever seen him in my life. His eyes were glassy. "I have to. Even knowing that you're not with Lance . . . my own situation hasn't changed. You wouldn't love me if I abandoned my child."

"You're right."

When he dropped to his knees, I gasped. He lifted my

shirt enough to kiss the tiny bow on the front waistband of my panties. My hands found his hair.

"Let me love you tonight, please, Penny?"

"But what about—"

"Shhh," he whispered against my belly. "We deserve this. We've been waiting so long."

"I don't know if I'll be able to let you go after this."

"Yes, you will. You're the strongest person I know."

When I lifted the T-shirt over my head, he ran his hands up my sides and found the tattoo. "On the ribs? Ouch, that hurts."

Not enough, I thought. He squinted to read the words under my left breast.

my breath
my joy
Milo Liam

He kissed it. "Beautiful," he said quietly. "I can't believe you inked your virgin skin. This is perfect, though." He kissed it again and made me squirm.

"I'm gonna light you up, Penny. We're gonna do this and then fall asleep together, and tomorrow, I'll wake you up gently."

"Oh my God . . ." I don't think anyone ever made me feel that way with words alone.

Pushing me onto the bed, he slid my panties down my legs. He kissed me between the thighs, making me writhe. Reaching back, he turned the dimmer up just enough so we could see each other. "I can't do this blind. You're too beautiful. I want to look at you," he said.

"Take your clothes off. There's clearly an imbalance here." I pointed to my naked body and then to his fully clothed self. He chuckled while he kicked off his shoes. A moment later, he was naked. I looked at his tall, tattooed frame: muscular, lean, and painfully turned on. I had never seen Gavin totally naked. He was impressive.

When he crawled onto the bed, slowly moving up my body, I started to panic. He kissed me but I was somewhere else, thinking about what I had done to my life.

"What's wrong?"

"Nothing."

"I can tell, P." He rolled onto his side and leaned up on his elbow.

"Can we just talk for a while? I'm sorry."

"Don't apologize. I understand. I'm scared, too. I'm terrified of everything that's happening. Here we are, finally being who we were meant to be, but tomorrow we have to go back to pretending . . . to living like we're other people."

"Gavin, why do you always sing that song to me? The Dylan song."

" 'Just Like a Woman'?"

"Yeah."

He looked thoughtfully at the blank wall across from us, remembering something as he absently traced circles on my belly with his index finger.

"They say Dylan wrote that song for Edie Sedgwick."

I knew the name but wasn't sure who she was. "Was that Andy Warhol's muse?"

"Yeah."

"And . . ."

"When I first met you, you were wearing black tights

and a short T-shirt. She always wore black tights. The way you danced was so captivating, like her. You still take my breath away. When I walk into a room, my eyes are immediately drawn to you. And back then I used to think you were so vulnerable. Like you would break. I saw a glimpse of that today, but you're not that girl anymore."

"What, am I hardened? Jaded? Sad?"

"No. You're strong."

Was he just telling me that because he knew I needed to be strong from now on?

"Maybe. I don't know how strong I can be now; this is just the beginning. My husband just divorced me, my son is going to college in a few months, and my best friend is leaving the country."

There was a sadness behind his smile. "You'll be fine. You've fought through worse."

"I always wondered why you had such a hard time with women. You're so loving and perceptive."

"I've never had a hard time with women." He smiled a full, cheesy grin. "If I had trouble with women, I wouldn't date, I'd just be single and pay for it every once in a while."

I socked him. "God, you're a pig sometimes."

"I'm being honest. You made me picky. I never felt as close to another woman as I do to you."

It was then that I finally noticed my name tattooed on his hip. I knew he had tattooed *Milo* on the inside of his upper bicep, but I didn't know about the *Penny* tattoo.

When I ran my finger over it, he shivered. "When did you get this?"

"The morning you got married. Imagine that."

I shook my head. "Why didn't you tell me?"

"I guess because it was for me, not you. I wanted it to hurt, but it wasn't enough."

I shimmied down the bed and kissed the word. His fingers got lost in my hair. "Gavin?"

"Penny."

"Can we just cuddle?"

I felt his body jerk with laughter. "Sure. I'm used to you teasing me to death."

I scooted up, lying on top of him, and wrapped my arms around his neck. My breasts were pressed to his chest, and his hands were around my waist. I looked into his sincere, warm eyes, crinkling at the corners. I knew he was trying to read my mind. Planting a soft, chaste kiss on his lips, I rolled off him and buried myself in the crook of his arm, where I had been so many times before.

AT FIVE A.M., I started awake to the sounds of Buckley scratching at the door. He wanted to be fed. I threw on Gavin's T-shirt and led Buckley to the kitchen, where I filled up his bowl. I was still exhausted and just wanted to climb back into bed. I went upstairs, brushed my teeth, and realized I had only a few more hours with Gavin. Back in the guest room, I tore my T-shirt off and crawled back into bed with him. His breathing was even, like he was still sleeping, but he stirred when I kissed his chest.

"Come here," he whispered. I had woken him with just a small kiss right over his heart.

Dawn filled the room with a pale, mystical light, cloaking us, letting us share a moment no one would ever know about but us.

I kissed him on the mouth, bracing his neck. He adjusted me so that I was straddling him. I bent and kissed him again.

"Are you sure?" he said.

"Yes."

With our mouths connected, he moved me to lie at his side. We were face-to-face as his hand snaked down between my thighs. He touched me gently, waking me, lighting me up. I pressed his hand to my body and said, "More, more."

The room was stifling from our movements and body heat. He tore the sheet off and got to his knees.

I reached up and wrapped my hand around him. He made a strangled sound. Breathing hard, he spread my legs so that he was nestled between them. He bent and kissed my belly, then lower and lower until I was squirming beneath him, beneath his mouth and his gentle, worshiping touch.

He sat back again. I felt cold and naked. "Come down here," I said.

Lifting my body with ease, he brought us together, to where we were going to connect. He placed a pillow under my lower back and slid in gracefully, carefully, with love in his eyes. His hands were so big on my waist that I could barely see my own body beneath them.

At first I was shy as he moved in and out. I kept my eyes closed and said, "Don't look at me."

"Ahh, Penny, I can't help it."

His movements got faster and faster; our breaths got louder and louder.

"Gavin, I can't believe you feel this way."

He covered my body with his, and he whispered near my ear, "We fit perfectly. I'm not going to last long."

"Let go," I said to him, but somehow my own body

responded to the demand and I felt the aching subside and the building, building, until I was trembling. "Don't stop, do exactly what you're doing. Don't—"

He smashed his mouth to mine and kissed me with such tortured passion, I fell apart beneath him. My back arched. I was frozen in that position as my body quaked. A second later, he thrust into me once more, pulled his mouth from mine, and said, "*God.*" The word was a prayer on his lips.

We were lifeless, limbs everywhere, not knowing which one of us they belonged to. Why had I waited so long to be with him? Why had I pushed him away all those years ago? I would never understand my twenty-one-year-old self or what she saw in other people. Why she chose Lance. I could list the reasons she gave, but they would all be overshadowed by how much I loved Gavin. How much I *still* loved Gavin.

MILO'S GAME WAS at one p.m., so we lay there, dozing in and out of sleep as Chet Baker played on the radio. We made love two more times in the guest bed, and once in the guest shower.

Later in the kitchen, as I made espresso for us, I asked him, "Do you feel bad for Briel?"

He pulled two espresso cups from the cabinet. "I should, but I don't. Selfishly, I still feel bad for us."

We were showered and dressed and it was just like any other time Gavin had sat at our breakfast bar and drank espresso. Except this time, memories of us together were rushing through me. I'd shiver, my body would react, and I'd try to push the thought away. But a part of me didn't want to let go; after all, I would never get to experience it again.

"Are we meeting Milo there?" he asked.

"Yeah, his friend Kale's mom is taking them. We should drive separately, though. Lance will probably be there, and I just don't want to deal with any drama right now."

"It's fine, I get it. Don't worry."

I gave him a grateful look and mouthed "Thank you." I downed the rest of my espresso quickly and stood up from the counter barstool. "We should get going. Are you leaving straight from the field?"

He nodded.

"And you have your guitar in your car?"

"Yeah, why?"

"Before we go, will you play our song? The one you wrote for me for my wedding?"

He smiled. "You want to see me fall apart, don't you, Penny?"

"No, I just . . . I don't know when I'll see you or hear you play again, in person."

His eyes turned glassy. "Okay." He went to his car and came back in with his acoustic guitar and started strumming the familiar chords. "I changed a few lyrics."

I laughed. "Just now?"

"Yep."

When he started singing, it looked like he was going to cry. I stood behind him and put my hand on his shoulder.

Tonight you are close to me,
I'm inside this time to pray.
Feeling everything I always knew and
All the reasons I want to stay.

A minute is forever.
A kiss left on your lips to remember.
I'm your lover, I'm your friend.
You're mine.
You were always my lover . . . for a lifetime in my
     mind.

Growing old like this . . . letting go and coming back
again.
Telling tales like this . . . of how it all began.

I'll hold your hand and your babies—I'll watch your
children grow—And one day you'll say, "Howdy, old
chum."
And I'll say, "No, I'm your lover . . . remember? And
     you're mine."
It's been this way forever. I've always been your
     lover . . . for a lifetime in my mind.

I kissed his neck from behind. "I love you."

"I love you, too," he said without turning around.

After he packed up his guitar, I walked him to the door and said, "I'll see you at the field."

He turned to me. "Close your eyes." He kissed me, and I put my hand on his heart the way he did fifteen years ago. We pulled away and, a moment later, he was gone.

AT THE FIELD, he cheered for Milo and exchanged a brief handshake with Lance, who ended up standing on the opposite side of the field from us. Gavin didn't say much to me. When the game was over, he congratulated Milo on scoring two goals. I overheard him apologize for having to leave right away, and then he came up to me and said, "I gotta go. I promise I'll call you as soon as I get to Paris."

But he didn't.

37. Two Months Later

GAVIN

I knew I needed to call her, but once we got to Paris, everything was chaotic. I had to meet Briel's family and find a place for us to live. Meanwhile, she was milking the pregnancy for all it was worth. She was incapable of doing anything. I thought back to that tiny house Lance and Penny lived in when she was about to pop with Milo. She used to dance and take long walks. She shot arrows with my dad and helped build a fence in her side yard. She was just a different kind of woman. But I had to stop comparing Briel to Penny; it wasn't fair, and it just made me an unhappy jerk.

Two months had passed since I had left. Finally, Penny broke down and texted me early one morning.

Penny: Forgot all about me already, huh?

Briel saw the text before I did. She liked to snoop. Before I even had a chance to respond, she came into the kitchen, where I was preparing breakfast, and said, "She knows manners?" She was holding my phone up, showing me the text.

"I thought we talked about this, Briel?"

"We are going to be a family now. Why this other woman going to be involved in our life?"

"She's not 'another woman.' She's my best friend. She's like a sister to me." Okay, that was a small white lie.

"I don't want it going on."

"I think maybe your hormones are getting the best of you. Penny and I are worlds apart now. She's going through a lot. She's in the middle of a divorce."

She threw the phone across the room.

"Oh my god, Briel. What are you doing?"

"Call your friend so she can leave you alone."

She left the room crying and slammed the bedroom door hard enough to shake our tiny apartment. I could hear her sobbing. I had never lived with a woman, and here I was confined to six hundred square feet of space, with one bathroom, a kitchen, and a woman I wasn't in love with. Meanwhile, I couldn't speak French to save my life; I had to rely on Briel for everything. I was suffocating after only two months.

I decided I wasn't going to let Briel boss me around. She had enough control. I walked out onto the cobblestone street and found a café, ordered an espresso, and called Penny. It was eight a.m. my time, eleven p.m. Penny's.

"Hi," she said.

"I'm so sorry I haven't called you."

"It okay," she said. "I figured you were busy getting settled in."

"God, I'm dying here. I hate it so much."

"I'm sorry, Gavin."

"What's going on? How are you and Lance?"

I could hear her take a deep breath. "We're not speaking. It makes the divorce proceedings easier. Milo arranges everything. What about you?"

"I don't know. I feel stuck here."

"You can't run now."

"That's not it. Briel's kind of a pain. I'm just trying to stay positive. She keeps threatening to leave me, and half the time I feel like saying, 'Go ahead,' but I desperately want to be a part of my daughter's life."

There was a long beat of silence. "You're having a girl?"

"Yes." I realized I hadn't told her. She was always the first to know everything, but I couldn't confide in her in this case. I was sure she was hurt. "I'm sorry, I meant to tell you right away."

"What will you name her?"

"We haven't chosen a name yet."

"It's okay. I have to get going anyway. Milo's waiting for dinner."

"Oh." I was caught off guard. "Well, I'll call you again soon."

"Settle into your life, Gavin. Try to accept it. I did."

I bristled. "Why am I sensing hostility?"

"It's nothing. I'll let you go."

ON MY WAY back, I picked up some lilies for Briel, hoping it would smooth things over. When I walked in and offered them to her, she jerked her head back. "Gaveen, I'm allergic."

"Fuck." Another thing I didn't know about her. I

dumped the flowers in the garbage outside and came back in to find her lying on the couch, thumbing through a magazine.

Without looking up, she said, "I want to name her Elodie, and I think she should take my last name. She'll fit in better here with the name Boucher."

"Why? Berninger is French, too."

"Kind of. I mean, she can have your last name, but I should take it too, in that case."

"Are you talking about marriage?"

She shrugged.

"Fine. Make a plan." I felt so beaten down, I couldn't even think for myself anymore.

38. Two Months Later

PENNY

I found out about Gavin's marriage via text and spent the next month drifting through my life. I bought college stuff for Milo—sheets, a shower caddy, an alarm clock, etc.—and imagined Gavin and Briel's wedding whenever I was alone: Briel in white, her belly swollen the way mine had been fifteen years ago; Gavin in black, exchanging vows in a French civil ceremony without a single friend or family member on his side.

A month later, I texted Lance.

> Me: I'm taking Milo to MIT in three weeks if you want to join.

> Lance: I'm slammed at work. I'm so sorry. But we need to talk before he leaves. I'd like us to have a family dinner on Sunday. Can we do that?

> Me: Sure, just let me know
> when and where and we'll
> be there.

> Lance: Sounds good. I'll keep
> you posted.

It's amazing what a positive effect divorce can have on a couple's ability to communicate clearly.

I texted Kiki and my mom next.

> Me: We're having a small party
> for Milo before we take him to
> MIT. I'll keep you posted.

A minute later, Kiki was calling. "Hello?" I said.

"Penny. I need to tell you something."

"What? Spit it out."

"I told Douche-face—"

"No more names, Keeks; that's Milo's dad."

"Listen, I promised I would let him tell you, but I don't want you to be shocked."

"What?!" I shouted impatiently.

"He was going to tell you and Milo over dinner. He has a girlfriend. I ran into them at the movies."

"Really?" I said quietly.

"Yes, a doctor. She's one of his clients."

"Is she pretty?"

Kiki paused for too long. "Never mind," I said. "Good for him."

"I'm sorry, Penny. I told him to just tell you over the

phone, that you don't like being put into uncomfortable situations."

"You're right, Keeks; thank you. I'm going to call him now."

"Don't tell him—"

"It doesn't matter anymore anyway."

I called him and told him I knew, and that the family dinner was unnecessary. He seemed relieved that he didn't have to tell me himself. He also admitted that it was early, but that he had known her for a while. I held it together. And then I called my mom.

"Mom," I said. Suddenly, I was crying.

She came straight over. I told her about Gavin getting married and Lance's new girlfriend.

Hugging and rocking me from side to side, she said, "Life will change and change again. You just have to find a port in this storm. It doesn't have to be another person, Penny. Find something just for you."

Weeks later, I texted Gavin that I'd dropped Milo off at MIT. Instead of responding to me, he called Milo directly.

I CAME BACK from Boston to Fort Collins to an eerily quiet house—and a package on my doorstep. Inside was a set of keys and a letter. I recognized Gavin's handwriting immediately.

Dear Penny,

This felt too personal for texting. Inside, you'll find a birth announcement. Elodie Adela Berninger came

into this world screaming bloody murder, but thankfully she was a perfectly healthy eight pounds four
ounces. She's beautiful, Penny. I wanted you to be her
godmother but Briel fought me on it until I finally
gave up. I'm sorry. In my heart you're her godmother—
please know that.

The keys belong to the four retail spaces located
in the strip mall where your old ballet studio was. I
bought the building and added your name next to
mine on the deed. I had a hefty chunk of cash after
selling the garage, and I needed to reinvest it.

If you wouldn't mind helping me manage the
property, it's all yours, rent-free. Fort Collins will be
lucky to have you teaching dance to their daughters.

I'm sorry I've been distant. Things have been rough
here. Let's talk soon.

Love, Gavin

39. Five Months After That

PENNY

Lance said he'd never get married again, but he said nothing about not having more kids. Deanna, his doctor girlfriend, was pregnant. I guess it was me all those years who couldn't conceive. I congratulated them. I didn't care anymore.

My dance studio was up and running. I put every ounce of energy I had into it. All my classes filled up so fast that I had to hire another teacher and a receptionist to help me run it. I talked to Gavin only when it concerned the building—just short, businesslike texts. Otherwise, I was left to fantasize about our last night together. I had accepted that he had moved on, and I was moving on, in my own way. Milo was doing wonderfully at school, my mother was dating a man from the lab, Kiki and Ling maintained their fierce independence, and I was . . . content. I got so much joy out of teaching—more than I thought I ever would.

But after a late night in the studio, I got a text from Gavin.

Gavin: I need you, P. Call me.

I called him immediately.

"Hello," he said.

"Hi."

"God, it's good to hear your voice."

"What's going on? Where are you?"

"I just left our apartment to take Elodie for a walk. I'm so miserable, P."

"I'm so sorry." But my tone was curt. My compassion for him was dwindling. He'd made his bed—now he needed to lie in it.

"Everything she does bugs me, even the way she says my name."

"I'm fine, too, by the way; Lance and his girlfriend are having a baby."

"Did you hear me? I said I'm miserable. I don't know what to do."

I could feel myself boiling over. "I'm sorry, Gavin. I'm sorry you got Briel pregnant and now you're stuck in France."

"Elodie is the best thing that's ever happened to me," he said defensively.

"Wonderful! Then why are you complaining?"

"Because I'm not in love with Briel, and having a child with someone you don't love is hard."

"Preaching to the fucking choir."

"Jesus, what's your problem?"

"I've just run out of solutions for you, and I can't bear to hear you talk about Briel that way. Leave her if you don't love her. You have options."

"No, I don't. You don't understand."

"Fine, then buck up. Be a father, be a husband. Life will change, Gavin, and then it will change again. Stop acting like your life is over."

"I can't talk to you anymore."

I took a deep breath. "Look, I'm so grateful to you for this studio. It saved me. But not having you in my life has been hard on me. You don't seem to mention that it's hard on you. All you talk about is how you don't get along with Briel."

"God, Penny, are you that dense?"

"Are you insulting me?"

"I don't get along with Briel because all I do is compare her to *you*."

I had no fight left in me. "But here we are, you and me, on opposite sides of the world."

He didn't respond.

"I hired an office manager." I said. "I'll text you her number. She's going to take over managing the strip mall properties. I'm gonna go, Gavin. I'm tired."

"I still love you, you know."

"I know," I said before hanging up.

40. Three Years Later

GAVIN

Peering through the floor-to-ceiling windows of the dance studio, I held my daughter's hand and watched Penny dance like I had when I first met her.

"That's her, Elodie. The most beautiful woman in the room. Do you see? Do you see the way she moves?"

"I do, Daddy. She's a very pretty dancer."

When Penny's routine ended and she excused her class, I led Elodie into the room. Penny and I hadn't spoken in three years. We needed space from each other. And watching her now, I knew I had made the right decision to stay away. She was vibrant and healthy looking. Her hair was up, and I noticed from across the room that she had a new tattoo on the back of her neck.

She still hadn't spotted us.

"Nice tights, Teach."

She spun around so quickly it made me dizzy. Those lips, those chocolatey eyes. "What the—" she started.

"This is Elodie. She wants to be a dancer." I shrugged. "I have no idea why."

Penny came toward us, ankles cracking and popping. I smiled at the familiar sound. She bent in front of Elodie and stuck her hand out. "I'm Penny."

"I know. My daddy shows me videos of you dancing."

"Does he?" she whispered. Her eyes misted over as she shook Elodie's hand.

"Why are you crying?" Elodie said.

"Because I'm happy to meet you. These are happy tears." They shook hands and then Penny stood, wiping the tears from her face, and stared at me. A small smile played on her lips.

"You here for a visit?"

I laughed. "I'm not fucking around this time."

"Daddy!" Elodie admonished.

"Sorry, baby girl. Elodie wants to take lessons here. We're moving back into my dad's house next Tuesday."

She stood there, blinking. "You and Elodie and . . . ?"

"Nope, just me and this little Tater Tot." I lowered my voice. "Briel wasn't cut out for it. Her band's second album hit it pretty big."

"I heard that."

"She was on the road a lot. I told her I didn't belong in Paris, raising our daughter alone."

"And . . ."

"She understood."

We spoke quietly, almost in code. She glanced down at Elodie and said, "But won't Briel—"

I shook my head. "Like I said, she wasn't cut out for it. Elodie, baby, go dance in front of the mirror. It's all yours."

Penny pressed a button on a remote and music came on. "That's it. Good girl," Penny said as Elodie danced around freely.

Now we had a little privacy. Penny leaned up on her toes, wrapped her arms around my neck, and whispered, "I'm going to hate-kiss you now for not talking to me for three years." I laughed but she stopped me with the kiss. I didn't feel hate in it at all.

When she pulled away, I said, "But you didn't talk to me, either."

"Fine, I take it back. Now close your eyes." I did and we kissed again. I placed her hand on my heart. We were back in the psychology room so many years ago, but this time we had a whole life shared between us. "Don't open your eyes," she said when she stepped away. "Now tell us, Gavin, what did you feel?"

"Love. What about you, Penny?"

"I felt everything."

"Yes, everything," I agreed.

"Now open your eyes."

When I did, she was staring at me curiously.

"Hi, beauty," I said.

"Hi."

Epilogue

Please write a little note to Penny and Gavin on their beautiful day . . .

To the bride and groom:

Even though you guys watched that video later, I don't think either one of you saw what we saw in the psychology room all those years ago. There was something we couldn't capture on film. Something we could all feel. You both know I'm not into that cheesy crap so it takes a lot for me to say this but . . . you two were made for each other. Love you and congrats!

—Ling

PS. Thanks for throwing the bouquet right at me and basically forcing me to catch it. Not funny.

To the bride and groom:

I like seeing you guys this happy. I hope someday I get to marry my best friend.
    I'm lucky I get to have you as a stepdad, Gavin.

                            Love you guys.
                                Milo

To the bride and groom:

We all knew there was something there. I can't believe you both fought it for so long. I already feel like Elodie is my new grandbaby. Thank you, Gavin, for always, always being such a wonderful addition to our family. And thank you for breathing new life into it.

                Love, Mom (Anne)

To the bride and groom:

You know how I feel about marriage, except maybe for you guys. This all finally makes sense now. Took you two long enough. Honestly, though, I've never seen the two of you so happy. You might make a believer out of me after all.

Congratulations!

Love, Keeks

To the bride and groom:

Gavin, I'm sorry I've missed so much. I hope to be a bigger part of your life. You married a lovely woman. I'm proud of you.

Love, Mom

P,

It's kind of pathetic but I would have waited forever for you. There's no other woman for me. There never has been. Will you wear those black tights again? I love

you in those tights. *Thanks for helping me raise Elodie. She's lucky to have you. I'm lucky to have you.*

I love you more than Charlize.

G

Gavin,

*Funny. I'm telling Charlize you said that. Listen,
though . . . I know you don't like being serious but
I wanted to tell you something: I don't think we're
exploding stars at all. I think we're constants. I know
because I've always loved you. And because you're different now. It's like your spirit has calmed. I see you
on the porch playing guitar and I know you're finally
content. I don't want to look back at the time when we
weren't a couple and have regrets. I have a lifetime of
wonderful, beautiful memories with you. This is just
the next chapter in our story.*

*All my love,
Penny*

Acknowledgments

I wrote this book a while back, and now I'm finally writing the acknowledgments after many months have gone by. Every time I go back through a book I remember the very small moments in my life that inspired whole scenes. Sometimes it's just a second, or a deep breath, or a sun flare on a photo, or words spoken to me by someone I love, or seeing someone's eyes well up with tears just because *I'm* crying. A scene will come to me and I'll think to myself, *I'm so lucky I get to do this for my job, even though it's not always easy.*

I wrote this book for my friends who have stuck around. I wrote it for myself, too. And of course I wrote it for the readers, the lovers, the dreamers, and if you're reading this now, I wrote it for you. Thank you for keeping me writing. It's my happy place.

Thank you to Allison Hunter, my agent, for taking me on, and actually liking the first draft, and also for a bunch of other awesome things you do.

Tara, you inspire me. Keep sending the music recs.

Rodrigo, thank you for the always amazing covers. YA YAs, always pushing me to be better, love you. John Snow Cash, please never stop sitting at my feet while I write. Whitney, what the hell would I do without you?

To my mom, dad, brother, sister, mother-in-law, and their families, thank you for sharing my books with your friends and family, and for your love and pride.

To this author and blogger community, I am so lucky to know so many of you. To Judith, Loan, Milena, and the Atria crew, thank you so much!

Jhanteigh, when I saw you last in New York and you came into the restaurant so jazzed, it put a huge smile on my face. You're a character. Keep laughing; it's contagious. Thank you as always for believing in me, trusting me as a writer, and for all your hard work on my books.

Ang, took a while to get a dedication, I know, but to me this book was more about friendship and trust than any other I've written. Thank you for being my best friend.

Sam, you amaze me. You're such a hard worker and so determined. Whenever I decide to let you read this book, you'll know by then that I couldn't care less about MIT. Your kindness and happiness is my biggest pride.

Tony, you are truly an original with the biggest heart, most clever one-liners, and great humor. I'm proud of your progress this year. You're still a messy eater, though. I hope that improves by the time you're an adult.

Anthony, our love tree still blooms every year, and your coffee-making skills have improved from year to year as well. Thank you for all you do for *all of us*.